This book is dedicated to my angel, Zalaya;
my little soldier, Zakari;
and everyone else who decided to read what is beyond this page.
I hope to have your eyes for life.
Thank you.
Enjoy

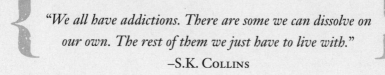

"We all have addictions. There are some we can dissolve on our own. The rest of them we just have to live with."
–S.K. COLLINS

ACKNOWLEDGMENTS

First, I want to thank the man above for giving me something that's worth more than any amount of gold, my mind.

I want to thank my parents for all their support. You made a lot of sacrifices to raise me and I've never taken that for granted. I'm glad to make you proud of my accomplishments. Maya, thank you for being perfect in nature. I couldn't ask for a better person to go through life lessons with. ZAKARI, you are the center of my motivation. My job is to provide you with all the tools and resources that will get you educated and be successful with anything you desire to pursue. You are a great son and I love you. To my sisters, Amicia and Cherise, The relationship between brother and sister is priceless. So is my love for both of you. Mary Jean, thank you for being my second mother. Corey and Kristen Nickens, thanks for being my extended family. You're always there when I need you. Kobe and Pat, thanks for always helping me get through the rough patches in my life. I really appreciate it.

To my Best Friends: Carl Clemons, Ricsheena Smith, and Ashley Guyton. We all have come a long way. I'm glad there was no time lost along our journey. Shadé, your dream is in progress! Keep working it! Gina Gee and Larnell Matthews, it's coming like I promised—*Wide Open 2!*

Special shout-out to the city of Pittsburgh, PA and the entire DMV area. Here comes another one!

Shout-out to Tawna Outler, Robin Brown, Shawn Hicks, Tanaill Wright, Shaunte Stieff, Rasheeda Brodus, Torrie Jones-Snyder, and all of the rest of the Nine-Six Clique. Thank you for your support! Ramina Foster, Sarah Jones, Brandy Garmon and Tracey Beddingfield. Your support has been much appreciated. Gene Wild'em, Tony Rome, Donald Patrick, and Kareem Smith. Thanks for keeping it real.

I want to thank the following book clubs: Black Faithful Sister and Brothers, Readers R Us, We Read Urban, My Urban Books, Diamond Eyes, Papaya Sisters, Classy Readers, Sistas of Essence, Ladies First, & New Beginnings.

Special book club member shout-outs: Carla "C Tizzy" Towns, India "Indy" Freeman, Monica Forbes, Sandy "The Late Night Chef" Barrett-Sims, Jeanette McMillan-James, Charlene Richardson, and Zaneta Powell.

Jennifer Rhynes, sis thank you for being one of the craziest individuals that I've ever met. Please take that as a compliment. Your lifestyle surely added some fuel to this story.

Thank you to my agent, Joylynn Ross. Thank you for believing in me and I hope we have a long business relationship. Thank you to my editor Khloe Cain for being so easy to work with. O.W.L. really has a jewel in their camp! I want to thank Keith Saunders of Marion Designs for taking my concepts and creating another dope cover.

I want to give a HUGE thank-you to Zane, Charmaine Parker, and Nakita! I love being a part of Strebor and Simon & Schuster! I hope I'm representing you well thus far.

Last but definitely not least, I want to thank Maurice "First" Tonia. You're one of a kind, homie. I appreciate all your support. It's only right that you close it out.

MESSAGE FROM MAURICE "FIRST" TONIA:

First, I would like to thank you Jesus Christ. You gave me grace and mercy and kept my kids, Jazmyn, Montre, Bryce, and Asia safe. Thank you Lord for giving me over 38 years with my mother, Yvetta Tonia. I also want to thank Pastor Michael L. Williams, First Lady Lisa Williams, Sharita Worlds, my three brothers Millz, Gary, and Big Mike. Thank you to my entire family and Facebook friends. Last, but not least, I would like to thank S.K. for being a true friend. Thank you and God bless.

All right, here we go! My second book! I consider this my hardmore novel because I never was a sophomore (DP insider).

Bayette Jackson, enjoy the storyline, cuz.

MESSAGE TO THE REAL SHAKITA AND LATRICE:

Your situation was grave. I prayed many nights that the outcome for both of your mistakes would be minimal, since you already lost so much. I know that the pain you now feel may burn deeper in your soul than anything you've ever held sorrow over. I'm here to tell you that everything will be all right. I wrote this story in the mindset that we would be parted from everyday life for a very long time. I wanted you to one day read this novel and know that our friendship was real... Our trust was real... And most importantly the lives we led were real. I hope you enjoy this story even if troubling memories are revisited. Remember it's okay to cry, especially if they're tears of redemption. I hope to see the both of you real soon. Until then...

A SPECIAL MESSAGE FROM THE AUTHOR:

I think no matter how many books I write this one will probably mean the most to me. A few years ago right before this book was written, I was having financial problems, and on top of that, a daughter on the way. My only goal was to make sure I could move to a big enough place so my daughter could have her own room.

I had a publisher who was lined up to purchase the author rights to the next book I wrote after I declined to sell them my first novel, *Wide Open*. I worked on this book day and night, determined to be a good provider for my daughter. A few days following the completion of *Crooked G's*, I received the worst news in my life. At six months in the womb, my daughter died from the result of an umbilical cord accident, and she was classified as stillborn. A part of me had been lost and I felt that writing this book was all for nothing. The only motivation I had to write this book was her, and now she was gone. There was no way I could sell this book to the publisher, especially if I would never be known as the author.

As time went on I continued to pray for a sign that life would get better. Then fourteen months later my son was born. My desire for writing had been ignited again. I decided to continue to keep writing and use my faith that my work would one day get into the right hands. My prayers were finally answered and now I get to write my own history.

S.K. COLLINS

INTRO

"This is it," Shakita whispered softly to herself. "This is my last fucking chance." She nervously exhaled as her sweaty palm gripped the last five-dollar bill that was once part of a thick bankroll. Shakita had been sitting at the same slot machine in Hollywood Casino for over three hours trying to get it to crack. The alluring sound of big payouts and jackpots being won all around her on the casino floor, kept her optimistic that she would soon be a part of that elite winning circle. She deliberated about all the thousands of dollars that she had dumped into the slot machine she sat in front of, and had a good feeling it would give it all back to her, and then some. Her last pull on the lever may be the one that would bring her riches beyond belief. For her sake, it had to be. If it wasn't, Shakita would be penniless. Shakita wished she could increase her odds of winning, but with no more money to spare, all she could do was pray for a fucking miracle.

She slid the crinkled bill into the machine and waited for it to register. She placed her trembling palm on the lever. Her heart began to pound at an enormous pace. She closed her eyes, not wanting to perceive what would ultimately happen next. Shakita pulled the lever down hard and intensely waited for the dramatic outcome.

She heard the reels spin in rapid succession until each one came to its own abrupt halt. Then there was complete silence, which scared the hell out of her. She slowly opened her eyes, hesitant to face the harsh reality of what she had already known. Shakita looked fearfully at the number 7's on the reels that failed to accurately line up. At that moment she wanted to die. It was now lucid in her mind that she had completely lost everything. She was now in a world of shit. Shakita's life literally flashed before her eyes knowing that all the money she lost never belonged to her in the first place. The money had been property of the notorious Bay Jackson, all two-hundred and fifty thousand dollars of it.

Bay Jackson was a ruthless hustler from the Northeast side of D.C. He'd grinded his way to the top all by himself to achieve the status he obtained before going to jail. He'd left his immense stash with his ex-girlfriend, Latrice. Bay didn't trust anyone but her and knew she would hold his money until he was finally freed. Bay planned on starting a rap label when he was released and Latrice was on board to be his trusted talent scout. Latrice was the only person Bay had in his corner, and she was also Shakita's best friend. Shakita didn't know how she would tell Latrice that she had blown all of his money, which Latrice never knew she had.

Shakita lit up a cigarette as tears rolled from her eyes. She smoked nervously as she reflected on how fucked up her situation had become. In two months she had gone through $250,000 and didn't have shit to show for it. She was well aware that Bay was a no-nonsense killer and would flip on anyone who played with his money; Latrice would be no exception. He would kill her, too, if it came down to his paper, and Shakita would be all to blame. Shakita had it etched in her mind that Bay was getting out of jail in less than four weeks. She had to find a way to get all his money back and she had to find a way to tell Latrice how badly she had betrayed her. Shakita smashed out her cigarette, grabbed her purse, and hurried out of the casino. She had no time to waste, because her and Latrice's lives were now on the line.

CHAPTER 1

TWO MONTHS EARLIER

J ust sit tight, lil' mama. I swear we're going to be in and out of this joint. All we need is five minutes," Kam assured Shakita. "Are you going to be cool?"

"Yeah, I'm fine," she said meekly as tension spread across her face.

Kam saw the strained look in her eyes and he had to console her.

"I know you're nervous as shit, but we're going to be straight. I promise. All right?"

Shakita quickly nodded her head as she fought to hide her anxiety. Kam touched her cheek and smiled before he exited the car. Shakita watched as Kam and three members of his crew casually walked into Montgomery Mall. To the average eye, Kam and his crew looked as if they were a group of regular browsers. They strolled across the mall floor not giving away any sign they were actually jewelry thieves. Montgomery Mall was set to be their fourth heist in the last eighty days. The only part Shakita had to play in the scheme was to get them out of the area before the police showed up.

Shakita pulled on her cigarette as she tapped her foot on the gas pedal. *Just chill, girl*, she said to herself, as she struggled to disband her paranoia of them getting caught. She suddenly got a bad feeling in the pit of her stomach that told her to get out of there. As much as she wanted to listen to her gut, she quickly shook the feeling off, and studied the exit doors, praying Kam would appear at any moment. She had to abandon her fear and remind herself the reason she was there. She needed money for gambling and selling stolen expensive jewelry was her way of making it happen. Shakita had promised herself that this would be her first and last time taking part in a jewelry heist. She would be one and done, never again allowing herself to descend so low out of monetary desperation. All she had to do was sell the jewelry and she would have enough money to get back to what she did best: gamble to win it big.

"Where the hell are they?" she wondered as she lit up another cigarette. Too much time had elapsed and Shakita was falling apart. Her protruding eyes fixated on the exit doors hoping Kam would emerge, yet her racing heart told her that he wouldn't.

Kam and his crew walked casually through the crowded mall and headed straight toward Bertzman Jewelers. Kam checked his watch and smiled knowing their timing was perfect for the security shift change. Now all they had to do was get in and get out. They stepped into the jewelry store and one of the sales associates' eyes beamed. He thought about the huge commission he would make from those he ignorantly assumed were rappers. He quickly dashed toward them eager to assist.

"Hello, gentlemen. Are any of you looking for something particular?" the sales associate asked as he displayed his preeminent charm.

"Yeah, I'm looking for a tennis bracelet or a pendant for my daughter. She just turned sixteen," one of Kam's crew members said. "I need something really special for my baby girl."

"I can certainly help you over here, sir," the sales associate said as he walked them to the other side of the store.

Kam walked over to a display case full of Cartier and Hublot watches. His eyes lit up green as he quickly added up the value of the watches in his head. He glanced up and saw that the other sales associates were assisting other customers. He knew his time was now and without warning he pulled his mini sledgehammer from his pocket and swung it heavily at the vulnerable glass.

Crack! Crack! Smash! Crack! Crack! Smash!

Glass flew in all directions as Kam reached in the smashed case and pulled out all the display trays full of watches. The rest of his crew followed suit and almost simultaneously smashed out three other cases full of diamond rings and bracelets. They quickly packed as much jewelry as they could fit in their bags and headed for the exit. The once helpful sales associate tried to intervene as he grabbed at Kam's arm. Kam cracked the sales associate in the head with the steel hammer leaving him bloody and disoriented. Kam then pushed him to the floor as they rushed out of the store.

"Security! We need security! We've just been robbed! Somebody stop them!" the sales associate yelled as he wiped blood out of his eyes while trying to catch his balance.

A security guard finally heard the sales associate call for help, but by the time he was ready to react, it was too late. They were gone.

Shakita's heart fluttered when Kam finally busted from out of the doors.

"Let's go!" he shouted as they quickly piled into the car.

Shakita took off so fast that she almost ran over someone in the parking lot. "What the hell took y'all so long? Y'all were in there for like twenty minutes. I was out here losing my fucking mind," Shakita emphasized as she put more distance between them and the mall.

"Girl, you tripping," Kam said as he shook his head. "We were only in there for four minutes...Five minutes tops. I told you we were going to be in and out."

"I swear this is some crazy-ass shit," Shakita said as her arms shook from the sudden rush of adrenaline. They were almost on the Beltway when Shakita realized that no one was coming after them; they made it. She fell back into the headrest and exhaled deeply. They had gotten away with grand theft and she felt like a true bad ass. The robbery put some hair on her chest as she felt bolder to take on the next challenge in her life.

"The spot's right there. Pull up in front of that Accord," Kam instructed as they made it to their destination. Shakita maneuvered the car into the tight space. She then smiled, happy that her required driving was finally over. Kam's men got out the car and then quickly entered into a small building while Kam waited behind. He opened up his bag giving Shakita a peek of what he had obtained.

"Damn," she said as her eyes marveled at all the diamond-clustered watches. She pulled one of them out of the bag and held it up to the light. The diamonds glistened so much that they looked wet.

"I see you got eyes for that one." Kam smiled. "It's perfect for a girl like you."

"The diamonds on this thing are crazy. This is like a twenty thousand-dollar watch."

"Try more like forty. That's a big-face Rolex. The diamonds alone are like ten stacks."

Shakita slipped the loose-fitting watch on her wrist and stared at it in admiration. The cold eighteen-karat gold band against her skin gave her the chills.

"This is so beautiful. I don't even want to take it off."

"You don't have to. Keep it," Kam replied.

"But don't you want to cash it in with the rest of them?"

"Don't even worry about it. Believe me, we have more than enough. We really made out on this heist. You'll still get your cut, too. Thank you for doing this for me. I really appreciate it."

"No problem." She smiled.

Kam returned her smile, then he opened the door. "I'll see you in a few minutes," he said as he placed his lips gently against hers. She tensed up from the sudden intimate gesture, but then pulled him in closer to her as her lips received his. The silent built-up tension between them had finally boiled over. The kiss had been long overdue, giving them clear indication that something was missing from their kinetic bond. The thought of them being together had often crossed her mind. They were both cut from the same cloth; they were reckless. They were outlaws in their own right, who made their own rules as they went along. They were supposed to happen and now that they did, together they would be even more dangerous.

"Can we celebrate tonight?" he asked as they clasped hands.

"Of course we can." She smiled.

"Okay, cool. I'll be back in a few. I got to get this money." He gave her a wink and got out the car.

Shakita blushed as she watched him walk into the building. A feeling of joy touched her heart. It had been awhile since someone had shown Shakita that they really cared about her. It was easy for her to get affection from men, but for them to actually care about her well-being was something totally different. When it came to Kam, there was no denying that she held a special place in his heart.

Shakita eagerly eyed the small store across the street and stepped out the car. She was out of cigarettes and needed a fresh pack. She figured by the time she got back from the store, the exchange would probably be done.

"Thank you," Shakita said to the clerk as she took her change. She placed the coins in her pocket and then retrieved her lighter. She stepped out the store and immediately lit her cigarette. She then headed back to the car but suddenly stopped in her tracks. The cigarette fell from her lips as she frantically watched the dramatic scene that emerged across the street. Police cars had completely surrounded the building. All three of Kam's crew members were being detained as they were being led out of the building. Shakita couldn't believe what was happening. She was confused to how they were found so quickly, or even at all. She had been convinced that they weren't tailed after leaving the mall. She had driven around in circles making sure that no one was behind them.

"Something isn't right," she whispered.

Police officers cleared onlookers from the street as a tactical team van pulled up to the scene. Shakita's heart started to pound as she thought about Kam still being in the building. She was convinced he wouldn't come out willingly and would fight to his last breath. Tears escaped her eyes as the tactical team entered the building with their guns drawn. She prayed that Kam could somehow find a way to escape the surefire ending. She wanted to help him any way possible. It was almost too late for him to surrender, and she was the only one he would listen to. Kam trusted her over anyone in the world. She was putting herself at risk of being caught, but she didn't care. She had to get to him.

She started to run toward the crowd of officers hoping she could stop them. Before she could even take a step, her ears informed her that she was too late. *Bang! Bang! Bang! Bang!* The erupting sound of guns being fired caused her heart to drop to her stomach. Gun blast after gun blast continued to echo from the building until they suddenly ceased.

"It's over. We got 'em," one of the officers said to his team after he received confirmation over his walkie-talkie. Shakita fell to her knees as pain flooded her heart.

Everything had happened too fast for Shakita to fully accept that it was real. Then the sight of a morgue van that pulled onto the scene undoubtedly let her know that Kam's existence had been lost forever. Shakita cried uncontrollably knowing that Kam had died for nothing. The heist had produced no winners, and Kam's tragic death made it completely evident. She then remembered the watch that was stuffed in her pocket. Shakita had the only unaccounted for piece of jewelry left from the heist, and had no choice but to get rid of it. She wiped her face and quickly got off the ground. She walked to her truck that was parked a few blocks away and never looked back.

The next morning, Shakita pulled up to Pawnbrokers Unlimited. She flipped down the visor and then sadly looked in the mirror. She moved her fingers through her blonde-highlighted hair and sighed at the thought of needing another color treatment. Her milky-tan skin felt slightly desiccated, so she reached in her purse to retrieve a container of Nivea moisturizing crème. She rejuvenated her skin and then placed her sunglasses over her sunken eyes. She stepped out of her truck and headed straight toward the entrance. The metal newspaper holder grabbed her attention before she entered the pawn shop. She kneeled down and read the top story on the *Washington Post.* "It was a setup," Shakita whispered in awe. The headlining article caused tears to stream down her cheeks.

"We were never supposed to make it."

Shakita continued to read the story. She was astonished to discover that the people Kam were supposed to make the exchange with were undercover cops. She finished reading the story and was assured that no other collaborators were being sought. She didn't understand how she avoided being caught, but she was extremely thankful.

"Can I help you?" the chubby, light-skinned owner of the shop asked as Shakita approached the counter.

"Yes you can. I want to get cash for a piece of jewelry I no longer have a need for."

"Sure thing, baby girl. What you got?"

Shakita pulled the watch out of her purse and placed it on the glass counter. The man curiously looked at the watch and then back at Shakita.

"This wouldn't happen to be stolen from anywhere, would it?" the man suspiciously asked. "If it is, I don't want any part of it."

"No, it's not stolen. It was a gift from my cheating ex-boyfriend. I don't want anything to do with him or this watch."

The man looked at Shakita with doubtful eyes. He was highly aware about all the jewelry store robberies over the past few weeks and didn't want any unnecessary attention drawn to his business. He quickly glanced at Shakita's overall appearance. He saw, without a doubt, her raw beauty had gotten her a lot of costly things. It was way too often that scorned women came into his shop to sell their once precious items. He saw that Shakita was another hurt soul trying to seek vengeance for her broken heart. He decided to help her. "I'll give you five thousand for it."

"You can't be serious. Five thousand dollars? Do you know how much this watch is worth?" she asked, feeling insulted by his offer.

"Yeah, I know how much it's worth. To me it's worth five thousand. To you it should be worth less than that. I think the cheaper you sell it, the more you'd piss your ex-boyfriend off. That is your purpose, right?"

"I know what you're trying to do and I won't let you take advantage of me. You can easily get twenty-five for this watch. I want ten or I'll just go somewhere else," Shakita threatened. She reached down to pick up the watch, but the owner quickly gave her a counter-offer.

"I'll give you eighty-five hundred. I respect your hustle, but that's the highest I can go. I guarantee you no one around will give anywhere near that much. Go 'head and shop it around, but if you come back here, my offer will go down to three thousand. The choice is yours."

Shakita didn't have time to hit every pawn shop in town hoping to get a better offer. She needed money fast and had to make a decision. The watch was the only thing that would forever connect her to Kam. If she parted ways with the watch, she would be left with nothing to symbolize their bond. All she would have left to remember him by were her cherished memories. She sighed deeply coming to terms with the choice she would have to make. If her conditions didn't progress, it would be inevitable for her to keep the watch regardless. If that happened, she'd be forced to sell it for an even lower amount.

She pushed the watch closer to him confirming her decision. He quickly picked up the watch and gave her a nod that she was doing the right thing.

"I'll be back with your cash and receipt," he said as he walked to the back of the shop.

Shakita rested her elbows on the glass counter and placed her hands under her chin. She felt stupid for what she'd done, but it was the only logical solution to fix her problem. The owner came back with her money along with the receipt. He counted every bill out loud to show her she wasn't getting cheated. "Thanks," she said placidly.

She hurried out of the shop not wanting to tear up in front of the store owner. She wiped her swollen eyes all the way until she got into her truck. She stared miserably at the shop as she thought of Kam. The keepsake that they briefly shared, which signified their irrefutable connection, would soon be sold to someone else. She assured herself that once she won a jackpot, she would return to reclaim the watch. Time was her only ally and she prayed she had enough of it to make all her efforts count. With a fresh stack of money in her possession, she felt the tide would surely turn in her glorious favor. She cracked a weak smile as she headed to Hollywood Casino.

Shakita pushed herself away from the crap table and rushed into one of the casino bathrooms. She screamed and pounded her fist against the wall, outraged and disillusioned about what had taken place. Two Caucasian women quickly exited the bathroom as Shakita continued her emotional rant. She was sickened to her stomach and heartbroken that she had failed to win once again. Not only had she sold the watch that Kam had given her, but the amount she received for it had been completely diminished. She was back to being broke and felt like the most ill-fated person in the world.

"If I would have just kept my stupid ass at the slot machines instead of fucking around with that damn crap table bullshit, I would still be out there fucking playing. I could be up right fucking now." She screamed in her head. Her chest heaved up and down as she paced the bathroom floor.

She then dug into her purse and pulled out a cigarette. Smoking had been prohibited in all non-gaming areas of the casino, but Shakita didn't care. Getting fined was the least of her worries. Her back slid down the cold wall as the nerve relaxant started to take effect.

She flicked her ashes onto the floor as she dwelled heavily on what she was going to do next. She needed money badly, and her avenues of opportunity were drying up fast. Now that she was without Kam, there were only two other people she could rely on. She would first go to her best friend, Latrice, for support. If and only if it really got chaotic for her, she would be forced to ask that certain individual for assistance. They would remain her ace-in-the-hole unless she was out of options. She swallowed hard, hoping that her predicament would never get to that drastic level.

"All I got to do is ask her to let me hold a few dollars until I get back up," Shakita said softly as she lifted herself off the floor.

She quickly headed to Latrice's house hoping her friend would be able to lend a helping hand. Her electricity had been disconnected in her apartment, and she had already been served an eviction notice on top of her other bills. Gambling had truly put everything she had in jeopardy, once again.

CHAPTER 2

Latrice stared blankly at the ceiling, as Bay dug into her flesh with his overbearing and powerful stroke. The harder he pumped, the more her face tensed in agony. She enjoyed rough sex, but not with Bay. He always unnecessarily took it to another level, somewhat violent. He was a sadist. Bruised knees, bite marks, and bleeding nipples were always part of the outcome. Whenever she complained, more intense pain would be inflicted upon her. Remaining silent and submissive would be her best option. All she ever wanted to do was survive the brutal sex acts, and make him content in the process.

"Open that pussy up for me, girl," Bay said as he pumped harder. He clasped his hand around her neck and then pinned her left leg up to her shoulder. Latrice grunted as her breathing became compromised. She started to drool all over Bay's hand, fighting to get air into her lungs.

"Come on, girl. If you could get this pussy as wet as your fucking mouth, I might be able to bust, damn!"

Latrice blocked out his callous insult, as she began to lose consciousness. Her eyes twitched, as she choked on the saliva that was trapped in her throat. Right before she blacked out, Bay released the grip on her neck.

"Roll over," he commanded as he wiped all the slobber off his hand and onto the sheets.

Latrice coughed uncontrollably as she fought to restore her breathing. Tears flooded her eyes as snot poured out of her nose.

"Come on, girl. Stop acting like you can't handle this shit. Now turn your ass over," he commanded, smacking her thigh.

Latrice slowly turned over on her back as she continued to cough. She had little time to recover, before Bay forced his length back inside her. He held her face down into the pillow as he punished her with strong back shots. Sweat poured off her brow as she continued to endure the severe pain. Bay grunted loudly as he compressed all his weight on top of Latrice's back. His massive frame suffocated her petite body. She felt as if her lungs were touching her spine. His deep groans signaled he was almost ready to bust. All she had to do was hold on a little bit longer, and the demoralizing act would be over.

"Here it comes, baby. Here it…" Bay's words trailed off as he released himself all over Latrice's backside. He slowly rolled off of her while trying to catch his breath. Latrice felt as if a car had merely been lifted off her body. She strived to revitalize herself.

"Damn. Doing three months in the shit hole is going to be rougher than a motherfucka for me. I've never gone that long without any pussy. I wish we could do it again, but I got to go," Bay stated as he reached on the floor for his jeans.

Latrice rejoiced quietly at the thought of Bay going to jail. Three months wasn't long enough for her, but any amount of time away from him, would help repair her battered core. Her love and detestation for him were equal. She wanted to be his only girl, but hated the level of degradation and womanizing that came along with the dramatized relationship. She hoped after their time apart, she would finally have enough strength to demand more from him.

Latrice's thoughts were interrupted when Bay's phone rang from on top of the nightstand. She grabbed the phone and tried to hand it to him, but without warning, her face met the back of his hand.

"Why the fuck you pick up my shit? Don't touch my shit. You don't know who could be hitting me up. Nosey-ass bitch." He shook his head and then answered the phone. "Hello. Yeah, what's up my, nigga. All right, I'll be down in a minute." He hung up the phone, then looked over at Latrice as blood trickled from her nose. "You brought that upon yourself. Nobody told you to touch my shit."

"I didn't even look at it. On top of that I don't care who calls you. You be the one tripping off of shit like that. Not me."

Bay put his shirt back on and waved her off, as if what she was saying didn't matter. Latrice felt slighted as blood continued to pour from her nose. She sighed out of frustration as blood droplets absorbed into her favorite silk sheets. She decided to use the tainted fabric to suppress the bleeding. She looked up at Bay as her eyes filled with tears.

"Why do you treat me like this? I do everything you ask of me, but yet, you treat me like I'm out to get you. I don't deserve this, Bay. Not at all."

Bay walked over to her and stood directly over top of her. He arched his brow as he stared into her saddened eyes. "You should be lucky with the amount of attention you get from me. Those other hoes don't get shit but dick and hair money. You don't have to remind me that you'll do anything for me. I already know that. I trust you like shit, girl. All the shit you did for me over the years to keep me out of prison, I respect that. I even trust you over my own niggas when it comes to my money. I don't ever have to worry about no snake shit with you. You're my little angel." He then brushed her face lightly with his hand, causing Latrice to tense up slightly.

"When I get out, we're going to start this label and everything is going to be straight. I need you to be strong right now. You're all I got to depend on. I'm sorry that I hit you, but don't make that an issue for us. You understand what I'm saying?"

Latrice nodded, confirming she understood. She hated his apology, but knew with Bay, that's the best she would get from him. He was a hardened thug and never displayed vulnerability to anyone. No matter how much he was at fault.

"A'ight, I got to get up out of here, so I can get this fucking time over with. I'm going to call you as often as I can. I need you to be here to catch my calls. Okay?"

"Yeah, I gotchu," she replied softly.

Bay kissed her forehead and then headed for the door. He turned around and gave her a fierce glare.

"Don't let anything happen to my money. You protect that shit with your life."

"Don't worry, Bay. Just go do your time and everything will be in order once you get out," Latrice assured.

Bay simply nodded and left out the door. Latrice didn't even wait long enough to see if he was really gone before she started to cry. Bay had completely destroyed her sense of worth. She didn't like the weak woman she had become. She prayed that during the time Bay was locked up, she would find herself again. She no longer wanted him to dictate her every decision. Latrice wanted to have as much power as Bay did with the record label. Some drastic changes in her life would have to be made, especially if she wanted to be a boss. She had to come up with a game plan.

Shakita walked into Latrice's apartment building right as Bay was leaving out. Their eyes coldly met as he descended down the steps. The abhorrence they shared for each other was clearly evident. She despised him for how he treated Latrice, and Bay hated her for how she played Latrice against him.

"Kita. Don't be having my girl out here fucking with no niggas while I'm gone. I know how your crazy ass gets down."

"Whatever, Bay." She rolled her eyes and tried to brush past him, but he grabbed her arm.

"Don't fuck with me, girl. I'll have your lil' dumb ass go missing," Bay hissed.

Shakita's heart pumped with fear. Bay had always threatened her but never to this extent. The thought of her getting killed for interfering with their relationship had gone way too far.

Bay finally released her arm and then laughed all the way out the door. *Damn, I hate that motherfucka*, she said to herself as she quickly climbed the steps. She reached Latrice's door and banged on it as hard as she could.

Bang! Bang! Bang! Bang!

"Bay must've forgot to tell me something," she said softly as she approached the door. When Latrice opened the door, she was surprised to see Shakita.

Shakita looked at Latrice's blood-smeared face in shock.

"What the fuck did he do to you?"

Latrice's face became flushed. Shakita was the last person she expected to see.

"Why did he hit you this time, Latrice?"

"I really don't want to talk about it," she cried softly. She covered her face and then sat on the couch. She was so embarrassed. She always had to make up an excuse for Bay's abusive behavior.

"Him hitting you every week is getting real old. You need to press charges on his ass like that other bitch, so he could stay in jail longer."

"I can't do that."

"Yes you can. Don't be scared. I'll even go down there with you."

"No, I can't do that. I need him to come out."

"Come out for what? He needs to stop hitting on you. Why do you feel like you need a man like him?"

"I don't need him for what you think. We're going to go ahead and start that record label together."

"You don't need him to start no label. You can do it by yourself. Damn that. You and me can start one if that's what it will take for you to leave him alone."

"You know we would not be good in business together. On top of that, neither one of us have any damn money like that to start a label."

"How do you even know Bay got money like that anymore? What if he's just trying to spin you to keep you around?" Shakita asked with concern.

"No, he has money. I know this for sure."

"And what makes you so certain of this? Just because he said so?"

"I'm holding his money here until he gets out. I'm the only one he trusts with it."

"For real? Did he give you a lot?"

"Let's just say he gave me enough. It's enough to make this thing really work."

"Girl, stop teasing me and tell me how much."

"Two hundred fifty thousand."

"Are you serious?"

"I'm so serious. I hid the money in the vent in my room. I'm only telling you this just in case someone comes looking for it. I'm not sure who Bay's enemies are, but if something ever happened to me, I want someone to know where it is." Latrice saw a diminutive glimmer in Shakita's eyes and could tell exactly what she was thinking. "Shakita. You can't use this money to gamble with. I want to make that very clear. My life depends on it." Latrice emphasized the seriousness of her situation. Shakita was an impulsive gambler and being around money was her Achilles' heel. Latrice really had no one else to trust with the money. She had no choice but to tell Shakita.

"Latrice, I would never do anything to jeopardize your life. I know how crazy Bay is. He just threatened to kill me over some bullshit, so I know what he'll do about his money," Shakita said with sincerity.

"He did? When?" Latrice asked in shock.

"I ran into him downstairs. He told me not to have any niggas around you. I blew him off and he grabbed me up and said he would kill me if I thought he was playing."

Latrice shook her head in sadness. She was hit with the realization that Bay had more control over her life than she did. Even in jail he would still be her oppressor. An impious puppeteer pulling her strings as he saw fit. She had to find a way to get the upper hand, or at least become his equal. Without her independence, she would be swallowed up in the music world. Bay's jealous and reckless temper would stop her from establishing any connections. No one would want to do deals with her if violence was how Bay conducted his business. She looked at Shakita as she thought about her future.

"That's why his money can't be touched under any circumstances. It's not ours to die over. Promise me you won't do anything stupid."

Shakita stared Latrice in the eyes and felt ashamed for even thinking about taking the money. As much as she would have loved to use it for her own personal gain, she couldn't go through with it. She hated Bay to the core, but crossing him would be death to both of them. She had to do what was right to keep Latrice out of harm's way. "I promise I won't touch the money. You have my word."

Latrice could tell that Shakita was being honest by the mood of her eyes. They were no longer narrow and filled with complicity. They had changed to being broad and lenient. Now that Latrice had Shakita's sworn word, she could focus on getting her life plan together. The record label was her main priority, and she had to learn more about the industry, she was so desperately trying to be a part of. She had to make moves quickly, so she would be at the top of her game by the time Bay got out. Swollen nose and all, she was determined to make every second count. She was ready to leave out since the bleeding had ceased, and remembered that Shakita must have stopped by to see her for a reason.

"So now that we have an understanding about the money, what made you stop by?"

Shakita wanted to tell Latrice everything she had gone through lately, but she wouldn't be the right person for that. Latrice was too critical about the way Shakita led her life. She could only tell Latrice bits and pieces, which would be more than enough information. She once again decided to tell her the half-truth.

"My air conditioner is broke, and I wanted to see if I could stay here until it gets fixed."

"Of course, girl, that's never a problem. It's been too hot this summer to be going without AC." Latrice grabbed her purse and headed to the door. She then stopped and turned to Shakita. "You already know my spare key is on top of the freezer. I'm about to go check some things out. I'll be back soon."

"Wait a minute. You don't want me to go with you?"

"No, that's okay. This is something I need to do by myself." Latrice smiled softly.

"Okay. Well, I'll be here. I'll see you when you get back. And don't worry about nothing, girl. We're going to get through this Bay situation together."

Latrice beamed as she looked gratefully at her best friend. All they had were each other, and it touched her heart to know that no matter what she went through, she was never alone. She valued their friendship more than anything in the world. Latrice was rest assured that she could leave Shakita alone with the money.

"Thanks, girl." She grinned as she left out the door.

Latrice had been long gone while Shakita lay jittery on the couch as she watched TV. She was alone with the money and couldn't stop thinking about it. She sporadically peered into Latrice's room where the large stash had been securely hidden.

I promised. I just have to find another way, she said to herself as guilt overshadowed her urge for deception. Time and time again Latrice had been her only benefactor. There was no one else willing to help advocate her struggle with addiction, which allowed loyalty to override her shameful obsession. Shakita vowed that she would do right by her friend this time, and find another alternative to get the money she needed.

As the days went on, Shakita still couldn't come up with a solution to resolve all her financial needs. When she went back to her apartment to get more clothes, she discovered that her water had been shut off. Shakita was now without electricity, water, and soon facing eviction. She now had her back completely against the wall. Her face grimaced as the thought of failure overwhelmed her mind. She withdrew her last cigarette from her pack as tension impeded on her emotions.

Latrice had started to leave her alone in the apartment more often than she should have. The more her trust was tested, the harder it became to resist temptation. She paced in front of Latrice's bedroom as the urge to enter heightened. Shakita swore that she wouldn't touch the money, but the more she stayed around it, the harder it became to resist. All she needed was to take enough to pay off her expenses and gamble with, then put it back once she won. She believed she was good for it, and decided to take a chance.

Her heart pounded as she crept toward the money. She removed the air vent cover, then reached inside and pulled out the heavy plastic bag. She feasted her eyes on the numerous bands of hundred-dollar bills as drool fell from her open mouth. The more she marveled over the bundles of cash, the less she felt guilty for going after it.

"All I got to do is win and put it back. Latrice will never know it was missing. I can do this," Shakita assured herself.

She quickly placed a total of ten bands in her purse that equaled ten thousand dollars. She then slid the plastic bag back in the vent, and then closed it up as if it never had been opened. Shakita sighed deeply as she closed Latrice's bedroom door. From that point on there was no turning back. Her time was now, and she felt confident in her decision to take a chance with Bay's money. She then walked out of the apartment unknowingly, that her life would be forever altered for the worst.

CHAPTER 3

"It's about to be on and popping for you, man. As soon as Bay gets out, we're going to have you in the studio the same day," Latrice promised Killa D, as she pitched to him over the phone. Killa D was one half of the gangster rap group that Bay had taken an interest in while he was still out on the street. Killa D and Piff were the best underground group in D.C., and Bay wanted them to be the first to sign to his label. Latrice handled all of Bay's business affairs while he was gone, and was instructed to keep the group attracted to the label. Latrice continued to spit game to Killa D over the phone making sure she kept his attention.

"You and Piff gonna be the biggest group to take over hip-hop in years. With the producers that we already have lined up to do your first album, ain't nobody gonna be able to fuck with you two."

"Who are the producers y'all got to work on it?"

"We got Butta Mo, Skip, The Go-Go Boyz, Chris Beats, Perry Mason, and Rooftop Productions just to name a few," Latrice happily informed him.

"Damn! That's enough already. With those cats doin' our production, we can't lose."

Latrice could tell by the way he reacted that he was smiling on the other end of the phone. She had him right where she wanted him.

"I told you. Getting down with Bangspot Records would be the best move you could make. We're gonna take over the whole fucking industry. With your kills and our marketing plan, you're guaranteed to at least go platinum. That's even with record sales slumping due to illegal downloading. None of your shit will even be affected."

Killa D thought about all the success they would have with Bangspot Records, and couldn't wait to get in the studio and put out their first hit single. Latrice couldn't wait either.

"So are you trying to get down with Bangspot or what?" Latrice asked, trying to close the deal.

Killa D didn't even have to think hard about it. He already knew what he wanted.

"We're down as long as you stay down."

"Cool. We gonna keep in touch, ya dig?"

"Gotchu."

Latrice got off the phone and started to attend to other matters. She had to hurry to get dressed, so she could get to the post office. She needed to mail off the copyright and business license materials Bay needed to officially register his company name in order to establish his business. She'd forged his signature on all of the documents precisely like Bay had instructed her so everything would run smooth.

Latrice needed to go purchase a ticket to see a female rapper named Clarity that she was hoping to sign to Bangspot Records. Clarity's style was the new hotness in D.C., and Latrice felt that everyone in the world needed to hear her. Clarity was performing that night at the Fantasy Lounge and Latrice had to be there. Latrice was confident she would be able to talk Clarity into signing with them. With Killa D, Piff and Clarity on the team, Latrice would get much praise from Bay.

After that night, Latrice hoped to have a lot of good news to tell Bay once he called in the morning. From their last conversation, Bay told her he would call her again Friday morning at eleven-thirty. She was going to make sure she didn't miss his call. She never knew the next time she would speak to him. But with Bay getting out of jail soon, Latrice felt that if she missed his call, he would call her every day until he found out how she was handling his business. She liked the way things had been going between them lately, and it was in her best interest to do anything to keep it that way. There was no way she would miss that call.

CHAPTER 4

Latrice danced in the bathroom mirror to Beyoncé's song "Upgrade U" that was playing out of her MP3 stereo docking system. She was putting the finishing touches on her hair. She spritzed her short hairstyle to give it a spiky look, as she bounced her ass to the music. Latrice -was a dark-chocolate baby doll with the toned, sculpted body of a fitness instructor. Although she had all the right moves and knew all of the latest dances, she still had no aspiration in being a video queen. Latrice's dream was to become a record executive and then transition into becoming her own boss. She wanted the big money and having her own label would get it for her. Latrice didn't want to be some ordinary chick floating around in the industry. She wanted to be that top bitch that made shit happen and everyone had no choice but to respect her.

Latrice sang out the words to the song as it brought more meaning to her life than it ever had before. She planned to upgrade Bay from a notorious street hustler to CEO of Bangspot Records. She had it all figured out and couldn't wait for him to get out of jail for everything to fall into place. With what she had planned, Latrice was going to take a start-up rap label from the bottom, to the pinnacle of the whole music industry. She continued to sing knowing that she would become a big part of Bangspot's success.

Latrice drove her midnight-blue Pontiac G6 down to the post office and did everything necessary to make sure her package would be delivered without incident. Latrice then left the post office and headed over to the Fantasy Lounge on K Street to purchase a ticket for Clarity's show. She didn't know if the club would be open this early, but she wanted to be assured that she was able to get into the venue tonight. When Latrice pulled up in front of the club, she couldn't tell if anyone was in there or not. She took a chance at the door handle and to her surprise, it was open. She walked in the dark club and didn't see anybody at the ticket window.

"Hellooo!" Latrice called out, after patiently waiting for someone to finally come up to the window. "I'm here to buy a ticket for tonight's show!" Latrice spoke out again hoping to get the attention of whoever was in there. "This is some bullshit," Latrice said under her breath as she became tired of waiting for someone to come up to the front. *Fuck this. I'll come back later.* She turned for the front door to leave, until she heard a noise coming from behind another door. As she walked closer to the door, she heard another noise. She assumed that the door led to the entrance of the club, and whoever was in there could sell her a ticket.

She walked into the lounge area and turned her nose up at the club's awful appearance. She looked at the scruffy-looking tables and the worn-out pleather that covered the booths. *This place is far from upscale,* Latrice thought as she continued to walk around the club. She didn't see how anyone would call this place the Fantasy Lounge when it was obviously far from that. *Maybe it was nice back in the day when it first opened, but it looks like some shit now.*

Latrice heard another noise coming from behind the curtain on the stage. "Hello!" Latrice hoped that the person behind the curtain heard her this time and would come out.

"Whatchu doin' in here?" a lady asked, quickly poking her head out of the curtain.

"I was trying to buy a ticket for tonight's show, but no one was up at the window. I thought I heard someone back here, so I came to see if someone could sell me one."

"That's cool," the lady said as she started to walk off the stage toward Latrice. "At first, by the way you were dressed, I thought you were the damn inspector people."

Latrice had on a white blouse, black skirt, and four-inch BCBG heels. She considered her wardrobe very classy but didn't think her outfit spelled out professional.

"I guess I'll take that as a compliment. My name is Latrice," she said as she extended her hand.

"Nice to meet you, Latrice. My name is Fantasy."

"You're Fantasy?" Latrice found it shocking as hell to find out that this light-skinned, overweight woman was the one and only Fantasy. But then again, Latrice took one look at Fantasy's matted hair and dingy clothes, and it became clear to her why the club had such a shabby appearance. "You got a nice spot here," Latrice said, not knowing what else nice to say about her.

Fantasy waved off her compliment. "Girl, you ain't gotta lie to me. I know this joint ain't nothin' but a damn hole in the wall. This place ain't been up to par in years."

"Why don't you fix it up?"

"I ain't got the money to do much of anything with this place now. Shit, I can't even change a light bulb in here without feeling it the next month."

"Well, if keeping this place is so much of a problem, then why don't you sell it?"

Fantasy sighed. "This place needs so much work done to it, I don't know who in their right mind would buy it. Besides, I couldn't sell it anyway. This used to be my daddy's place. He named it after me and this was the only thing he had to give me before he died. He loved me and this club. I just don't have it in my heart to ever sell it."

Latrice felt sorry for Fantasy and knew first-hand what she was going through. When Latrice was fourteen, she'd lost her mother to ovarian cancer, and the only thing she had to pass down was her old engagement ring. Latrice's father had broken off their engagement, and as a result of a broken heart, her mother kept the ring. Latrice's mother was a strong believer that if a man gave a woman something, she should never have to give it back. While on her deathbed, she made Latrice promise to never let a man take anything away from her. As long as it was in her possession, then it was considered hers. Latrice made the vow to one day live by her mother's words.

"Don't you have a lot of acts that come here every month?" Latrice asked. "I heard the shows be sold out all the time."

"They do, but I still got bills to pay. The lights don't stay on for free, ya know," Fantasy said with her hands on her hips, as she looked at Latrice with a *duh* expression on her face.

Latrice didn't know how much Fantasy's electric bill or anything else she paid was, but she was damn sure smart enough to know that Fantasy was barely breaking even each month. Latrice felt there was something suspect about Fantasy but didn't know exactly what. She decided to forget about what was really up with Fantasy and changed the subject.

"What time does the show start?"

"It starts at eight, but we start letting people in at seven-thirty."

"Okay. I just need one ticket, please. How much are they?"

"Twenty before the show and thirty at the door." Latrice reached in her purse and pulled out a twenty-dollar bill.

"The tickets are behind the window. Let's take a walk up front."

Latrice followed Fantasy to the front of the club. Fantasy walked inside the window booth and handed Latrice a ticket. "Thank you," Latrice said as she put the ticket in her purse. "One more thing before I go, Fantasy. Do you think there's a way you could introduce me to Clarity tonight? I'm starting up a label and I wanted to holler at her about it."

"I could do that, but you know help ain't always free these days," Fantasy said as she raised her left eyebrow. Latrice understood what she was getting at and had no problem paying her for a favor. She had to sign Clarity. She reached in her purse once more and pulled out a hundred-dollar bill.

"Will this do?" Latrice asked as she gave Fantasy the money.

"This'll do just fine." Fantasy smiled as she clutched the money in her hand. "I'll make sure you get a one-on-one with Clarity after the show."

"Good looking out. I got to be going now. I'll see you later." Latrice waved goodbye to Fantasy and walked out the door. Now she was on to the next order of business.

CHAPTER 5

Shakita quickly took her eyes off the road to look down at her ringing cell phone and saw that Latrice was calling her. She decided not to answer the phone. She didn't know how to tell her she'd blown away all of Bay's money. She felt bad for putting her friend in a bad situation, but she couldn't do any apologizing yet. She had one more scheme she had to try first before she went to Latrice. If she could get all the money back, then she wouldn't have to tell Latrice anything. She needed some fast cash and the person she could turn to during extremely rough times was Eric.

Eric had been so many things to her long before Kam. She used to work for him prior to becoming his lover. She wanted to leave her troubled past behind but couldn't yet. She needed Eric more than ever and couldn't afford to be foolish by being stubborn. She made the call to Eric and he picked up on the third ring.

"Hello."

"Is this Eric?" she asked softly.

"Who is this?"

"It's Shakita."

"What's up, Petita Shakita? How are you doing?" he said in a playful tone.

Shakita hated when he called her Petita Shakita. She knew he only called her that because it rhymed, but she still thought it was corny of him to say. Shakita was built extremely well and was damn sure far from being petite.

"I'm okay, but I need to talk to you about something. Is there a place I could meet you?" she asked anxiously.

"There sure is. You know where I'm at."

"You know my door is always open for you."

"That's what I was hoping. I'll be there as soon as I can." Shakita hung up the phone and started concentrating on driving again.

She lit up another cigarette attempting to soothe her nerves. Shakita hated stooping low to work for Eric, but she had to until she made enough money to go gambling again. She figured once she made it back to the casino, she could win big. She believed it in her heart and no one could tell her any different. She was born a risk-taker and that's what risk-takers did.

Shakita parked her green Explorer in a parking garage on Nineteenth Street NW. Eric owned The Black Emporium, which was on the same street. The Black Emporium was an upscale gentleman spa that serviced from getting a massage to having your wildest sexual fantasy fulfilled. Shakita hated to come to this place. It absolutely wasn't for her. She was much more of a mover and shaker than waiting to play someone's submissive whore. Yet, she had to revert back to her past in order to fix her future. She sighed deeply and then thought back on the day she first met Eric.

Three Years Earlier

Shakita stuffed her hands in her jacket as the sudden drop in temperature caught her offguard. She continued to step carefully through the snow as she headed to her bank's automatic teller machine. "Please let me have something in here," she said as she placed the card into the machine. Her face quickly drooped as she stared at the screen. *Two dollars and thirty cents? I can't do shit with that*, she stressed.

Anxiety had started to get the best of her as she yearned for a cigarette. She had no more money on her, and would have to endure the long bus ride home before she would be able to smoke again. She started to stomp toward the bus stop as the cold air nipped at her ears. There was a small blue-and-orange object in the snow that managed to get her attention. She leaned over to get a closer look, and to her surprise it was a PNC debit card. She picked it up and felt that the card was still warm, and guessed that it had been dropped recently. *It might not have been canceled yet*, she thought to herself.

She quickly looked around to see if anyone had seen her pick up the card. She saw no one in the area, so she placed the card in her pocket and rushed down the street to 7-Eleven. She didn't want to use the card to do big shopping. She only wanted to make a few small purchases and throw it away. She didn't know how much was in the account and didn't care either. Stealing money from a regular individual wasn't what she was into. She needed to get by for the moment. "Can I have two packs of Newports in a box, please," she said to the clerk.

When the total displayed on the screen, she nervously swiped the card and then pressed "cancel" to give her the pay-by-credit option. She was relieved when the transaction was completed. She placed the cigarettes in her purse and headed for the door. The blue-and-red scratch-off lottery ticket machine by the door stopped her in her tracks.

"One or two tickets won't hurt," she whispered as she made her selection and then swiped the card. She removed the two five-dollar Winner Take All scratch-offs from the machine and then left the store.

"Excuse me, miss," Shakita heard a man call her from behind. She presumed it was a homeless person asking for change. She was ready to tell them she didn't have anything to spare and then be on her way.

When she turned around to speak, her words got caught in her throat, as she stared at the extremely eye-catching man before her. She knew right away from his burnt-orange, custom-made leather jacket, and one-karat diamond earring that he couldn't have been impoverished. His facial features were carved to perfection making him one of the most attractive men she had ever seen. He was Reggie Bush brown with hazel eyes. He was any woman's fantasy and every man's nightmare. No man could trust their woman enough to even ask him for driving directions if they were lost. Any woman had no other choice but to be captivated by his lure and presence, Shakita being no exception.

"I dropped my card at the ATM machines around the corner and I saw you pick it up. Can I have it back, please?"

"And your name is?" she asked timidly, wanting to make sure the name he said matched the card.

"Eric. Eric Falls."

Oh shit, she said to herself. "I'm so sorry. Here you go," she said as she handed him his card.

"Thank you." He quickly smiled. "So do you always use people's cards you don't know to buy cigarettes and scratch-offs?"

"I swear I've never done anything like this before. I was out of money. I needed a cigarette really bad. Oh my God, this is so embarrassing," she said, covering her face with her hands. "I can pay you back. I really didn't mean for this to happen."

Eric sensed her reaction was real. He didn't see her to be the conniving type. What he saw was a beautiful young woman who had fallen on rough times. He presumed all she needed was a break—an opportunity that he could effortlessly provide. That was if she wanted it.

"Instead of paying me back I have a small proposition for you."

Shakita looked at him sideways and placed her hand on her hip. "Please don't tell me you want me to have sex with you, so I can avoid you pressing charges? I don't get down like that."

He grinned. "That's not what I had in mind. I want you to see if you won anything with the scratch-offs. If so, you can pay me back that way."

"And what if I don't win anything?"

"Then you let me take you to dinner. Is that a deal?"

"Just dinner?"

"Just dinner and good conversation. I promise."

Okay, Mr. Eric Falls. Either way it looks like the odds are in your favor, she said to herself as she reached in her purse for the tickets.

She used the tip of her nail and scratched away at the first ticket until all the numbers were visible. "Nothing on this one." She frowned. "Let's see about this other one." She started to scratch away on the second ticket as Eric looked on. Her eyes grew wide at the results. "I won ten dollars. Wow, I never win with these things," she exclaimed.

"Well, maybe I'm your lucky charm."

"Maybe you are. It's all yours now," she said, handing him the ticket.

"Thank you," he said, putting it in his pocket. "I still want to take you to dinner, if that's all right with you."

Her hunger pangs kicked in with the simple mention of food. She thought Eric was a nice guy and probably good company to be around. She had nothing to lose, and going to dinner with him would give her a chance to prove she wasn't a bad person, either. She smiled. "Dinner is fine."

"Great. So would you like to go now, or should I pick you up later?"

"We can go now," she said as her stomach lightly growled.

"Perfect. I have a good place in mind. It's actually not too far from here. We can walk there if you don't mind."

"Okay."

"First, before we go, I would like to start over. We need to have a formal introduction." He extended his hand. "Hello, my name is Eric. It's nice to meet you."

"Hello, Eric. My name is Shakita. It's nice to meet you as well." She smiled as she clasped his hand. They both started walking and getting to know each other. This was the beginning of their remarkable relationship.

"Good evening, Mr. Falls. We have a table ready for you," the maître d' greeted as they stepped inside The Palm Restaurant. Shakita was surprised that the host knew Eric by name. As they were led to their table, Eric engaged in short conversations with very distinguished-looking male patrons. She realized Eric had to be someone of importance. They were finally seated in a glass-enclosed private room. Shakita sat at the table in awe as she took in the panoramic city view. She had never been in such a classy setting and started to feel out of place. She tugged at her clothes as Eric took notice.

"Are you all right?"

"I've never been in a restaurant like this before. When you said dinner, I thought you were talking about a diner or somewhere like that. I'm so underdressed. Everything on this menu is so expensive. The sauce for the steaks is fifteen dollars. That's crazy. Fifteen dollars for sauce?"

Eric chuckled at Shakita's innocent concerns. He found it attractive that such a pretty girl had yet to really experience life. She was so unaccustomed to the fine conditions he was easily privileged to that he instinctively wanted to spoil her. He looked at her like she was a warm ball of clay that could be molded to his liking. He could put her on an elite status like he had done for so many women before her, only if she were willing.

"It's okay. You're dressed fine. Don't be afraid of the prices. Please order whatever makes your stomach happy. If I were you, I would get the filet mignon. It's amazing."

"Okay." She then checked the price of the steak. She shook her head realizing she had never eaten anything that expensive. The waiter came to the table and took their order. Shakita took a deep breath and smiled at Eric as their dinner date began.

After a few glasses of merlot, Shakita was completely at ease. Her stomach was full of the best-tasting steak she'd ever had, as well as being completely saturated by Eric's nifty charm. She loved how his words flowed from his mouth so smooth and effortlessly. She was so intrigued with Eric that she wanted to know everything about him, most importantly, what type of work he was into.

"So Eric, tell me. What profession are you in? And how do you know these people that are in here?" she asked as she sipped her wine.

Eric grinned as he placed his glass down on the table. "Well, I'm actually in a few professions. Those gentlemen you saw were clients of mine. I provide them special services."

"And what special services would those be?"

"Let me ask you this first. Have you ever heard of The Black Emporium?"

"No. What is that?"

"It's a spa that provides female companionship."

Shakita was in shock. "You run an escort service?"

"Not just an escort service. I like to call it an upscale pampering shop."

"Oh my God. I thought you were a lawyer or something."

"I was a lawyer, but now I'm an entrepreneur that serves the whole district. And those men you saw me talking to, guess what they do? They're members of Congress."

"Are you serious? You're involved in some straight-up *Scandal*-type shit. Have you met the real Olivia Pope?"

"Nope, and I'm not trying to either."

"Wow. What you do is so mind-blowing. I would have never imagined. How long have you been doing this?"

"I'll be celebrating five years in February. This business has been really good to me. I've been blessed with a great staff."

"So I guess your girls do pretty well for themselves?"

"They most certainly do." He grinned, taking notice of Shakita's increased curiosity.

"Let me ask you a question, Shakita. Have you ever stripped before?"

"No, but the way they be balling, I can honestly say I've thought about it plenty of times. Those hoes are out here winning."

"Believe me. My girls do more than ball out. They make more money in one month than most people make in a whole year. I think you should come check the spot out and see what you think about it. I guarantee with your raw beauty, you could do really well there."

Shakita never thought about working in a sex shop. Having sex for money was something that she always frowned upon. Now that she was eighteen, she'd started looking at the world in a whole new scope. Everyone that she knew with money was getting it the fast way. She was tired of struggling to keep her lights on while the hustlers thrived on the streets. Playing scratch-off lottery tickets wouldn't get her any real money, unless she was lucky. She figured working in a sex shop would get her in a better place, at least financially. She looked at Eric with hungry eyes as her curiosity continued to peak.

"So tell me more about The Black Emporium."

"I honestly would rather show you than tell you. Would you like to see it?"

"I think so." She scrunched up her face as nervous energy flowed through her.

"Well, let me take you there and if you don't like it, we can leave. Is that a deal?"

"I guess so." She smiled as she shrugged her shoulders.

"Okay then. Let's finish up this wine and be off."

Shakita didn't have any clue about the type of environment Eric would take her into, but felt he could be trusted. Eric filled up her glass as he prepared her for a life-changing experience.

Nine months had gone by and Shakita had quit working at The Black Emporium five times already. What she encountered there was too much for her to handle. Eric paid her well exactly like he'd promised, but it was what he didn't mention up front that made her detest his entire establishment. Not only was Eric a business owner, but he was also a drug dealer and pimp. He made his girls do drug runs all across the country. His girls had to have sex with the drug bosses, and then with the hustlers to whom delivered the product. Eric wanted to please his clientele on both ends, which he felt represented a superior business model.

Eric had as many clients coming through The Black Emporium as he did out in the streets. He controlled a sizeable prostitution ring that stretched all the way to Pittsburgh. Eric sought after clients who were too ashamed, or feared being seen by someone they knew walking into a sex shop. Eric understood that discretion was every customer's number one demand, and he was more than willing to fulfill their request, as long as a dollar amount was attached.

Shakita's gambling addiction got worse once she started working at The Black Emporium. Some of the other girls took weekly trips to Atlantic City and Shakita started going with them. The rush she got after winning five thousand dollars from a slot machine sent her over the edge. Scratch-off tickets were a thing of the past as she graduated to where the real money was being won: high-stakes gambling. The more she played, the further her addiction took control of her unbalanced life. She never wanted to return to the one place that had given her so much, but so little at the same time. Shakita declared that the last time she left The Black Emporium, it would be wiped clean from her memory, but once again she was back.

Shakita walked into the front door and saw that everything was actually the same as it was when she'd left there nine months ago. As she opened up the custom-made, wrought-iron door, she could smell the aroma of fresh-cut roses that were neatly dispersed throughout the structure. The scent from the roses interlaced with the perfume selection of the day that was used to increase the arousal of all male suitors. The walls in the spa were made of white marble with a fourteen-karat, gold-speckled pattern. All the decorations and furniture were inspired by ancient Rome with Julius Caesar-accented affiliations. The Black Emporium was the most beautiful, devilish nirvana that was wrapped up in four walls, and Shakita simply despised it.

Shakita walked past rows and rows of waiting clients as she walked to the receptionist desk. All the men looked at her with wondering eyes hoping she would be the girl whose services they would pay for. Shakita could feel their eyes on her, but she intentionally avoided looking at them, not wanting to provoke their yearning. The men continued to stare at her ass as she stood at the counter in her Lucky Brand jeans.

"I'm here to see Eric," Shakita said to the unfamiliar female receptionist.

"May I have your name?" the receptionist politely asked.

"It's Shakita. He's expecting me."

"Okay. One moment, Shakita," the receptionist said, as she picked up her phone to dial Eric's extension. "Eric. There is a Miss Shakita here to see you." The receptionist waited for his response and then hung up the phone. "All right, here's your card. He told me you know where his office is," the receptionist said, as she handed Shakita a silver access card.

The Black Emporium offered eight different service levels, which were all categorized by colored access cards. The cards came in pink, red, blue, yellow, orange, gold, purple, and black. The pink card was the lowest-level service card and the black was the highest. The silver card wasn't a service card at all and was only given out if a person were going to Eric's floor.

Shakita took her card and walked over to the elevator where she then flashed it at the guard who would allow her to get on the elevator. Once in the elevator, Shakita inserted her card into the access panel. "You are going to Level-Silver," the voice prompter informed her as the elevator began to move. The elevator passed all the other colored floors as it was programmed not to stop until it got to the silver level. "You are at Level-Silver. Please take your card," the voice prompter informed her again as the silver card was ejected right before the doors opened. Shakita took the card and stepped out of the elevator and was now in the center of Eric's office.

"Petita Shakita," Eric said as Shakita approached his desk. He had a lit cigar in his hand, but put it down in his ivory marble ashtray once Shakita was before him. He got up to give her a hug. It had been such a long time since he had seen her. "How are you?" he said as he held her tightly to his tall and well-groomed frame.

He was draped in a sandy, linen, custom-made Armani suit and wore a diamond-and-platinum Audemars Piguet watch. He always smelled of high-quality scents and looked even better.

"I'm not doing too good," Shakita said sadly, as she tightly embraced him.

"What's going on?"

"I'm in a little trouble, Eric."

"What kind of trouble?"

"I owe somebody a lot of money."

"What happened and how much?"

"I can't tell you what happened right now, but I owe them two hundred and fifty thousand."

Eric shook his head in disappointment. "How do you manage to get yourself in situations like this?"

Shakita dropped her head down in shame. "Just being stupid, I guess. I didn't mean for it to happen this way and now I really jammed myself up. You were the only one I could turn to for help."

Eric broke their clasp and moved himself away from her. "So I guess you want me to give you the money?"

"Not exactly give me the money. I mean I can pay you back any way I can. Just consider it a loan."

Eric positioned himself on top of his desk with his left arm resting on his thigh, while his right foot was still on the floor. "A loan?"

"Yes, a loan."

"If I can recall correctly, I've given you a loan before. Matter of fact, quite a few of them, and you've never paid me back. You always up and disappear and come back whenever you run into another problem. I don't know if I can do it anymore."

He was right, but Shakita still had to find a way to convince him that this time would be different.

"Look, Eric. I know I haven't made good on my promises in the past. But this time is different." Her eyes started to moisten. "This time I put other people in danger and it might cost us our lives. If you help me, I promise I will pay you back every dime. Please help me, Eric. I really need you more than ever right now."

Eric dropped his head to weigh out his options. He didn't know whether to believe Shakita this time or not. He had trusted her many times in the past and each time, she had abandoned her obligation to him. Yet, he had an emotional connection to her that he couldn't let go of. Not only did he feel deeply sorry for her, but also he was still secretly in love with her.

Eric loved so many qualities about Shakita and wished she could be his perfect lady, but her body and soul were too badly tainted. Shakita wasn't the right woman for him to risk his reputation and everything he'd worked hard for. Unfortunately, he was a glutton for punishment and couldn't help but to woo her every chance he got.

"All right, Shakita, I'll help you. I can't give you what you're asking for. A lot of my assets are tied up in investments, along with the development of four more Black Emporiums. But I can give you something."

Shakita felt relieved and wanted to stroke his ego a little, hoping to get him to change his mind and give her the full amount.

"Thank you so much. I really appreciate it. Only if you could really know how much I do." She looked around at her surroundings. "I can't believe you're adding on to what you built here so far. Are your new locations going to be in the city?"

"Not hardly, I'm thinking bigger than D.C. I'm opening up in Atlanta, Las Vegas, L.A., and Hong Kong."

"You're opening one in Hong Kong? Why there?"

"Hong Kong is a very rich region with a low taxation policy. It's a golden opportunity to start a global network from there. With Hong Kong's strong economic influence on Europe, the UK, Germany, France, and Italy will soon want a Black Emporium of their own."

"You are a marketing genius," Shakita said as she walked over to him and stood in between his legs. "You are so brilliant and you know exactly what you want in life. I wish I could be more like you," she said as she glided her hand across his firm chest.

Eric became weak when Shakita touched him, but he had to be strong and not give in to her flirtatious manner. He felt what she was doing and couldn't let her continue with her advances. "I can only give you ten thousand," he said as he stopped her hand from moving up his chest, then stared into her eyes. He waited for her reaction to see how grateful she was.

"Thank you so much, Eric. That really helps out a whole lot, but honestly, I need to find a way to get more. My life depends on it."

"I'm sorry, but that's the best I can do for now."

"How about workin' for you? Can I work for you, so I can get the rest of the money I need?"

"Do you really want to go back to tricking?"

"No. But right now I have no other choice. I need to get that money."

"Okay. You can work here until you get the money you need."

"In here? I can't work in here. You know I work better in the streets."

"True indeed, but you can make more money in here than you can make out there and with less risk. You already know the high-paying clients that come through here so this would be your best situation. If you're trying to make some big money quick, then I suggest that you do it."

"What about drug runs? Can I do those for you?"

"I'm fully legit now, baby. I've been out of the drug game for months now. The only thing I can offer you is in here."

Shakita didn't want to work under Eric's roof, but he was right. She could make more money working at the spa and avoid having to do illegal prostitution on the streets. She took Eric up on his offer. "Okay. I'll work here, but I really got to make some money."

"No problem. I'll put you on the gold floor. You should do well there."

"How come I can't be on the black or purple floor? Don't those floors make the most money?"

"Yes. But those floors are off-limits to you."

"I don't understand. Why can't I go on those floors?"

"I don't want you up there and that's the only explanation I'm going to give you."

Shakita wanted to know what was Eric's reasoning for not allowing her onto the floors, but she didn't want to aggravate him. "I'm sorry, Eric. I stepped out of line. It won't happen again."

"Don't apologize for what you said, just don't question me."

Shakita nodded her head making it clear that she understood.

"Now when do you want to start?"

"I wanna start now. I gotta make some money today."

"Do you have anything to wear?"

"Yeah. I have a few of my old lingerie sets at home. I could go get them."

"Don't bother. I want you to go shopping for some new pieces." He pulled a money clip full of hundreds out of his pocket. He removed the clip and gave her ten bills. She quickly stuffed them in her tight pants pocket and then gave him a hug. She wanted to tell him how thankful she was for the extra money, but before she could, he placed his fingers over her lips.

"Before you go shopping and start on the gold floor, I need to have you before anyone else does."

Shakita's pussy instantly became sodden from the slightest touch of his finger. She loved the way Eric desired her. She followed him into his master bedroom suite that connected to his office. Shakita had been in this room many times and everything still looked the same.

Shakita saw that the walls in the room were still painted burgundy as she walked across the glossy hardwood floor. The room was very well shaded by the drapes that kept the sun's rays from coming in. The plasma television was turned on with the volume muted as jazz music played low throughout the surround-sound theater system. Eric always had the mood set and that drove Shakita crazy. She stripped out of her clothes as Eric did the same. Shakita hadn't been with Eric in so long, and it felt good to be caught up in the moment with him again.

They found their way onto his king-sized bed as they passionately kissed. His warm mouth kissed lightly on her neck while his hands explored her endless curves. She was captivated by his touch and wanted him even more. He then cupped her soft breasts together and sucked her swollen nipples simultaneously. She arched her back as a sharp tingle traveled down her spine. He grabbed a condom from on top of the nightstand and quickly rolled it over his large mass. He circled his dick around her glazed lips several times and then entered her slowly.

She gasped as his thickness rippled in and out of her tight walls. Shakita dug her nails into Eric's hard muscles as he gave her more than she could handle. He was by far the best lover she ever had, and didn't know how a man could make her feel so damn good. Eric's dick was a diamond, and any woman in the world would want it to be their best friend. Every inch of his flawless stone graciously drilled out her insides. Her body soon fell into an enhanced state of ecstasy that released a sexual eruption, over and over again.

CHAPTER 6

After several hours of window shopping, and trying on outfits and dresses she couldn't afford, Latrice decided to call Shakita back. Shakita's phone continued to ring and then went to voicemail again. Latrice still didn't think anything of it, and went to her favorite restaurant, Tara Thai, to have a late lunch. Before Latrice had left the mall, she'd decided to buy one particular item, a pair of Oakley sunglasses. She thought she needed a pair of hot sunglasses, so she could look trendier, and wanted to be taken more seriously by Clarity. The success of Bangspot Records was highly riding on having Clarity sign to the label. Without Clarity, Latrice didn't know if she had enough time to secure another artist by Bay's release. Latrice needed her to get on board badly.

Latrice had a little over an hour left before she needed to be at the club. She decided to go back home to freshen up before the show. She had been trying on clothes all day and wanted to take a quick shower. When she got out of the shower, she touched up her hair, put on a red Bebe side-cutout mini dress, then picked out a pair of black pumps to match. She sprayed herself with her sweet-smelling Lancôme Miracle perfume, then looked in the mirror and hoped for a miracle tonight. Latrice put in her small, white-gold diamond hoop earrings and was now looking like she had money in the bank.

Latrice got down to the club at seven-thirty p.m., and noticed that there was already a long line that had formed outside the club. She had figured this would happen since Clarity was such a hot artist. She parked in the parking garage across the street from the Fantasy Lounge and walked over to the club. Latrice patiently stood in line, and waited for her turn to get in the club, as the line continued to wrap around the corner. At seven forty-five the doors opened and everyone started to pour in rapidly. Latrice's stomach knotted up as she anticipated the beginning of an interesting night.

The bartenders were busy serving up drinks to the rowdy crowd that waited for the first act to come on stage. A few minutes later the lights got low indicating that the show was about to start. Right before the first act made it to the stage, someone tapped Latrice on her shoulder. She turned around and saw that it was a guy that she had never seen.

"How are you doing tonight?" the tall, dark-skinned guy asked.

She smiled. "I'm doing good."

"I bought you a drink," he said as he held out a Long Island Iced Tea.

Latrice was confused. "You bought me a drink? But I don't even know you. I'm sorry, but I can't accept that."

"Why not?"

"I don't know you. You could have put some date rape drug in there, for all I know."

He raised the glass up to his mouth and took a big gulp from it. "Well, if it affects you, then it'll affect me." He smiled and held the drink out to her again.

Latrice liked his smile and charm but still couldn't take the drink from him. She didn't know him well enough.

"I'm sorry, but I still can't take the drink from you."

"Do you still think I put something in it?"

"Maybe, but even if I watched you get it from the bar, I still wouldn't drink it. I decided not to drink tonight. Now if you want me to pay you for the drink, I can do that, so you won't feel some type of way about it."

"No, it's okay. I wouldn't want it to go to waste. I'll just drink it myself," he said as he took a sip of the drink with the straw this time.

Latrice found him very attractive and didn't want him to think she was a stuck-up bitch. She decided to talk to him. "So what's your name?"

"Teyron. What's yours?"

"Latrice."

"It's nice to meet you, Latrice." Teyron extended his hand for her to shake it.

"It's nice to meet you as well."

"If you don't mind me asking, why aren't you drinking tonight?"

"I'm meeting with…wait a minute, what type of business are you in?" She didn't know if he might have been there to sign Clarity, too. Latrice had to choose her words carefully.

"I'm a singer."

Latrice gave out a silent sigh of relief. "What type of singer are you?"

"R and B, baby."

"That's very interesting. Are you signed to a label?"

"Not yet. But I will be."

"Are you in a group or are you solo?"

"I'm solo. I used to be in a group, but they didn't have the same focus as I did."

"And what focus is that?"

"To be number one. I'm gonna be the future of R and B."

"Have you met with any labels yet?"

"Not yet. But once they hear my demo, they're gonna be all on ya boy."

"Well, I'm starting a label soon. I would like to hear your demo."

"You're gonna start a label? Really?"

"Yes. I'm actually here to see Clarity. I'm trying to sign her to my label."

"Are you serious? I'm tryna to get her to rap on one of my songs."

"Maybe that could be possible. Have you heard of Killa D and Piff?"

"Hell yeah. Who haven't?"

"Well, they're already signed. You never know, they could be on one of your songs, too." Latrice could see she had his interest and Teyron thought him meeting her was too good to be true.

"So Teyron. When can I get one of your demos?"

Teyron only had one demo CD with him and he was planning on giving it to Clarity. He really wanted to get Clarity on a track with him, but if he could get a deal and have Clarity as a possible label mate, then he would have a double win. Teyron had to take a chance with Latrice. He reached in his back pocket and handed her his CD.

"Now that's the only copy I have on me. I was gonna give it to Clarity, so I hope you take the music serious."

"Believe me. I definitely will." She gave him a small smirk. "If I don't like your music, then I'll still pass it on to Clarity. Even if she does not sign to my label, having me give her your demo would be a better look for you. Ya dig?"

Teyron felt confident he'd made the right choice by giving Latrice his demo, but he needed to ask her one question.

"What is the name of your label?" Latrice could've been blowing smoke up his ass and he needed to know who he was handing his work over to. Latrice could be a *crook*.

"Bangspot Records. We're going to be the biggest thing in hip-hop."

"I'm feeling that name. Do you have a business card?"

"You know I do." She handed him the card and he studied the information on it.

He liked what he saw and could tell Latrice was the real deal. "So if you like my sound, do you really think you can make me a star?"

"Baby boy, if I like you, then you ain't just gonna be a star; you're goin' shine like a mothafucker. Ya dig? Bangspot is going to take over shit. You can believe that."

Teyron and Latrice continued to talk about the business as the two rappers performed. Neither group was anything out of the ordinary to boast about, and was only a reminder of how good Clarity really was. The crowd went crazy once Clarity's hype man, Dull, hit the stage.

"What's up, D.C.?" The crowd continued to holler and scream. "I said what the fuck is up, D.C.!" The crowd got even louder. "Tonight! The realest bitch in the world is about to rip this motha-fucka up! Are y'all ready?" The crowd continued to scream. "I said, are y'all fuckin' ready?" The crowd got so loud that the whole club felt like it was shaking. "D.C.! Here she is! It's Clarity!"

The instrumental from Jay-Z's song "Can I Live" came on and Clarity hit the stage. Clarity was a sexy, thick redbone with long, curly hair that stopped at the middle of her back. She was rocking a tight, black cotton mini dress that easily flaunted her well-shaped figure. She strutted across the stage wearing some black Gucci frames and black three-inch heels. Latrice had never seen Clarity and didn't know how pretty she was. There was no doubt that Clarity would be very marketable and that the fellas would be all over her, too. Latrice wanted to sign her even more now.

Clarity started to spit. "Y'all know fake-bitches be makin' me sick—So when they see me, I don't see 'em in the Benz, 'cause my tints be extra thick—I'm on some killer, I'ma murder shit—I bust my gun, I got 'em —I don't run, I get my nigga Dull to scoop me quick—I'm really 'bout my paper, bitch!—You betta pay me, Poppo/ For that brick—Or I'll send el goupo to come bust ya 'shit—I'm the topic of a lot of shit—Like who's money she's stuffing—Who's she fucking—And who's the bitch she's mean mugging—I'm the shit and I'm loving it—I'm the best bitch in the game—Ain't even playing with the cards I get—So when they deal—And say you gotta play that shit—Just say fuck 'em—Make something from nothing—And get it how you live, youngin'."

Latrice was blown away by Clarity's lyrics. She thought she could rap better than most guys and thought her delivery was crazy. She hadn't seen a female rapper with her type of intensity and caliber since Lil' Kim. If Clarity was on her label, other rappers in the game would seriously have to step their shit up. Clarity performed for another half hour doing songs that no one had ever heard. The crowd went crazy when Clarity finally left the stage. Latrice couldn't wait to talk to her. The music came back on and everyone started dancing and going back to the bar again to get more drinks.

"Damn. Her performance was something else. Her ass made me wanna try to rap," Teyron proclaimed.

"Hell yeah. She's the hottest bitch out right now," Latrice replied.

Without Latrice even noticing, Fantasy came up behind her and tapped her on her shoulder.

"Latrice, right?"

"Hey, Fantasy." Latrice looked at Fantasy and saw she still had on the same raggedy clothes that she'd had on earlier. The only thing Fantasy did differently to herself was change her shoes. She replaced her old beat-up Reeboks with some flat dress shoes. Latrice knew that Fantasy looked like a hot ghetto-ass mess, and thought that saying "fuck it" was her style.

"Did you enjoy the show?" Fantasy asked.

"Hell yeah. Clarity is like that, for real."

"So are you ready to meet her?"

Latrice was so excited that she couldn't even talk. All she could do was nod her head yes. "All right, follow me."

Latrice looked over at Teyron. "If I don't see you before the club let out, call me in a few days so I can tell you what I think of your demo." Teyron assured her he would call as he watched her follow Fantasy onto the crowded dance floor.

Fantasy took Latrice to the back of the club. Clarity was waiting for her in a private room. Latrice was getting nervous and didn't know what she was going to say to Clarity when she finally met her. She had a one-shot deal to sign Clarity and didn't want to say anything stupid to fuck up her chances.

I got Killa D and Piff to sign with me. But that was done over the phone. I gotta do this shit face-to-face now, Latrice said to herself hoping she could get over her anxiety.

Fantasy knocked on Clarity's private room and waited for someone to come to the door. Latrice's heart was beating fast as hell when Dull opened the door. Dull was a tall, brown-skinned cat with a goatee and long dreads. He looked just as intimidating on the stage to Latrice as he did off of it.

"What's up, Fantasy?" Dull said as he pulled the door back to let them both in. Dull licked his lips as he looked at Latrice when she walked past him. She noticed and gave him a wink to get on his good side. Latrice had a strategy of her own. Whose opinion did Clarity admire more than Dull's? If Dull liked Latrice, that would give Clarity all more of a reason to sign with her. When Latrice got around the corner, Clarity was in her clear view.

Clarity was leaned back in a leather chair in front of a square table smoking a blunt, as she sipped on a cup of peach Cîroc.

"Yo, Clare. This is the girl I was tellin' you about," Fantasy informed her as they walked over to the table.

Clarity put down her blunt and got up to shake Latrice's hand. "How you doing?"

"I'm doing good now that I finally got the chance to meet you."

"I don't know about that. The pleasure might be mine." Clarity gave Latrice a slight grin. "Please have a seat so we can talk." Clarity pulled out a chair for Latrice to sit in. Fantasy saw it was time to make her exit and let Latrice know she was leaving.

"I'm outta here. You got it from here? You got me later, right?"

"Whatchu mean?"

Fantasy gave her that *"come on now, bitch, you should already know"* look, and waited for Latrice to comprehend. *Damn. I just gave this bitch a hundred dollars. Now she wants more.*

Latrice was going to pay her again for the services, since she did set up the meeting, but was only going to compensate her on how well the meeting turned out. "I gotchu," Latrice replied.

After Fantasy knew she was getting some more money out of Latrice, she quickly left the room smiling. Shortly after Fantasy was gone, Clarity gave Dull the sign to leave them alone as she passed him the blunt.

"I'm gonna go see what's up with these bitches out there," Dull said as he departed smoothly.

"So what's ya name?" Clarity asked as she lit up another blunt.

"Latrice."

Clarity smiled. "That's cute."

"Thank you, Clarity."

"My real name is Claretta, but you can just call me Clare."

Latrice started to relax knowing that Clarity was chilled and not boisterous now that she was offstage.

"Where are you from?" Clarity asked.

"I'm from Northwest, Seventh and P. What about you?"

Clarity blew out smoke. "I'm straight up Potomac Gardens." Clarity was all about business and wanted to get straight to the point. "So you here to see about signing me?"

"Yes. But first I want to say, I love your music and I'm a big fan."

Clarity nodded her head and smiled, showing Latrice that she'd accepted her compliment. "You're the best thing out and you know how to give the crowd what they want. Latrice felt she had Clarity's attention and continued to go for it. "I'm about to build the biggest label that anyone has ever seen. I got some of the best producers and marketing concepts that will be sure to put any artist that signs with me guaranteed platinum success. The label I'm talking about is Bangspot...Bangspot Records."

"It sounds good and all, but how someone who's about to start a label do something that the majors can't even do? With all the downloading ring tones, and all that other bullshit that's happening. How can you guarantee platinum?"

"It's quite simple. Bangspot is not only going to be a label, but it's going to be a distribution company as well. My business partner discovered that there is a ROM company in Sweden that manufactures CDs that can only be burned once, and are not rewriteable. Not only that, but there is no downloading software available that can override the disk and force them to rewrite."

"Okay. I see how that stops the bootlegs from happening, but what about radio play and ring tones? How can I still benefit off of that?"

"The CDs that get sent to the radio stations will be edited versions on the same type of disk, and with ring tones, fans will only be able to download a portion of a song. Nothing can be copied, only produced. And everybody still makes money. The only ones who don't get shit are the *crooks*."

Clarity was pretty much sold now, but she had one more question. "What happens when someone creates software that can override the CDs and copy 'em?"

"They already have. As a matter of fact, several companies have found solutions, but by law they aren't allowed to use them since the ROM Company has a patent protection on their product that lasts for the next eleven years. By then you'll be rich as hell and out the game and you wouldn't be affected. So if you want to get down with a sure thing, the time is now."

Clarity was feeling everything Latrice was saying and wanted to find out where she should sign her name on the contract. She wanted to have all the platinum success that Latrice had talked about and more. Since Latrice promised to bring her more money and fame, she was willing to take a risk of a lifetime. But before she signed her life away, only going off of Latrice's vision alone, Clarity had a little proposition of her own—one that Latrice never saw coming.

"All right, ma. I'm with everything you saying; you talking big shit and I like it. So as long as all the advance money and royalties are right, we got a deal."

"Thank you so much. You made the right choice. I won't let you down." Latrice was so ecstatic that she wanted to jump on Clarity and hug her.

"Hold up, doe, mommi. I agreed to get down with you and all. But for it to really happen, I need you to do a little somethin' for me."

At this point in the game, if Clarity needed a special favor, Latrice was willing to do it. She was willing to do anything to secure her artist.

Latrice smiled. "You name it and it's done."

"I want you to come home with me," Clarity said, giving her a devilish grin.

"Excuse me?" Latrice said, wanting to make sure she'd heard her correctly.

"I said I want you to spend the night with me. Did you hear that clear enough?"

"I had no idea you were a lesbian."

"I'm not a lesbian. I'm bi. There's a big difference. Don't get it twisted. I still love dick."

"I'm sorry. I didn't mean to offend you. I just don't usually have this type of conversation."

"It's all right. I ain't taking that shit to heart. I know you look at me and think there's no way this bitch could like pussy. But I do. I'm feeling you like that and I know what I want. So what's it going to be?"

"I'm sorry, Clare. But I don't get down like that."

Clarity shrugged her shoulders. "All right then. It was nice to meet you."

Latrice was confused. "Wait a minute. Since I won't fuck you, then you're not signing with me?"

"Look, baby. You're not the only one that's trying to sign my ass. It is what it is," Clarity said, giving Latrice a devilish smirk.

Latrice couldn't believe what the fuck was going on right now. Clarity had given her an ultimatum in which she could never imagine happening. All of the hard work and sacrifice that she had put into chasing "The Dream" had been tested. Latrice need-ed to sign Clarity bad and couldn't believe that the tables had turned on her severely. She had to make the best decision even if it went against everything she believed in. Latrice was now on the verge of being desperate.

"So let's say I do decide to be with you tonight," Latrice said meekly. "Does that mean you're definitely going to sign with me?"

Clarity moved in closer to Latrice and gave her a serious look. "If you allow what I want to happen tonight, I promise you on everything I love that I will sign with you. You have my word on it."

Latrice rested her hand on her forehead, and couldn't believe that she was actually considering going home with another woman. That shit completely boggled her mind to no end. But unfortu-nately, she had to conform and do what had to be done, especially if she wanted Clarity to be on her team.

"All right, I guess I got to do what I got to do, right?" Latrice said unhappily as she started to feel sick to her stomach.

"Nobody has a perfect situation, mommi. You just got to make the best of ya own."

Latrice understood exactly what she meant. Clarity had to trust Latrice with her career, hoping she would do the right thing. Latrice realized they both had something to lose and gain by dealing with each other, and she could afford to take a gamble.

"If we're going to do this, I got to get drunk and high first. I need to really be fucked up for this one."

Clarity opened up the bottle of Cîroc and then filled up a cup with ice. She filled up Latrice's cup to the rim and placed it in her hand.

"Drink as much as you think you can handle," Clarity said, passionately wrapping her hands around Latrice's hand. Latrice anticipated running through the entire bottle, just so she could make it through the night.

CHAPTER 7

Latrice rushed into the bathroom and quickly sat down on the toilet seat. She had drunk so much vodka and felt like her bladder was about to burst. After she was done, she wobbled over to the sink to wash her hands, and started to fumble with the liquid soap dispenser.

"I'ma real drunk bitch right now," Latrice said out loud to herself. She looked in the mirror and laughed nonstop. While she was washing her hands, she noticed that the bathroom she was in didn't belong to her. In fact, she didn't know whose bathroom she was using, or how she'd managed to get there. Latrice came out of the bathroom looking for a clue to where she was, and that's when she saw Clarity lying on the bed.

"What took you so long to come out? Come here."

"I don't know," Latrice said, continuing to laugh as Clarity laid her down.

"I thought you were scared of me. Are you scared of me, mommi?" Clarity asked as she rubbed on Latrice's leg.

"I'm not scared of you," Latrice said after she became comfortable with Clarity caressing her ass and thighs. Clarity kissed all over Latrice's neck as she slowly lifted up her dress. Latrice began to breathe heavily and that's when Clarity realized she had her.

Clarity kissed Latrice's soft lips repeatedly, until Latrice allowed her to place her tongue in her mouth. They started to kiss passionately as Clarity undid her bra, massaging Latrice's hard nipples. Clarity yielded from sucking on Latrice's lips so she could finish undressing her. Latrice arched her back so that Clarity could remove her dress and panties. Clarity stepped off the bed and slipped her dress over her head. She threw her bra and let her thong fall to the floor. Now they were both completely naked and Clarity's box was starting to throb.

Clarity climbed on top of Latrice and quickly slid her tongue in her mouth. Latrice's body was feeling like it was on fire, which she had never felt before. Every part of her body was tingling and Clarity's slightest touch caused her body to vibrate. Latrice didn't know if this unusual sensation was coming from her having her first female experience or something else. Whatever it was, she couldn't help feeling all giddy inside, as Clarity rolled her tongue down her stomach. Clarity loved her dark-chocolate skin and continued to maneuver her way down Latrice's love trail until she was face-to-face with her lotus flower.

Clarity licked her lips eager to get a taste of Latrice's juicy melt. This is what she had wanted to do ever since she'd first laid eyes on Latrice.

If she didn't plan on making good on her promises before, I know after tonight she will, Clarity said as she spread Latrice's wet hairless lips. She plunged her face into her flowing, warm mass and felt like she had died and gone to heaven once she tasted the sweet and slick nectar. Clarity became more aroused after swallowing Latrice's flavor and didn't want to stop until her well was completely dry.

But instead of Latrice drying out, she did the opposite and got even wetter as her walls tightened, releasing a force that made her momentarily paralyzed. The only thing Latrice could do was scream as Clarity continued to please her. Once Clarity finally released

Latrice's pleasure button, she sat back and watched the after-effects of her sex therapy. Latrice gasped for air and felt dehydrated as she became extremely sleepy from all the alcohol she'd consumed. She closed her eyes and didn't want the tingly feeling to stop racing all through her body. Latrice soothingly drifted off to sleep.

CHAPTER 8

atrice's head was throbbing so badly that she didn't even want to open her eyes. She could feel the light coming from the blinds burning her brow and realized it was morning. She felt fatigued and icky, and could feel the hands of another touching her body. She struggled to open her eyes so she could get a peek at who was with her. She took a faint look and made out that it was Clarity who was between her legs. Latrice felt horrible and resentful about what was going on, and wanted Clarity to stop what she was doing to her. Latrice scooted away from her so she could stop licking on her body.

"Please stop," Latrice said as she leaned up against the headboard.

"What's wrong? You don't like it no more?" Clarity asked as she wiped her mouth clean of all Latrice's juices.

"I don't know. I just want you to stop. I feel sick as hell."

"I'm sorry. I'll stop. I can't help it, you taste so good, mommi."

Latrice cringed at the sight of another female in between her legs, and wished she could forget what happened the night before. She felt so disgusted.

Latrice held her aching head. "Can I have some water or something? I feel dehydrated like shit."

"I got you, baby." Clarity walked to the kitchen completely naked and came back with a tall glass of ice water and some aspirin. Clarity had no doubt that Latrice was definitely going to need the aspirin.

"Here you go." Clarity handed her the glass of water and two capsules. Latrice swallowed the two capsules and quickly drank all the water. "Wow, I really needed that. Can I have some more water, please?"

"That 'E' makes you thirsty, don't it?"

Latrice gave her a puzzled look. "What 'E'?"

"Ecstasy. What else, baby?"

"You had me taking fucking Ecstasy? Why would you do that?"

"I offered it and you took it. You said you wanted to be completely out of it, remember?"

Latrice felt stupid for taking the drug and wanted to get the hell out of there.

"What time is it?" Latrice asked, looking around for a clock.

"It's ten thirty-eight."

"Oh shit! I gotta go." Latrice hopped up to put on her clothes. She felt sharp pains in her head after every movement she made.

"What's wrong? Why you got to leave so quickly?"

"I got to catch a call that I'm supposed to get at eleven. I can't miss that shit."

"I need to get your number before you go." Clarity walked over to her purse to retrieve her cell phone.

Once Latrice was dressed, they both exchanged numbers, and promised they would keep in touch and talk about doing business.

Latrice got in her car and found it very difficult to drive with her excruciating headache. By the time she pulled up to her apartment building, it was 11:02 a.m. She hoped Bay hadn't called yet and hurried to get out of the car. As she ran through the entrance doors, she heard the phone ringing. She skipped steps trying to make it to the third floor in time. She quickly put her keys in the door, and once she was running over to the phone, it had stopped ringing. Latrice was devastated.

Latrice was so blown that she missed Bay's call that she plopped down in a chair and threw her purse across the room. She knew Bay could easily try to call back again, but the amount of anger he would have when he did wasn't worth the stress. Bay hated when his instructions weren't followed through correctly, and those who didn't follow them received heavy consequences due to their error. He was very violent and Latrice didn't want to have anything to do with making him upset, and taking out his rage on her when he came out, but it may have been too late. Latrice thought about everything she'd accomplished the day before and hoped it was enough to keep Bay off her ass. She had successfully secured the signing of two diffcrent acts and the possibility of a third. She had everything set in place to establish the record label and now only needed Bay's approval. But she wouldn't know how Bay would perceive her efforts until he called back again.

CHAPTER 9

Shakita woke up to the smell of coffee and a fully dressed Eric, sitting on his sofa and staring at her. She didn't realize she had slept through the night, but appreciated how refreshed she felt as her eyes adjusted to the light.

"Did you sleep good?" Eric asked as he spun his coffee cup around in his hand on the table in front of him.

"Yes. It felt like the best sleep ever." Shakita stretched and then rolled out of bed before she wrapped the satin sheet around her. She walked over to Eric and sat beside him.

"I got you some coffee." Eric peered his eyes down at the other cup that was on the table.

Shakita picked up the cup and smelled the aroma coming from the lip opening. "I love Saxby's coffee."

"I remember. How could I forget?"

Eric had known so much about Shakita that sometimes it scared her. He was aware what could make her laugh, make her cry, and everything else in between. He was like her unclaimed soul mate. Shakita took a sip of the coffee and savored the taste of the caramel, espresso, and white chocolate blend. It was exactly what she needed after an incredible night of sex.

"After you drink your coffee, you can get dressed and go shopping."

Shakita nodded her head yes as she took another sip of the hot delicious brew.

Eric then rose to his feet. "I'll give you the money after you finish working tonight."

"Thank you so much, Eric. I appreciate everything you're doing for me."

"It's no problem. It's no problem at all." Eric started to walk away but stopped and turned to her. "Oh yeah. You start on the gold floor at eight p.m." He then looked at his watch. "So that gives you ten hours to roam. Don't be late."

"I won't."

He gave her a wink and then walked out of the room as he sipped his coffee.

Shakita curled up on the couch and thought about the night ahead of her. She had never worked on the gold floor and didn't know what to expect. She hoped to get the money she needed for Latrice really fast. She didn't know what she was going to be doing on the gold level but was so curious to find out. She needed to get herself ready so she could go shopping to get some outfits to wear for work.

She got in the shower and put on the same clothes once she stepped out, except for her bra and underwear. She threw her undergarments in the wastebasket knowing she was about to get all brand-new stuff. She pressed the button for the elevator and once it arrived, she inserted her card again. The elevator took her directly to the lobby where she passed the guard again, and then walked over to the receptionist to turn in her card.

"Thank you. And I will have your gold card for you when you return."

Shakita wasn't surprised that the receptionist was already aware of who she was. Eric had a keen way of keeping all his people informed about everything that was going on. Eric loved to keep his operation running smoothly.

"Thank you," Shakita said as she smiled at the receptionist before walking out the door.

Shakita's first stop was Victoria's Secret. She needed to get all the right outfits so that the customers would spend more money with her. Victoria's Secret was the perfect place. Since the floor she was working on had the gold theme, she needed to get all matching accessories. She picked out some white, black, and gold teddies and baby-doll halters.

When she was finally done shopping, she managed to still have one hundred and eighty-five dollars left from the thousand that Eric had given her. She wished she wouldn't have spent that much money, but she strongly believed that it took money to make money. The new wardrobe was an investment for all the money she would make the rest of the week. The money she had left and the money she planned to make tonight would be used to go gambling. She had to make as much as she could in hopes to win everything back that she'd lost.

Shakita had time to kill after she was done shopping and wanted to drop off all of her bags at her apartment before she went to work. As she was en route to her house, her phone started to ring. She looked at her phone and saw that Latrice was calling her again. "Damn!" Shakita said as she put her phone back in her purse. She thought that maybe Latrice knew that the money was missing and was trying to question her about it. Latrice already told her that she couldn't flip any of the money and would be the first person to come to if the shit came up missing.

When her phone stopped ringing, she reached back in her purse and pulled out a cigarette. She lit up the cigarette and turned up the stereo on full blast. She drove nervously trying to think of a way to tell Latrice what had happened to the money if she were accused of taking it. She couldn't think of a more logical way of explaining than simply telling the truth. Shakita was only willing to do that if she were caught in the act. Shakita planned to avoid Latrice as long as she could in order to stall for more time. She only had a month to make it all happen.

Shakita arrived back at the spa around 7:30 p.m. That gave her a good half hour to get comfortable before she started working. When she walked through the door, she could see dozens of men waiting for their appointments. She quickly eyeballed all the customers wondering which one of them would be her first client. She thought that he might not even be there yet, so she continued to the receptionist area.

"Welcome back," the receptionist said, giving her a bright smile.

"Thanks." Shakita wondered if the lady were very happy to see her or really loved her job.

"Here's your card."

Shakita looked at the two-toned gold card as it sparkled in her hand. "Thank you."

"You're welcome. My name is Monique. If you need any assistance from me, just pick up any phone on the floor and dial one."

"Okay, Monique. Thank you."

"You're welcome. Please have a good night."

"One more thing, Monique, before I go. Are any of these men here my first appointment?" Shakita whispered.

Monique looked over the sign-in sheet before she could give Shakita an answer. "No. He hasn't arrived yet."

Shakita became relaxed and no longer had a problem looking at the men now.

"Thanks. I'll see you later, Monique."

"Okay. Remember to call me if you need anything."

Shakita nodded her head and smiled while walking to the elevator. She once again flashed her card at the guard before he let her pass. She pressed the button and within seconds the doors opened. She inserted her card into the panel and the voice prompter told her she was going to the gold level.

When she stepped onto the gold marble floor, she was amazed at how glamorous everything looked. Shakita was overwhelmed with all the great designer features that the floor had to offer. In the foyer there were white leather sofas with matching coffee and end tables. Each coffee table had a large oval gold bowl filled with water and white floating candles. The end tables had clear Duncan & Miller footed vases on them filled with white roses. There were tall bronze statues of angels and knights that were spaced out along the floor. The entire area smelled of cinnamon and lilac, which was a pleasant combination to anyone who came on the floor.

Shakita began to walk the hall as crystal chandeliers hung over her head. The walls were painted metallic gold with expensive paintings that hung from them that Shakita couldn't help to look at as she passed. She then looked on the bottom of her card to see what room she would be working out of tonight. She saw that the card had "G8" on the bottom of it and began looking for that room. She was almost at the end of the hallway and saw the door with "G8." She inserted her card in the door and waited for the green light to flash allowing her entrance. The green light flashed and Shakita made her way into the room. She was more than impressed with the complete layout of the huge suite. To the left of the room there was a square-shaped Jacuzzi with a wet bar surrounding it. On the other side of the room there was a living room with a white fluffy sectional, a large glass table, along with a sixty-inch flat-screen television.

Behind the living room, there was a massage table and directly in the center at the end of the dining area was the bedroom. Shakita walked through the sheer gold curtains and walked into the white and gold heavily decorated bedroom. Inside the bedroom there was a bathroom that Shakita walked into so she could change her clothes. The bathroom had a round tub with a walk-in shower. Shakita set her bag down on the sink and gazed into the mirror. She looked at how pretty she was and felt confident she would do good tonight. Her first client was going to be there shortly so she had to get dressed.

Shakita looked herself over in the mirror once more as she sprayed on her perfume. She was applying some lip gloss when she heard the front door open. Her heart started to flutter, as being face to face with her first client was becoming a reality. She took a deep breath and strutted slowly out of the bathroom.

Shakita separated the curtains and saw her client sitting down in the living room. She could only see the back of him and was curious to know what he looked like. The man heard Shakita approaching and he turned around to see her. His eyes were as amazed at what he saw like Shakita's were. He was a tall, fair-skinned man wearing a gray suit with a black dress shirt. He was damn sure easy on the eyes, which made Shakita want to fuck him for the hell of it. If they would have met on different circumstances, she probably would have, but since it was about getting money, she couldn't afford to give away any free pussy.

The man looked Shakita up and down from head to toe and was marveled by her good looks and amazing body. Shakita was wearing a white lace teddy and gold heels with her hair pinned up in a bun. The man couldn't help himself to say something to her.

"Hey. How are you doing?" he asked smoothly.

n your company," Shakita spoke seduc-

t's funny. I was feeling the same way
ne, sweetheart?"

imp." It was for the girls' protection
nes to try and avoid stalkers.

can call me Danny."

ou like me to do for you first?"

rt off by telling me how you got

s your favorite game to play?"

te."

g with my life."

but I gamble with my life
e good at it," Danny said,

in bad at it."

hing? We have to pin-
e were born to do."

ving her a life lesson.

g?"

ead a lot of motiva-

w what book he was
he last time I read a

whole world of information that's right at your fingertips. Y

could help you with your life gamblin

"That's a good idea. Maybe I'll look

"If I can be of any assistance, let me

"I certainly will." Shakita didn't wa

more and wanted to move on to other

my name, can I make you a drink?"

"Yes, you may."

"What would you like?" Shak

the refrigerator that was part of

"How about starting off with

Shakita opened up the fridge

chill. The red level only stocke

to this type of treatment. She

champagne flutes from the r

the middle of both glasses a

thing else that piqued her i

Shakita grabbed a small

were in a bowl on the botto

Shakita thought that add

icing on the cake. She

as possible.

Make that money, gi

herself walking back

ish smile on her fa

"I'm good now that I'm i tively.

The man laughed. "That about you. What's your na

"You can call me Miss Tr not to give out their real nar

"And your name?"

"My name is Daniel, but you

"Okay, Danny. What would yo

"Well, Miss Trump. You can sta that name."

"I love to gamble."

"You love to gamble, huh? What'

"My favorites are slots and roulet

"Then what is your worst?"

"My worst are keno…and gamblin

"I never tried my luck with keno, every day, and so far I've become qui laughing.

"Well, right now, I'm doing pretty dam

"You know we all can't be good at everyt point our talents and be the best at what w

Shakita thought it was cute that he was "Are you some type of professor or somet

"No. Actually I'm an investment banke tional books during my down time."

Shakita didn't read much so she didn't referencing from. "I don't read that ofte book was in high school."

"That's too bad. You're missing out o

ou should find a book that

g problem."

for one."

know."

ht to talk about herself any-
subjects. "Now that you know

ita asked, as she walked over to
the wet bar.

a little bit of champagne?"

and saw three bottles of Cristal on
d Moët in which Shakita wasn't use
took out a bottle and removed two
ack. She filled the champagne up to
nd went back in the fridge for some-
nterest.

handful of fresh-cut strawberries that
om shelf, and placed some in both glasses.
ing the strawberries was like putting the
was going to get Danny to spend as much

Make that mothafucking money, she said to
him and carrying both glasses with a devil-

sleep after missing Bay's call since
an excruciating headache. It was
awakened by her hungry stom-
to eat. She walked slowly into
she struggled to put a frozen
ate her pizza and drank some
ill couldn't believe what she'd
the deed served its purpose.
ut so that Clarity would be
d out before she was able to
have is a wet pussy to show
that so she needed to keep
nt through.

trice remembered that she
Teyron's music was what she
ty for a minute, and on to
d his CD out of her purse
ayer. She plugged in some
o she could get comfortable.
was struck by the sound of the
ittle louder so she could really
back of the CD case to see if

there were any song titles. She was plea

so she could familiarize herself with the

of five songs and the first track was enti

thought that Teyron was some ordina

started to sing on, she was blown awa

As Teyron sang, Latrice thought h

tween Raheem DeVaughn and Tre

own unique style. Latrice closely lis

stood he was talking about how

with his girlfriend. She thought

his girl was so damn sexy in her

her to leave. He wanted to us

wanted them to start over fres

good to be the sexy woman t

fuck'em dresses and loved pu

time was right. Latrice could

song.

The next track was so goo

heat between her legs. Each

his girlfriend was the same

nipples started to harden, i

her body. Latrice was so mu

eyes and found her hand lost

on by Teyron's aggressive ly

with herself. Latrice licke

waited for the next one to

turn-on, which caused her

fingered herself forcefully. L

jumped up when the CD abru

believe that she'd gotten so cau

atrice had gone back to
she was tired and still had
late evening when she was
ach and needed to get something
the kitchen still feeling out of it, as
pizza in the microwave. After Latrice
juice, she started to feel better. She st
done the previous night and hoped
She couldn't wait for Bay to get o
locked into her deal. If Clarity backe
sign a contract, then all Latrice woul
for it. Latrice definitely didn't want
close tabs on Clarity until the deal we

While thinking about Clarity, La
still had Teyron's demo. Hopefully, T
needed to get her mind off of Clari
other potential artists. Latrice grabbe
and put it into her portable DVD pl
headphones and lay back in her bed s
The first song came on and Latrice
beat. She turned the volume up a l
hear the music. She looked on the

sed to see that there were

e music. There were a total

led "Krispy Klean." Latrice

ry singer, but when Teyron

y by his sound.

e sounded like a cross be-

y Songz, yet still having his

tened to the lyrics and under-

he'd gotten into an argument

about leaving him. He thought

fuck'em dress that he didn't want

e sex to save his relationship. He

n. "Krispy Klean" made Latrice feel

nat she was. She had a full closet of

ting each one of them on when the

relate oh so well to this make-up sex

d it started to make Latrice feel the

spot that Teyron said he touched on

places that made Latrice weak. Her

magining that Teyron was touching

ch into the hook that she closed her

in her boy shorts. She was so turned

rics that she began to be aggressive

her lips as the song faded out and

start. Latrice found his confidence a

o become wetter and wetter as she

atrice was so into herself that she

ptly stopped playing. She couldn't

ght up in his music that it had led

her to masturbate. This was a first for her and she was convinced something had to be special about Teyron and his music. Teyron was going to be a rare commodity in the music business, and Latrice was going to make sure that she signed him as soon as she could.

With three hot artists in the game, Bangspot would be moving units like no other label had been able to do in months. Latrice could see the big picture clearly and immediately saw dollar signs in her eyes. She liked his demo so much that she started the CD over so she could hear it again. This time, she was going to try not to play with herself again. Now knowing what she knew about Teyron, she now had two reasons to be looking forward to his call.

CHAPTER 11

Shakita's last client threw a large amount of money on the bed to show his great generosity for her pleasurable service. He left out the door grinning, as Shakita lay wrapped up in the sheets waving and blowing kisses, giving him a sweet farewell. She indeed left a long-lasting impression on him that would force his return. Once the door shut, she rested her head on a pillow, and eyeballed the pile of money, wondering what her total in tips added up to for the night. Her 8 pm start time had came and went. It was well past four in the morning and Shakita had finished with her sixth and final client of the night. She'd had two two-hour sessions and four one-hour sessions and was totally worn out.

Shakita pussy was so sore that she thought she might need to pack herself with ice. It'd been a long time since she'd had more than five clients in one day, and she'd forgotten how painful the aftermath was. She already had taken six showers and was too tired to take another one, but she had to get the dried-up sweat from the last client off of her body. Shakita gathered up all her tips to see how well she'd done. She counted and was completely satisfied with the amount she held in her hand. In one night she'd racked up $3,200 in tips, which didn't include the percentage she would get from each service that the clients paid for.

She had no idea what that percentage would be. She'd never made tips like this. She was looking to cash a pretty fat check.

Shakita reflected on her first night of work and smiled thinking about all the nice gentlemen that filled up her pockets. Some of them got more than their money's worth by asking for strange requests that Shakita didn't mind fulfilling. The customers knew exactly how far they were allowed to go.

Out of all the men she had been with tonight, the one who'd struck a chord with her the most was Danny. Danny was attractive, well dressed, and intelligent. He knew how to please her in the most sensual way. He wasn't too rough or too gentle and knew how to use his hands. He was the only one that night who was able to find her "spot" and keep "it" there. All the other men came to please themselves and ignored any desires that she may have wanted. Shakita thought that she might have been feeling Danny so much, for the fact he was her first of the night. He helped ease her into the groove. However, she still felt tense with her second and third client. She concluded that Danny was different.

Danny reminded her of Eric in so many ways that she felt they were both somehow related. They were the same complexion, about the same height and build, and looked to be close in age. They even had similar mannerisms that could imply that they knew each other well. Whenever the time was right, Shakita would later ask Eric if he were related to Danny. For now she was going to merely enjoy the thoughts of them both. She was almost on her way to the bathroom when the phone that was hanging on the living room wall rang.

She wasn't expecting anyone to call her but decided to answer it anyway thinking it may be housekeeping.

"Hello."

"I was calling to see if you were done for the night?" Eric asked inquisitively.

Shakita was relieved it was him. "Yeah. I got finished not too long ago."

"What are you doing now?"

"I was just about to get in the shower when you called."

"Okay. Get in the shower and then come up and see me. I'll be out on the balcony."

"How am I gonna do that? I don't have a silver card to get to your floor."

"When you get in the elevator. Insert your card and immediately press sixteen thirty-eight pound. The elevator will bring you up. I'll see you in a few."

After her shower, she got dressed and left out the room and motioned toward the elevator. When she was on the elevator she inserted her card and quickly pressed 1638#. *"Special request,"* the voice prompter said as the elevator began to lift up.

She got off the elevator and walked past his office, and through his formal room to get to the balcony. Eric was leaning on the railing as he looked out into the night when Shakita was now only a few feet behind him. He could hear the tap of her heels against the hardwood floor as she walked her way onto the balcony.

Shakita walked over to the right side of him and rubbed his left shoulder.

"How are you?"

"I'm good," he said, not giving her any eye contact. "I love this city. Besides Honolulu or Las Vegas, there's not too many other places that I'd rather be," he said, still not looking at her, as he breathed in the city's night air.

Shakita hated living in D.C. and believed it wouldn't be long before she hit the jackpot, and was able to flee the city she'd had so much bad luck in.

He turned around and looked at her. "If you could go anywhere in the world right now, where would you go?"

"Shit. The way things been going for me lately, I would sneak over the border and hide out in Mexico."

"You're so funny to me. For a girl to be so damn pretty, I don't get how you run into so many pitfalls. You have to stop running from your problems and straighten your life out."

Shakita understood his words but didn't know how to apply them to the situation she was in now. If she could get Bay's money back and enough money for herself, then her life would be straightened out. But until then, she was going to run into the pitfall of death if she didn't get Bay's money by the end of the month. Without Eric's help she might as well go jump in a casket and get it over with. She needed to find a way to persuade Eric to give her some more money than what he was offering.

"I'm trying, Eric. I stayed at work all day. I don't know why I keep getting myself jammed up. I'm not strong like you, but I want to be." She looked deeply into his eyes. "I need your help. I gotta get that money I need."

Eric refused to fall into her trap. "Well. You keep coming to work and you'll earn more than enough. Now here's the ten grand I promised you." Eric reached into the pocket of his dress pants and pulled out a large stack and handed it to her.

Shakita took the money but was disappointed that she couldn't demand more from him. She figured she was losing her touch or that Eric was not buying any of her bullshit anymore. When Eric kissed her on her forehead, she knew right then that he was dismissing her and that she had no more control over him.

Shakita slowly walked away from him with her head slightly down.

"Hey," Eric called out to her. She turned around to see what he wanted. "Will I see you at work tomorrow?"

Shakita nodded her head yes and gave him a fake smile without saying anything. She started to walk away but didn't know how to get out.

"How do I get down?" she asked with a little attitude.

"The same way. Sixteen thirty-eight pound."

"Thanks. And thank you for the money."

Eric nodded his head and Shakita stomped across the hardwood floor until she couldn't be heard anymore.

Eric made sure she was on the elevator and out of listening distance before he busted out laughing. Shakita was mad as hell at him and he thought that shit was the funniest thing in the world. Eric hadn't laughed this hard in so long, he almost forgot what it felt like. Shakita was the only girl who could get Eric to bend over backward. He laughed because he didn't let her get into his feelings. And she was mad she couldn't get it her way this time. He was winning—finally.

CHAPTER 12

Another day had gone by and Latrice still had yet to hear from Shakita. She didn't know what was going on with her, but it wasn't like Shakita to go two days without talking to her. Latrice decided to call her again. Shakita's phone continued to ring until the voicemail came on. This time Latrice left a message:

"Hey you! Remember me? I'm your best friend in case you forgot you had one. I know you're probably laid up with some bama-ass nigga, and that's why you ain't been getting back at me. At least you could call me back and let me know you're still alive. You could be dead for all I know. I ain't heard from you in like a month. Hit me back, I'm bored as hell and I'm trying to go out. Make sure you call me back, hoe. I'm just playing. Love you, girl. But fo'real. Call me back, bitch. Bye."

Latrice ended her message and waited for Shakita to call. She hadn't heard from Teyron yet either and was waiting for him to call also. She didn't understand for someone to want a record deal so bad to not follow up like they were supposed to. Latrice understood that it took more than being a good artist; you had to be reliable and show persistence, and Teyron was demonstrating neither right now. Latrice hoped he wasn't a lazy singer. She'd seen so much potential in him and believed he could go a long way. Latrice then thought that maybe he didn't want to seem pressed, so she decided to wait a few more days before she formed her own opinion. Yet, it was in her right mind to think the worst of him. She would be shit out of luck if Teyron wasn't whom she thought: one who sang his songs with so much emotion and pride, and who easily would move on someday to become legendary status. She hoped he was still that man.

Shakita placed her foot up on the toilet seat and was attempting to make the adjustments on her garter belt, when she heard her phone ringing in her purse. She ignored it, thinking it was probably Latrice trying to call her again. She was about to start working and didn't need to deal with her right now. Her phone had stopped ringing and a minute later, it beeped. She stopped fooling with her belt and became curious of who had left her a message. She pulled out her phone and as she suspected, it was a missed call from Latrice. She wanted to know what Latrice had to say, but didn't want to hear shit right now about Bay's money being missing. She still wasn't ready to deal with that and had no idea when she would be.

Shakita had less than ten minutes before she started working and didn't want to become stressed out by her message, so she dropped her phone back in her purse. She started to walk away, but couldn't help to think that maybe she should hear the message anyway. She pulled out her phone again. She waited nervously to hear her only message. Shakita started to ease up when she found out her friend wasn't mad and only wanted to talk to her. *This girl is crazy.* Shakita laughed to herself. "It ain't been a month since I talked to your ass. Quit faking; it's only been like two days," Shakita said into the phone.

Shakita finished listening to her message and decided to call Latrice back. Latrice didn't know shit about the money missing, and Shakita wanted to replace it fast before she did.

"Well, if it isn't the bald bitch of Christmas Past. Girl-la, where the hell you been?" Latrice asked, happy to finally hear from her friend.

"I've been a little busy lately, but I've been around."

"Why haven't you called me back?"

"I just told you I was busy. I didn't have time."

"You could have at least sent me a text message or something, girl. Even if it was just to tell me you were all right."

"I'm sorry, damn. You're questioning me like you my man or something."

"No, if I was ya man, I'd be whooping your mothafucking ass for getting out of pocket." Shakita took her ear off the phone and shook her head thinking about how retarded and silly her friend was. "Where are we going tonight?" Latrice asked.

"I can't go out tonight."

"And why not?"

"I got something to do."

"Like what?"

"Whatever I got to do bitch, damn."

"You can't tell me what you got going on? When has the shit ever been like that?" Shakita heard someone at the door and had to get off the phone.

"Look, girl. Shit is complicated right now. I can't hook up with you tonight, but meet me at Afterwords for breakfast tomorrow morning."

"All right, I'll meet you at ten," Latrice slowly responded.

"Okay. I got to go. Bye."

Shakita hung up the phone and put her purse under the bed. She hurried out of the bedroom so she could greet her guest.

"Hello. How are you, mister?" Shakita said, making her dark-skinned, overweight client comfortable. The man took one look at Shakita and thought he was in for a treat. Shakita looked at the size of her first client and realized she was in for another long night.

Latrice was so pissed that she and Shakita weren't going out that she leaned up against the headboard and pouted. Shakita was acting strange and Latrice was going to find out why. But in the meantime she was stuck at home without shit to do. Her phone rang and she thought it was Shakita calling her back telling her to get ready. She looked at the number and didn't recognize it. "Hello," she spoke hesitantly.

"Hello. Is this Latrice?"

"Yes. This is she."

"This is Teyron. I gave you my demo last night."

Latrice was so happy that he called that she was momentarily speechless.

He thought she hung up. "Hello."

"Yes, I'm still here. I'm so glad you called. How are you?"

"I'm good. I know I just gave you my demo yesterday, and I'm not even sure if you had a chance to listen to it yet, but I am going out of town tomorrow morning, and I really wanted to touch bases with you before I left."

"No, I did listen to it and I thought the whole thing was incredible."

"So you really liked it?"

"Woo. You have no idea how much I enjoyed it," Latrice said, fanning herself.

Teyron was so excited he wanted to know what she really thought of it. "What are you doing tonight?"

"Nothing. I thought me and my girl were going out tonight, but we're not. I was actually sitting here not doing shit before you called."

"Well. I don't have anything going on either. How about we get together tonight so we can talk about my demo?"

"Okay. I'm feeling that. Where would you like to meet?"

"I'm not really hungry and I don't feel like hitting the club either. But if you want to go dancing, I don't mind going out with you."

"I don't have to go out. It's whatever."

"How about coming out my way? I got some new stuff I would like you to hear."

This was the invitation she had been waiting for. She had to take it.

"If you got new songs I definitely want to hear 'em. Where are you at?"

"I'm over in Southwest. I stay at Eagles Crossing Apartments. You familiar?"

"Yeah, I know where that's at."

"I'm on the Joliet side."

"Okay. I got to get dressed. I'll be there in the next forty-five minutes."

"All right. I'll be waiting for you."

Latrice hung up the phone and shuffled through her closet looking for the right outfit to wear—something that wasn't too slutty or too conservative. She didn't want to go for the same executive look she'd had on the previous night, but surely wanted to wear something that would get his attention. She then found exactly what she needed. She pulled out a tangerine-colored halter top and some black Rock & Republic jeans. "He's gonna like me in these," she said, holding the jeans up to her butt. Latrice put her clothes on the bed and skipped to the shower. She was up to no good.

CHAPTER 13

Latrice turned onto Joliet Street once she arrived at the Eagles Crossing Apartments. She used to have an aunt who stayed in the same complex, so Teyron's spot was easy to find. She thought that it was a good time to call him.

"Hello."

"Hey, it's me. I just pulled up."

Teyron peered through the blinds and saw Latrice's car. "I see you. You can park where you're at. I'll be right out."

"Okay." Latrice hung up the phone and waited for him. When he was finally in view, she got out the car and walked across the street.

Teyron came out the house wearing a wife beater, gray sweatpants, and some house shoes. Latrice could see that he had a nice body and his tattoos were still visible under the complex's lighting. She was even more intrigued with him.

"What's up, baby girl?" Teyron asked, giving her a hug.

"Nothing much." Latrice took in the scent of his cologne. "Whatchu got on smelling all good?"

"I was about to ask you the same thing," Teyron said, laughing. "I got on some D and G. What about you?"

"I'm wearing Valentino," Latrice said as they started to walk into the building.

"Valentino, huh? I was wondering why you smelled as good as I did."

Latrice was definitely turned on by his cockiness. She loved that in a man. She walked into Teyron's apartment and noticed that his place had a modest look. There was no clutter and everything was well put together. In his living room there was one long couch and beside it was a tall protruding floor lamp. There was also a round coffee table in front of the couch with magazines neatly arranged on it. On the other side of the room, there was a small dining room table with a ceiling fan spinning slowly above. Latrice presumed he had a bachelor's pad judging by the simplicity of his dwelling décor.

"Have a seat," Teyron insisted.

"You have a nice spot," Latrice said as she took a seat on the couch.

"Thank you. Now can I get you anything to drink?"

"Sure. What do you have?"

"Bottled water, orange soda, grape juice, white zinfandel in a box, and Hennessy."

"Boy, whatchu doing with some wine?" Latrice asked flirtatiously.

"I don't drink it. It's only for whenever I have company."

"You know how much *us* girls like to drink. Are you sure you have any left?"

"Yes. It's not even opened yet, smart ass." Latrice laughed. "I'll get you some water since you like to tell jokes."

"Nooo. I was just playing. Can I have some wine, please?"

Teyron smiled and rolled his eyes at her as he walked to the kitchen. While Latrice waited for him to return, she noticed that there wasn't a television in the living room. She would ask him why when he returned and decided to pick up a magazine in the meantime.

Teyron's magazine selection ranged from *Bizarre*, *XXL*, *F.E.D.S.*, *Entertainment Weekly*, and *Don Diva*.

"I'm going to be on this cover one day," Latrice said as she picked up an *XXL* issue. By the time she was able to flip through a couple of pages, Teyron was back. He handed her a glass of wine.

"Thank you. I noticed that you don't have a TV in here. What's up with that?"

"My TV's in my bedroom."

"Is that where you entertain your guests?"

He shook his head. "I'm not even going to answer that."

"I think you already did."

"Whatever. I'm not in here that much. That's why I don't have one in here."

"Whatever. You know you do that so you can lure innocent girls to your room."

"For your information, whoever goes in my room ain't innocent."

"Well, excuse me, playa playa. I guess I'll never be watching anything in your room, huh?"

"I guess not. I only mess with innocent girls now," Teyron said, giving her a wink.

"You know what? I'm not even going to comment on that," Latrice said, refraining from not saying what was really on her mind. She was as freaky as the next girl but didn't want Teyron to know that about her yet.

He sat down beside her as he cracked the top off his bottled water. "So you really like my demo, huh?"

"Do I?" She turned to face him and got more comfortable on the couch. "That thing cranked. I couldn't believe that every song on that joint was like that…And 'Teyronimo.' That shit right there was off the hook. Whenever girls hear that song you're going to have panties wet all over the world."

Teyron laughed at her exaggerated compliment of his work. He believed he would do some damage but not like she was saying.

"I have to ask you something. Did you write all those songs yourself?"

"Yes. I wrote and produced them."

Latrice was shocked. "You made those beats yourself?"

"Yeap. All by myself."

"What studio do you record at?"

"I got my own studio here."

"You do?"

"Yeah. It's in the back room."

"Wow. You really got your shit together, don't you?"

"Not quite. I still don't have a deal."

"Yes you do," Latrice assured him.

"Are you serious?"

"Hell yeah. I'm offering you a deal with Bangspot. I don't have a contract prepared yet, but I know we can get everything worked out. Do you accept?"

"I can't believe this is happening."

"Believe it, boo. Everything I say is real. So do you want the deal?"

"Yes," Teyron said, struggling to hold his composure.

"Then it's settled. Welcome to Bangspot." Latrice extended her hand for him to shake.

Teyron grabbed her hand and pulled her in close for a hug.

"I won't let you down."

"I know you won't. I believe in you."

Teyron still couldn't believe he'd gotten a record deal. After dozens of major labels closed the door in his face telling him his style wouldn't work, and that his voice wasn't good enough, Teyron still didn't stop at accomplishing his dream. He was determined to be a singer amongst the best of them, despite what the majors thought of him. He knew in his heart that he was a star in the making and was going to do everything in his power to prove them all wrong. After four years of hustling, grinding, and dedication, he'd finally gotten a shot to show the world who he was. Teyron had Latrice and Bangspot to thank for that. He realized Bangspot was up and coming but so was he, and he believed that they could make it happen for him, and for that reason alone he was going to take a chance.

"As soon as my business partner gets out of jail, you can sign a contract. He'll be home in less than thirty days."

"Cool. I'll be ready. Did you ever talk Clarity into signing, too?"

"Matter of fact, I did, and she'll be your label mate."

"That's what I'm talking about." Teyron was charged up and saw bigger things for Bangspot knowing that they were going to both be on the same team. "I got this track that I want Clarity to spit on. I want you to come hear it." Teyron stood up and reached out for Latrice's hand.

Latrice grabbed his hand as she carried her wineglass in the other one. They began to walk down the hallway to his studio room. Teyron didn't have all the state-of-the-art equipment like a real studio, but he had what was necessary to produce good music. He had a Yamaha AW 2400 and an 808 machine. He had a laptop that stored all his music and he used his closet as the recording booth with the microphone connected to the inside wall. Latrice was impressed with his little mini hit factory.

"All right. Let me play this track." Teyron sat down at his desk and searched for the song he was looking for on his computer. He quickly found the track and Latrice started to listen.

Latrice was feeling the song and thought the beat sounded like something that Drake would use. As the music played, Teyron had the lights in the room synced together with certain instruments, making everything look like a flashing disco. Latrice liked Teyron's uniqueness and could definitely hear Clarity spitting over the track.

"That shit was like that," Latrice informed him when he stopped playing the track. "Thanks. With Clarity and me on that track, we'll tear it up. If you like that…Believe me, I got a whole lot more for you to hear." He then looked for another track to play.

Latrice indeed wanted to hear more of his music, but she also wanted to hear more about him.

"Teyron. Do you have a girlfriend?"

"No. I'm afraid I don't."

"You know. I find that quite odd. You make all this baby-making music and you don't have a girl? What's up with that? I mean, if you don't want no main chick and just want to have your friends, I can understand."

"It's not that. I'm not out to get a bunch of hoes, if that's what you're thinking. I wouldn't mind having a girl, but most women can't vibe with me."

Latrice twisted her lips. "Are you trying to say that most women aren't on your level?"

"It's not that," Teyron said as he went back to searching through tracks, leaving the conversation still open.

"Then what is it?"

He sighed. "Okay. You really want to know?"

Latrice nodded her head yes as she waited.

"When I first meet a girl and she listens to my music, she wants to know the person singing the songs instead of me. They get so caught up in the music that they don't have a clue who I really am. They don't understand what I'm saying at all. They only hear how I'm saying it. All I want is for someone to know me."

Latrice was touched by what he said and felt remorseful, for she, too, was also drawn to him by his music. She relived hours ago when she was listening to his demo in her bed, as she pleased herself with the help from his words and rhythm. Latrice was suddenly speechless and had to break her stare from him as she became guilty of what all the other women that he met shared.

"Listen to this track," Teyron said, changing the subject to ease the awkwardness that suddenly came between them.

The beat came on and it revamped her emotions again. She got a chill down her back as he broke the song in with his notes. Latrice was perplexed by what she was feeling, as it reminded her of how she felt in her bedroom earlier. She wanted Teyron more by the second and wanted him to know as well. She walked up to him and stood in front of him as she stared into his eyes.

Teyron's heart started to beat faster now that he knew what was about to happen. His first encounter with Latrice at the club was no accident. He wanted her as soon as he saw her, but didn't think they would both end up where they were now. Latrice stared into his timid eyes and didn't see him making the first move. If anything was going to happen between them, she would have to initiate the act. Without warning, she grabbed his face and they started to kiss heavily. She climbed up on his lap and began to grind on him intensely. They both began to peel their top layers off as the rubbing and kissing heightened. Teyron picked Latrice up and carried her over to the wall. He managed to quickly get both of their pants down. He then picked her up and engulfed her wet insides with himself.

Latrice's eyes rolled to the back of her head as she blinked heavily as the flashing lights toyed with her vision. All Teyron could hear were her loud seductive moans, as he attempted to feed her mind with his sexy wordplay, while his lips nuzzled her earlobe. But all Latrice could hear was his music beyond everything else, only further proving that Teyron was right about why he was single. They never could hear his real song; they never could hear him.

CHAPTER 14

"**G**ood morning. My name is Bev and I'll be your waitress. Is there anything I can get for you?"

Latrice quickly browsed over the menu. "Yes. Can I have an orange juice for now? I'm still waiting for my friend to arrive."

"No problem. We'll give 'em a few more minutes. I'll be back," Bev said with a smile, as she walked off to go wait on another table.

Latrice tried to study the menu, but the thoughts of her and Teyron kept filling her mind. Her experience with him completely overshadowed the one she'd had with Clarity. The sex was so good that she was almost able to block that aspect about Clarity out of her mind. The special moment that she and Clarity had was a bust and would never be retried again.

Shakita walked casually into Afterwords Café. She was wearing her sunglasses to hide the bags under her eyes from getting only a minimal amount of sleep. She didn't get home until five in the morning after another great night at work. She'd made another three thousand-plus in tips and was feeling good about her earning potential.

"Hello, miss. Will it be just you today?" the hostess asked.

"No. My friend should already be here."

"Do you know the name she would be under?"

"Probably under… Never mind. I see her," Shakita said as she spotted Latrice. Latrice got up to greet her as Shakita walked down the steps.

"What up, girl?" Latrice said, hugging her tightly.

Shakita rocked her back and forth. "What's going on?"

"I feel like I ain't seen you in like two months."

"It does seem that way, don't it?"

Shakita tried to hide her uncomfortable disposition of what she was doing with most of her time from Latrice. So far she was doing a good job with the help of her glasses. They both sat down and started looking at their menus.

"Nice shades, by the way," Latrice said, complimenting Shakita on her stylish frames.

"Thank you. So what's new?" Shakita quickly asked, changing the subject to keep Latrice from asking her to take her glasses off.

Latrice couldn't help but to tell Shakita about her new-found friend, but since the waitress came back around, it would have to wait.

"Hi. Are you two ready?"

"Yes, I would like the Nouvelle Leo, please," Latrice said before closing her menu.

"And you, miss?"

"I'll have the Soho Omelet with an order of turkey sausage and wheat toast."

"And what would you like to drink?" she asked Shakita.

"I'll have a cappuccino and an iced coffee."

"Okay. I'll be right back with your drinks," Bev said as she took both of their menus and walked off.

Latrice gave Shakita a puzzled look. "When did you start drinking coffee?"

"I'm trying something new, that's all." She really needed the caffeine to keep herself awake.

Latrice didn't want to spend too much time trying to figure Shakita out. She thought she was going through her usual phase and wanted to talk about something more important.

"Girl, I gotta tell you about what I was doing last night," Latrice said, with a glow on her face.

"What happened?" Shakita asked, gladly to keep the spotlight off of her.

"I met this dude, right. Well... he's this new artist I'm signing to our label. I was listening to his demo and that shit was cranking. So he invited me to his house so I could listen to more of his music, right? Then one thing led to another. And girl, it was so so good," Latrice said, covering up her face as she reminisced.

Shakita shook her head and was not amused by Latrice's story.

"Don't you find it funny that you always end up fucking all the artists you meet?"

Before Latrice could defend herself, the waitress came back with Shakita's coffee.

"Here you go." Bev set both of her beverages on the table. "Your meals should be out shortly." Bev then walked away to assist another table.

"I don't fuck all the artists I meet," Latrice said to Shakita as she was adding sugar to her iced coffee.

Shakita sucked her teeth. "Latrice, please. Every artist you always take interest in, you end up fucking them."

Latrice became bashful when Shakita called her out on the way she was.

"If you want to be the best in the biz, you can't go around fucking all your artists. Then they won't just be calling you a CEO. The whole industry will be calling you the CEO Hoe. You don't want that, do you?"

The waitress came with their food giving Latrice a minute to think about what Shakita had said. She was always attracted to talented singers and rappers and couldn't deny that Shakita was telling the truth. She knew right then that she had to be taken more seriously and would stop her naive ways.

"Damn, girl. You really put that shit in perspective for me. I got to stop being stupid. I should've never fucked youngin' last night."

"Don't even worry about it. So what, you fucked him. What's done is done. Besides, it's not too often you get good dick anyway." Shakita smiled.

They both broke out in laughter as they continued eating their food. This was what true friendship was all about, they both thought to themselves. They knew each other so well that they never took it to heart when they were called out on their foolish habits. It was all love between them, and that alone outshined any character flaw that caused them to make bad decisions.

"Is there anything else I can get you ladies?" Bev asked, picking up their empty plates.

"Just the check, please. Thank you." Shakita took the bill from Bev and dug into her purse for her money.

"How much is it?" Latrice asked.

"Don't worry about it. I got it."

Latrice was shocked.

"That's a first."

"Like I said earlier, I'm trying something new."

"Ain't nothing wrong with that," Latrice said as Shakita handed Bev the money.

"I'll be right back with your change."

"Don't worry about it. Keep it," Shakita informed her.

"Well, thank you. You two have a nice day," Bev said as she walked off with a big smile.

"All right. So what you about to get into?" Shakita asked.

"I was about to ask if you wanted to go to the mall with me?"

"Nah, homie. I got something I got to do."

"Aw, come on, Kita. You can go to the mall with me. That's the least you could do since you carried me like shit by not going to the club last night."

"I'm sorry about that. I wish I could go with you, but I really can't." Latrice knew something wasn't right.

"What is going on with you? You ain't acting yourself."

"I'm good. I really got some important things I got to handle right now. I'm the same old me."

"Is everything okay? Do you need me to go with you?"

"No. I'll be fine." Shakita's conscience was starting to get to her and she needed to leave. "Look. I got to go," Shakita said as she rose out her seat.

"Tomorrow I'm not doing anything. We can get together then. Okay?"

"Whatever," Latrice said with an attitude. "Well then, answer me this. Are you in some type of trouble?"

"No, everything is straight, okay? I'll call you later." Shakita quickly left the restaurant leaving her friend still sitting at the table. Her emotions were starting to get to her and she had to leave before she started crying. Holding on to the secret was starting to become all too much for her.

She hated lying to her best friend, but it was the wisest thing to do right now. Shakita couldn't tell her about the money. She got in her car and removed her sunglasses. She cracked open a Red Bull that was in the cup holder and took a few sips. Shakita had money in her pocket and was going to go put it to good use. She was off to Hollywood Casino to add interest to the money she already had. Shakita was feeling lucky and didn't think that losing was going to be a part of her day; she was ready to gamble.

CHAPTER 15

Shakita arrived at Hollywood Casino in exactly one hour and a few Red Bulls later. Charles Town, West Virginia had the closest casino to D.C. until Maryland Live! opened up in the next few weeks. She wanted to get a few hours of gambling in before she started work so for now, Hollywood Casino served its purpose. Shakita lost her last dollar here a few days ago, and hoped to win some of her money back, hopefully all of it. She sat down right beside a lady who looked like she had been at the same machine for hours. Shakita thought the lady was playing away her pension by the way she hesitated to put dollars in the machine.

Her strategy was to take over the machine if the lady left without any winnings. Shakita inserted a hundred-dollar bill into the five-dollar play Triple Bonanza machine. She selected all three lines and pulled the lever. The reels started to spin and then quickly stopped on all odd symbols. Having no winnings on the first pull didn't discourage her at all. She had enough money with her to potentially secure a big win.

After an hour of senseless betting, Shakita had lost way more than she'd won. She was looking for a break that would end her losing streak and get her a big payout. Her opportunity finally came when the lady sitting next to her decided to leave, after her machine neglected to return any of her hard-earned money, or anybody else's. Shakita didn't even wait until the lady was out of sight before she started loading the machine up with bills. She pulled the reel down on the Mardi Gras Madness machine and waited to see what happened. The reels stopped spinning and Shakita was still not a winner.

Shakita continued to play both machines simultaneously hoping to increase her winning probability. She pulled the lever down on the Mardi Gras Madness machine and waited for the reels to stop. Three babies lined up on the middle line, sending the sirens off. Shakita couldn't believe her eyes as she stared at the loud and flashing digital screen. She pictured herself cracking the machine but didn't think she would win like this.

"All right. Here's your money, ma'am. Come back and see us now," the deep-voiced cashier said as he handed Shakita her payout.

"I most certainly will." Shakita smiled, pleased to do business with their establishment. She took the stacks of money and put them in her purse as she made her exit out of the casino. Shakita had won twenty thousand dollars from the same slot machine that was abandoned by the poor lady. If the older woman would have stayed a little longer and played, that would have been her jackpot to take home instead of Shakita doing so. Shakita had over thirty thousand dollars toward the money she owed to Bay. With the amount of money she was making at the spa, she would be guaranteed to have all of Bay's money before he got out.

The only problem was that Shakita didn't plan on working at the spa any longer than she had to, which meant she was going to have to take another trip to Atlantic City. The casinos in Atlantic City had blackjack and roulette tables that would bring in the big bucks, giving her a jump start to riches. Shakita was feeling luckier than ever, and would be coming back this time from Atlantic City with all Bay's money and more. Shakita was going to leave for

Atlantic City right after she got off work. All she needed to do was run home real quick to gather up an overnight bag before she saw her first client. She had the whole thing figured out and now she was off to get some more Red Bulls.

Shakita was so tired after she had finished with her last client that she wanted to lay down and take a short nap. She didn't want to go to sleep and risk not being able to wake up in time to leave for Atlantic City, so she stayed up, and drank another Red Bull to keep her energy level high. It was 4:30 a.m. when she got in her truck and was on her way to 295-N en route to Atlantic City. She drove with the music blasting loud and the windows rolled down, so the cool morning air could blow in her face to help keep her alert. Shakita was exhausted but was going off of pure adrenaline from being so eager to make it to Atlantic City in good time.

Three-and-a-half hours later, Shakita was getting off the Atlantic City Expressway and could see the beautiful Atlantic City strip clearly. She loved Atlantic City and her heart started to race every time she came here. She could smell the salt from the ocean and felt like she was coming back home. She set her eyes on the beautiful Taj casino that always amazed her whenever she saw it. The Taj was the biggest and tallest hotel and casino on the whole entire strip and she only wanted to play in the best. The Taj was the color of pure white sand with gold domes that made it resemble a Hindu Temple. She couldn't wait to get inside.

Shakita walked onto the casino floor and was relieved that the casino wasn't crowded at this time of morning like usual. She had every slot machine and gaming table at her disposal and didn't know where she wanted to start first. She decided to get warmed up by playing slots, and later move on to some table games. Besides, she was hoping to collect all the money that patrons dropped in the machines on Friday and Saturday nights that hadn't been recovered. She inserted a hundred-dollar bill in a five-dollar Triple Sevens machine and began to play. After a while, Shakita hadn't found any luck from the Triple Sevens machine, so she started playing two other Black Cherry machines right beside it.

As she continued to play all three machines at the same time, she realized she was losing money three times as fast. After dumping a thousand dollars in all three machines and seeing no returns, she decided the hell with them and wanted to try the roulette table. She went to the cashier booth so she could get five thousand dollars' worth of chips. She put all her chips in a bucket and proceeded to the roulette tables.

Shakita went over to a roulette table where the minimum bet was a hundred dollars for each game and the maximum was five hundred. She needed to pay to get into the game, and couldn't use the same chips from the cashier booth. She had to use the different color chips the dealer had so they could know who was winning what. She paid two thousand dollars to get in the game and the dealer gave her twenty pink chips. Shakita was only going to do inside bets knowing that the odds of winning and payout were better than safer outside bets if she won.

Shakita positioned four chips on space 23 and waited for the rest of the players to place their bets. When the dealer yelled "no more bets," he tossed the ball on the wheel so it could spin around. She eagerly watched as the wheel went around and around hoping it would land in her pocket. The ball started to bounce around and then finally fell in the 35 black pocket. "Damn it," Shakita said, as the dealer took away her chips. Shakita was pissed but wasn't going to let that one loss make her quit. She'd come there to make money and that's what she was going to do. She continued to play until tragedy struck again.

Shakita was so fucking angry that she walked away from the table and straight out of the casino. "Fuck! Fuck! Fuck!" Shakita yelled outside of the Taj's parking garage as she kicked the wall. She couldn't believe she'd lost so much damn money and without even being there a whole day yet. She slid down the wall and tucked her head between her knees wanting to cry. Her phone suddenly started to ring while she still had her head down. She initially ignored the first couple of rings not wanting to deal with anybody, but then got irritated by the ringing so she looked at the phone to see who it was. It was Latrice calling and she became even more frustrated.

"Leave me the fuck alone! I don't have time for your shit right now!" Shakita screamed, slamming her phone back in her purse. She went back in her purse to retrieve a cigarette as her phone continued to ring. By the time she had her cigarette lit, her phone had silenced.

Shakita was so upset that she'd lost all that money, and with Latrice calling at the wrong time again didn't help much either.

"I'm about to say fuck it and tell her ass. This shit is too much work," Shakita shouted.

Shakita's nerves were wearing thin and her conscience was heavily weighing on her. Shakita was feeling defeated and was ready to give up. She was going to give Latrice whatever money she had left and deal with the consequences, even if that meant death. No matter what happened, she was ready to go home.

She smashed her cigarette on the ground and grabbed her purse. As she was getting up, her purse bumped her bucket and knocked her chips over. Shakita looked at the spilled chips and started to get second thoughts about leaving. Shakita was about to turn her chips in so she could get her money back, but the sound that the chips made as they hit the concrete, gave her a rush. She couldn't go home yet. There was no way in hell she was going to travel all that way to go back home to say she'd broke even.

Shakita was a born hustler and gambling was in her blood. Gambling was her addiction, and the only way she knew how to suppress it was by blowing everything she had, so she didn't have anything else to risk. She was either going to leave Atlantic City richer or poorer. There was no room for in between. She was going to go back in the Taj and try to break the casino for everything it had. Shakita's palm started to itch and she predicted that luck was coming back on her side again.

CHAPTER 16

Shakita walked back in the casino with her head held high and confidence in her stride. She walked to the far end of the casino to go where the high-rollers played. She was going to step up her shit and play a game that showed who had the biggest balls at the table. Shakita was going to play Texas Hold'em. Along with craps, she'd learned this style of poker from her Uncle Bunny that used to play with mobsters in Reno, and would always walk away with a large pot. If there was any game in the casino she could play well it would be this one.

Shakita began to yawn as she looked for the right table. She was extremely tired but couldn't afford to sleep right now. She had to get rich first. It was a little past noon, and the poker tables were filled with blood-sucking card sharks looking for the weakest fish at the table. She then noticed one of the high-stakes tables had an open seat with her name on it. She quickly made her move before it was taken. The table was full of men and she hoped they would be warm to her company. If they weren't, then fuck'em. She was going to play anyway.

"Excuse me, gentlemen. Do you mind if I join your game?" Shakita asked the three white men at the table.

All three looked at Shakita and then at each other and started to laugh hysterically. Shakita didn't see a damn thing funny but presumed they were laughing at her because she was a woman.

"Did I say something funny?" Shakita asked as she placed her hand on her hip.

"We don't mean to laugh at cha, doll," a country-talking man said as he tried to control his laughter. "But you sure you wanna play wit' us?" He wiped the tears from his eyes and now rosy red cheeks.

She looked hard at the chubby guy with the thick, fuzzy sideburns. "Yes. Why wouldn't I?"

"You know this is a high-stakes table, aye? If you're looking for cheesesteaks, you're in the wrong part of the casino, honey," said the older, skinny man wearing a black cowboy hat and a brown suede sports jacket. Shakita thought the way he dressed was whack as hell and so were his corny-ass jokes.

"I didn't come here to eat. I came here to make money," Shakita responded.

"Well. It takes money to make money. Ya have any?" the chubby guy asked her.

"Yeah, I have it. What's y'all usual low bid?"

"About a thousand," the chubby guy answered.

Shakita reached in her bucket and dug out ten chips and slammed them down on the table. "Does this sound like I have enough?" she asked as she swirled around her bucket so they would know she had a lot of chips in it.

All three men looked at each other cunningly. The chubby guy then gave the skinny man with the hat a signal.

"All right, sweet tits. I guess you can have a seat," the skinny white man said. Shakita scooped up her chips as she smiled walking over to her seat.

"So where are you boys from?" Shakita asked, trying to make small talk while the cards were being shuffled.

"We're from Upstate New York. Elmira, to be exact," the third man said, making his presence known as he shuffled the cards. He was a young, rusty-haired kid with freckles. Shakita thought the trio seemed to be a son, dad, and grandfather group with each one closely resembling each other.

"What 'bout yourself?" the young man asked with a slight grin on his face.

"D.C.," she said with pride.

"Oh, you're one of them ol' city women, aye?" the man with the hat asked.

"Yes I am, fella," Shakita answered, mocking the way he talked.

"Well. Don't start crying like a baby when ya candy money get took. This is a man's game and we play like men. There will be none of that sissy shit at this table," the old man informed her.

"After I win... And best believe, I will win. After I take all your money, I may find it in my heart to give you enough money so y'all can make it back to Upstate New York. Elmira, to be exact," Shakita said, putting on her game face.

The old man didn't like her smart-ass comment but decided not to say anything about it. The rest of his shit-talking was going to be done with action.

Shakita began to yawn again as the cards were being dealt. The young man dealt everyone two cards faced down and then they were able to do the first round of bidding. Since the initial bid was a thousand dollars, Shakita had to put that in the pot so she could play. The initial bids were always half of the regular bid, and were both forced bets that were put in the pot before the deal started, so that the players would have something to play for. Shakita peeked at her cards and saw she had two jacks. She was now ready to see the "flop," or the three community cards that are placed face up for all players to see. These cards were matched with the cards in your hand to try and create a poker combination.

The young man revealed the top card to show everyone he wasn't cheating, and then turned over the community cards to let everyone see that there was a two of hearts, a queen of diamonds, and a ten of clubs. Since Shakita was sitting beside the player who put out the "big blind," she was to start off the next round of betting. She felt good about her pair of jacks but looked at the other players to see how they felt about their hand. Shakita didn't notice any cockiness so she assumed she had the better hand so far. She put in another thousand dollars as her bid for this round. The three men put in their bids and were now ready to see the next community card which was called "the turn." The turn card was a six of spades.

Shakita still felt confident about her two jacks and put in a bid for another thousand dollars. The three men bid the same amount as well. They all turned over their cards to reveal to each other what they had. Shakita put down her two jacks and the young man put down a six of hearts and a nine of spades. He ended up with a pair of sixes but wasn't good enough to beat Shakita's two jacks. The old man had a ten of diamonds and a four of hearts. He ended up with a pair of tens but wasn't good enough to beat Shakita's hand either. Shakita leaned over and swooped up the pile of chips in her hands. She'd won fourteen thousand dollars.

The old man was the dealer in the second round and took the dealer button from the young man grandson, and placed it in front of him on the table. The old man dealt out everyone's cards and was now ready to get the betting started. Shakita had a five of hearts and an ace of spades. She was the "high blind" and was prepared to put down her two grand to play. Everyone else put down their bets and was ready to see the community cards. The old man burnt the first card and then turned over an eight of clubs, a three of spades, and a two of hearts. Shakita thought she could be able to pull off a straight and was waiting for a four to do so. When it was her turn to bet, she raised her bet by a thousand.

The other players raised one thousand also except for the old man. He had to fold and was pissed for doing so. He hated losing and getting put down by some little black woman was an insult to all his gaming experience. He was going to have to find a way to take her out of the game, but for now he was left frustrated with a weak hand. The old man turned over the second card, since he was still the dealer, and allowed everyone to see that "the turn" card was a king of clubs. Shakita couldn't use a king with the cards she had, but still felt confident about her hand. She called her two thousand like the rest of them and waited for "the river" card to be revealed.

"The river" card was turned over and Shakita saw that the four she needed wasn't there. Instead, it was an ace of hearts. She didn't get her straight she was looking for, but she did get a pair of aces. She didn't know if it was enough to win, but she still was going to bet on it anyway. Whenever it was her turn to bet, she put in another two grand to match the chubby man's bet. The young man then folded not wanting to lose any more money, leaving Shakita and the chubby man to go one on one over the pot. They both revealed their hands and Shakita saw that the chubby man had only a pair of kings. Shakita's face lit up with a grin. She pulled her forty-three thousand dollars pot closer to her and couldn't believe she had won two times in a row. The next win would put her on a winning streak.

After playing for two hours and some odd minutes, Shakita had over $250,000 in chips, and had enough money to give back to Latrice with a little left over for herself. This was going to be her last hand and wanted to get the men for as much money as she could before she split. She also wanted to get some real sleep since she'd been going on only a few hours of rest. She was yawning every ten seconds now, and her eyes felt extremely hard to keep open. A headache was starting to form and she wanted to get this hand over with as soon as possible, so she could climb into one of the queen-sized beds at the Taj, and dream about her money. Shakita hoped that the men wouldn't try to take her tiredness for a weakness.

"Shit. Shit. Shit" was the only thing Shakita could say to herself as the three men were continuing to raise the bet on her. She was overly confident with the king of diamonds and ace of hearts she had in her hand, and with the community cards being a ten of hearts, a king of hearts, and an ace of hearts, she had her two pairs already secured. All she needed now was to get another king or ace to appear from out of "the turn" or "the river" and then she would have a full house. If she was able to pull off a four of a kind somehow, that would be even better. She didn't know whether any of the men were bluffing with their hands or not, but they were really starting to piss her off. She had $75,000 of her earnings in the pot already and they hadn't even gotten to the second round of bidding yet. She had no idea where the game was going.

"The turn" card was a four of spades, which did nothing to enhance Shakita's hand at all. She put in her usual two thousand-dollar bet and it was matched and then raised $25,000 by the young man. Shakita looked at him funny wondering why he'd never taken a big risk the entire game until now. She tried to read the young man's facial expressions but couldn't get anything. The old man then matched the younger man's bet and then raised it by $10,000. Shakita took her focus off of the young man to follow what was going on around the table. The betting was getting worse. The chubby man matched the $35,000 that the older man added to the pot and raised him another $15,000. Shakita couldn't believe what the hell was going on. If she wanted to play this hand, she would have to put in another $50,000 or fold her hand.

She thought her hand was probably better than the three assholes that were playing with bullshit hands, and didn't want to lose all the money she'd put out thus far. All the men had more money to gamble than she did. She couldn't afford to lose any of it. She decided to match the $50,000 and hope the betting would stop. Finally, everyone was satisfied with what was in the pot and was now ready to move on to "the river." The last card was turned over and it was an ace of clubs. It was the exact card Shakita needed to get a full house. She felt that there was no way any of the bastards could beat her hand now and was more than ready to collect all her money once the last round of bidding was over.

Fuck! Shakita said to herself, as she tried to place another safe bet of two grand, but was raised $50,000 by the young man, which really put her on the ropes. The old man matched the young man and raised him another twenty grand. The chubby man folded his hand leaving Shakita with a whole lot to think about. *What the fuck is going on?* Shakita said to herself, looking down at her lonely three thousand dollars' worth of chips. She couldn't afford to fold her hand nor did she have enough money to continue. Shakita was caught up in a tough situation.

"So whatcha gonna do, darlin'? We ain't got all day," the old man said, easily antagonizing her, knowing she was backed in a corner.

Shakita didn't have a clue what she was going to do, but she had to think fast. That's when she realized she had to use what she had to get what she wanted.

"I only have three thousand left. Can I play with whatever I got and count it as a match?"

"Are you sure you wanna do that?" the old man asked. He then gave her a stern look. "Don't think you're winning none of that money on that there table. If I were you, I'd lay those cards down and use that pocket change to get back home with."

Shakita couldn't tell if the old-timer was bluffing or not, but leaving the table with three grand wasn't shit. Even if she did fold on this hand, she didn't have enough money to play through the next one.

She had been at this table too long to walk away with nothing, and Shakita was going to either win it all or lose everything. She felt good about her hand and was going to try them head-on for the whole pot. She had no other choice but to bet.

"I don't need any of this to get home. I came here with a full tank," Shakita said with a straight face, as she pushed her little three thousand in chips over to the rest of the pile.

The old man thought the idea over as he bit down on his bottom lip. Her three thousand meant diddly-squat to him at this point, but it was worth almost the whole pot when it came down to principle. He wanted to teach her little black ass a lesson, so she could remember this ass-whooping for the rest of her life. He gladly accepted her bid.

It was time for them all to lay out their hands, and Shakita couldn't wait to see the look on their ugly white faces when they laid eyes on her pretty full house. Her three aces and two kings could not be beat and she was going to prove that right now. She put down her cards and waited for the country bumpkins to read 'em and weep. The young man put down his cards to show that he had a jack of spades and a queen of diamonds, giving him two pairs, which still wasn't enough to beat Shakita's hand. The old man then put down his cards and caused Shakita's mouth to hit the floor. All of them started to laugh at her when she was able to piece together his card combination. The motherfucker had a royal flush. This was the highest and rarest combo one could ever get, and Shakita's full house couldn't do shit with it. Confusion came over her face as the old man hugged the massive pile of chips into his arms and pulled them close to him.

Shakita couldn't believe what had happened and became disoriented when she realized she'd lost all her money *again*. The men continued to laugh as her humiliation and frustration grew, sending her into a state of shock.

"If you play with us, we send 'em packing," the old man said as he tipped his hat. "Now if you decide to give up some of that sweet black cunt of yours, I might be willing to throw you back enough coins to getcha self a sandwich."

The other two men both laughed at the old man's joke, which made Shakita feel like crying.

"Fuck y'all hillbillies," Shakita said as she walked over to the old man and knocked off his cowboy hat onto the floor and kept walking.

"You fuckin' lil' bitch!" the old man yelled after picking up his hat and placing it back on his head lopsided.

The old man calmed down after Shakita was out of sight, knowing that they all had gotten the bigger laugh on her, and that she would be even madder than he was if she knew what they had done to her. During the last couple of hands, the men noticed Shakita dozing off on several occasions. They secretly came up with a plan to set the deck and force her out of all her money. After Shakita lost all her money to the old man, they all split her part of the pot three ways, giving them $90,000 each of her $270,000 that she had obtained throughout the course of the game. The three men really caught her sleeping and took her for everything she had.

Shakita sat on a bench along the boardwalk and cried her little heart out. She felt so brainless for losing all her money that she wanted to knock herself in the damn head for being so stupid. She'd had all the money she needed to get her out of the jam she was in and she'd blown it all in a punk-ass poker game. If she could turn back the hands of time, she would have gotten up from the table before the last hand even started. Now she had nothing to play for and not a cent to even go back home with. She was all fucked up and had no one to blame but herself. Shakita was so tired and emotionally drained that she couldn't help but to cry herself to sleep. Her heavy head crashed on her shoulder, and she suddenly went into a deep slumber. She snored away heavily right along the boardwalk.

CHAPTER 17

"Why the fuck you ain't catch my call, you stupid-ass bitch?" was all Latrice heard when she accepted Bay's collect call.

She had accidentally missed his call on Friday messing around with Clarity, and now he was calling her back at ten a.m. on Monday morning mad as hell. "My bad, Bay. I was trying to make it to the phone on time. I thought you were going to call back."

"Why couldn't you get to the damn phone? Did you have a nigga over there or somethin'?"

"No I didn't, and why are you all in my business anyway? You ain't my man no more."

"Whatever, bitch. You know you lying like shit. I know you had a nigga over that mothafucka. That's why ya lil' dumb ass ain't pick up the jack, 'cause you was too busy fuckin'."

"Whatever, Bay," Latrice said with attitude. "You can believe whatever the fuck you want. I do me out here and you do your jailbird shit up in there."

"You got a lot of tough talk in you over the phone, huh? Don't make me bank on ya lil' ass when I get out."

I wish you would hit me again. I'll kill ya bama ass, Latrice said to herself, becoming fed up with his ill ways.

She didn't want Bay to start beating her ass again when he got out, so she bit her tongue and kept what she really was feeling to herself. Instead, she sucked her teeth, letting Bay know he still had control over her.

"That's what I thought, bitch," Bay said, further intimidating. "Now did you handle any of my business like I told you to?"

"Yes, Bay. I got everything done for you."

"Even the company logo?"

"Yes, Bay, that too. I did everything you asked of me when you asked me to do it. Everything is set up."

Bay was pleased with her work and realized he didn't have to question his trust in her. She was his little soldier and without her, he would have no one to hold him down. Bay needed her.

"Good work, baby girl. You know I'm gonna take care of you when this thing blow up, right?" Bay said, finding a gangster way of thanking her.

"I know you will," Latrice said unenthused.

She didn't like how Bay talked to her at times, but she couldn't really do anything about it, unless she gained another hundred pounds, and was able to knock a nigga out in one punch. Bay was indeed a brawler who had a huge temper and Latrice couldn't do much of anything when he got a hold of her. Bay had as much of a grip on her life in jail, as he did when he was out. She felt there was no escaping from him. Latrice continued to go along with whatever he said to make their business relationship run smoothly. That way she would keep herself from geting harmed.

Bay was temporarily distracted by another inmate who was walking nearby. The inmate gave Bay a hard look which he happily returned. There was bad blood between these two men and Bay had to let Latrice know who appeared before his eyes.

"I just seen ya lil' bitch-ass boyfriend walk by here."

"Who you talking about?"

"You know who the fuck I'm talking about. Ya boy, Timbo."

"That is not my boyfriend. It could have been, but you made sure he wasn't, remember?"

"You damn right. And I'll bring it to any nigga you ever try to fuck with."

Latrice shook her head in disgust. "Why do you have to keep doing this to me? I'm not with you anymore and I should be allowed to talk to whoever I want. Do I go off on those disrespectful-ass bitches you be having me call on three-way all the time?"

"This ain't got nothing to do with them and you know better than to do that shit anyway. As long as me and you doing business together, I don't want no niggas around my shit, period. I can't trust nobody and with you fucking around with some dumb-ass nigga, my whole shit could get all fucked up! And I can't be having that! 'Cause if that happen, then somebody gotta…" Bay realized he was getting heated and didn't want to risk saying something he would regret over the phone. "Anyway. I gotta get off this jack. I'll tell Timbo you said hello."

"Bay, please don't do anything dumb to get yourself more time. Remember you'll be out in less than a month."

"I ain't going to let that little bitch-ass nigga keep me up in here. He definitely don't want that."

"And neither do you. We have a record label to run and I need you out here."

"Aight, man. I gotchu. I'm getting off. Now you remember to keep them niggas out ya bed and the money in ya head. Feel me?"

"Yeah, I feel you," Latrice said nonchalantly.

Bay smiled. "Aight. I'm out."

"Bye." *Click.* They both hung up the phone.

Latrice became depressed thinking about how Bay continued

to try and control her life. The mention of Timbo made her feel that Bay would risk himself getting out for handling their beef. She flashed back to last summer, which was the last time she'd seen Timbo.

"Hey, baby girl. I'm outside," Timbo said as he pulled up to Latrice's apartment.

"Okay. I'll be right down in a minute."

Latrice hung up the phone as nervous energy flowed through her body. It was her first date with Timbo and she didn't know what to expect. Her relationship with Bay had ended terribly two months ago and she was still trying to pick up the pieces. The sexual abuse from Bay had become so horrific that she definitely had to get away and find herself again. She moved out of her apartment and relocated across town where she hoped Bay wouldn't find her. Timbo was a breath of fresh air and a potential romantic prospect.

She'd met him a few months back when she was at the hair salon. While she was getting her hair trimmed and styled, Timbo walked in and approached her. She'd never had someone walk into a crowded hair salon and try his hand at getting her attention. She'd found it very sexy that he would go to such lengths to try and win her heart. Her stylist had forced her to take his number after he'd paid for Latrice's hair to get done.

She took a deep breath and walked out of her door as she anticipated their first date.

When Latrice exited her apartment building, she was in shock to see how Timbo greeted her.

He sat on the hood of his new moonlight-white Infiniti M56 holding a dozen white long-stemmed roses.

"You got those for me?" she asked, beaming.

"Of course they are, beautiful." He smiled. He lifted up his tall and slender frame and handed them to her. His sexy swag and golden-brown complexion caused Latrice's stomach to flutter.

She took in the sweet aroma of the heavily scented flowers and started to blush.

"I never had white ones before."

"I got you the white ones. They symbolize innocence, and that's how I see you."

Latrice smiled from the unexpected compliment. It had been so long since someone tried to make her feel special. Bay never said anything endearing to her, or gave her flowers, or took her out to make her feel appreciated. Timbo was a thug and a gentleman wrapped in one, and Latrice was feeling on top of the world. She stepped into his car and smiled as they drove off. On the way to their destination, she couldn't help but think that Timbo may possibly be the one to help change her life, and she was looking forward to it.

Latrice and Timbo held hands as they walked out of the restaurant after enjoying a wonderful dinner. Timbo wrapped his arm around Latrice as they waited for valet to bring his car around. They both agreed to meet up again the next night and didn't want the night to end. Timbo's car finally arrived, and he made sure she was secured in her seat before walking over to his side of the car. He was about to pull off and saw a figure quickly approach his window.

"So, Latrice, this is the type of yellow bitch-ass niggas you into? Get the fuck out of the car," Bay barked.

Latrice's heart dropped not expecting Bay to show up out of nowhere. She was so scared that she couldn't even move.

"Look here, homeboy. I don't appreciate your level of disrespect.

I advise you to back your ass up away from my window before you have a real problem," Timbo threatened.

When Latrice didn't move fast enough, Bay pulled his 9 millimeter from his waistband and shot Timbo in his abdomen. Latrice screamed as blood quickly soaked up Timbo's gray Polo shirt.

"Get the fuck out the car!" He pulled her through the window. "You thought I wouldn't find you, huh? You were trying to leave me for this bitch-ass nigga?"

"Bay, stop. I don't want to go with you. Somebody help me," she screamed as her feet dragged across the ground.

Timbo was slumped over in pain as he reached for his gun that was stashed inside the glove compartment. He opened the door and slowly crawled to the ground. He saw Bay dragging Latrice across the street and wanted to stop him. He raised his gun as his shaking hand tried to get a clear shot at Bay, but fired wildly missing all three times. There was no real chance of him dropping Bay without risking Latrice getting hit. He started to fade as sirens were heard faintly in the back ground. Before he could discard his weapon, he quickly blacked out on the ground. Bay had forced Latrice into his car and driven off before the police made it to the scene. Timbo was later charged for reckless endangerment with a firearm and sent to jail.

Latrice cried thinking how terrible she'd left things with Timbo. She never called him out of embarrassment and thought it wouldn't work out between them. Bay hated seeing her with another man. He would always go to great lengths to make sure she wouldn't be happy without him. Latrice hated getting to know new people. She was always afraid that Bay would chase them away, like Timbo. There was no way he could ever find out about her and Teyron. If he did, he would kill his own artist. Latrice prayed that she was doing everything she could to keep Teyron out of harm's way. She hoped Teyron would understand why.

"Who the fuck was you lookin' at like that, nigga?" Bay said to Timbo, as he approached him in the phone line.

Timbo was the same height as Bay and was able to look straight into his dark eyes. Timbo was light-skinned and slenderly built with tattoos on both sides of his neck and his arms. He wasn't scared of Bay and was waiting to pay him back for shooting him in the abdomen last summer. Now wasn't the best place to get revenge, but it was a good place to start.

"I was lookin' at ya bitch ass. What you tryin' to do, young?" Timbo backed up and threw up his guard. He wanted to beat Bay's ass for shooting him and making him look like a bitch in front of everyone.

"You lil' bitch-ass, piss-colored nigga. I know you ain't trying to see me like that. You sure you wanna get knocked out in front of all these niggas?"

"Stop talkin' and bring it, nigga!" Timbo yelled, accidentally alerting the guards.

The guards ran over and stepped in between Bay and Timbo.

"I ain't do nothing wrong, yo. I just came over here to give him a message and he started bugging the fuck out," Bay said, putting his hands up while taking the innocent role.

"Yo, don't believe this pussy-ass nigga. He came over here and started talking shit."

"I don't give a damn what happened," one of the guards said. "If I see you two assholes at it again, I'm going to throw both of you in isolation. Now break this shit up!"

Bay listened to the officer and walked away, but not before giving Timbo a clever smile. What had happened between Timbo and him was far from over, and he would have to end it before Timbo tried to catch him offguard. Timbo looked at Bay walking away from him and thought the very same thing. One of them would have to die.

CHAPTER 18

Shakita was back in the city and was still broken by all the money she had lost. She didn't want to go to work feeling all depressed, but she had no choice. She had to keep getting money, hoping to make enough to resolve her problem. She walked into the spa with her sunglasses on not wanting to look at anybody until the receptionist, Monique, called her over. Shakita didn't want to be bothered but went over to see what she wanted anyway. When Shakita got close to her, Monique handed her an envelope.

"What's this?" Shakita asked, confused.

Monique smiled. "It's your check."

Shakita had forgotten that they got paid every week and needed this money more than Monique knew. She quickly tore open the envelope so she could see the amount.

What the fuck is this? Shakita said to herself as frustration spread across her face. "Is Eric up there?"

"Yes he is. Would you like me to call him for you?"

"Please do."

Monique smiled, paying Shakita's anger no mind and placed the call for her. "Yes, Eric. Shakita is here to see you. Okay… No problem."

Shakita was going to be pissed off if Eric dismissed her visit.

"Here's your card."

"Thank you, Mo," Shakita said as she walked away in a hurry. Shakita couldn't wait to get off that elevator so she could tell Eric what she really thought about her check. She arrived and entered.

"Eric. What the hell is this?" Shakita said as she held out the check.

Eric leaned back in his chair. "It's your check. I'm not understanding what the problem is."

"Eight hundred dollars, Eric! What am I supposed to do with this? You told me I would be making more money than this."

"Relax, girl. The pay period cut-off day was Friday. That means that check is only for two days. Don't worry; they get bigger."

"I can't tell. I did all that work and this is all I get?"

"You just started back. If you want more money, you're going to have to rely on your recurring clients. Those men alone should provide you with all the money you need." Eric spoke unflustered, hoping that Shakita would calm down and see his point.

"What about putting me on the damn purple or black floors? I don't have time to be depending on tips!" Shakita shouted while Eric remained cool.

"I told you already. Those rooms are not for you."

"You keep saying that and not telling me why. I need to know why."

Eric thought for a second about what Shakita asked him before he answered. "Didn't I give you ten grand the other night?"

"Yeah. But I asked you for two hundred and fifty."

"What I'm getting at is if I gave you ten and you have been making good tips, you should have close to twenty thousand or more right now."

Shakita gave him an uneasy look as he continued to talk.

"And if you still had twenty thousand now, you and I both know that you would reach your mark right when you need it. So that makes me wonder if you still have the money."

Shakita became stumped by Eric's assumption of her and didn't feel comfortable being in his presence any longer. She rolled her eyes at him and then walked away. She realized he may have been on to her and needed to do something else to make that money back. If Eric wasn't going to let her in the purple and black rooms, then she was going to have to get it another way. She was going to have to work the corners even though Eric didn't want her to. Yet, it wasn't Eric's life that was on the line. It was hers. If Eric wasn't going to ensure her life, she had to go against him and do it herself. Shakita would hit the streets and start hoeing. She had to make that money.

Eric watched as Shakita left his suite and couldn't understand why she had so many problems with saving money. If he didn't know any better, he would have presumed she had a drug problem. But he knew Shakita better than that and realized she must have still been gambling. He didn't understand why she kept putting herself through the misery of losing. Eric was a risk taker himself but never spent everything he had on only one investment. He was convinced that it didn't matter if Shakita were on the purple or black floors. If she was gambling again, she would still find a way to lose all her money. Even if he gave her the two hundred and fifty thousand that she had asked for, he wasn't sure she would do the right thing with it. Shakita was going to have to make that decision on her own.

Shakita got off work an hour earlier and hit the streets to make more money. She made four thousand in tips for the night but still wasn't satisfied. She left her car parked in the garage and walked up to Logan Circle. This was one of the hot strips that Eric had his girls work on. When Shakita got on the strip, she didn't recognize any of the hoes except for one, Cotton, a thick white girl who wore her long black hair in a ponytail. Her diamond-studded earrings, electric-pink lipstick, and ultra-short mini dress was her winning formula to getting paid. Cotton labored the corners because Eric wouldn't let her work in the spa. He wanted to keep an environment with only women of color and Cotton's white ass wasn't dark enough.

"What's going on, Cotton? I didn't think you would still be out here."

"Well, everybody ain't got privileges like you to work in the spa," Cotton said sarcastically.

"How you know I'm back over there?"

"You know how. We in the hoe business and hoes talk." Cotton took a pull from her cigarette. "Since you working at the spa, what brings your ass out here?"

"Times are rough."

"You got some nerve talking about times are rough? At least you get to work on the fucking inside. I'm a rain, sleet, or snow bitch. If anybody got it rough, it's my ass."

Cotton was very bitter about not being able to work at the spa. The spa bitches had it three times as good as the strip hoes and had no risks to take. Shakita always thought Cotton was jealous when it came to her position, but she couldn't care less. It wasn't her fault that Cotton was born white.

"So how many johns you have tonight?" Shakita asked.

Cotton gave her a nasty look. "Ain't you making enough money at the pussy palace already?"

"No, bitch. Didn't I just tell you that times were rough?"

Cotton raised her eyebrow. "Does Eric know you're out here?"

"No he doesn't and I plan to keep it that way."

"Well, bitches talk so you better be careful," Cotton said, giving her fair warning to stay off her block.

"Well, if I find out that one of them bitches is you, then you are the one that will need to be careful."

Cotton couldn't do anything but suck her teeth at Shakita, and then responded to a trick that had pulled over for her. "You looking for a good time, baby?" Cotton said as she stuck her head in the passenger-side window. The trick agreed with her price and Cotton rolled her eyes again at Shakita before she got in the car and was off.

Shakita knew that Cotton wasn't a fighter and really didn't want any problems with her. Cotton was only mad at her circumstances and not with Shakita. She believed Cotton wouldn't say a word to Eric. If she did, her ass was going down. Even if it did get back to Eric that she was tricking, she really didn't care. He wasn't willing to help her more than he was. She was the only one who cared if she lived or died, and that's why she was out working the corners. Shakita wore a silk violet-colored halter and a black mini skirt as she strutted in her four-inch heels. She was determined to get some money out there and she had three hours to do it before the sun came up.

Shakita was walking hard, trying to get the attention of every car that rode past until one of them finally stopped.

"Hey, baby? You looking for a good time?"

"What can I pay for?" the middle-aged black man asked.

"Two hundred for pussy and fifty for head," Shakita said as she leaned in the window. "Get in," the man told her as he unlocked the door to his Camaro.

Shakita got in and they both were off. The man parked his car in a quiet alley that was across from the House of Kabob on N Street, so that they could get it on. The man only wanted to pay for sex so that's what she was going to give him once he paid up front. She rolled the condom down on his dick until it reached the bottom of his shaft and then climbed on top of him in his seat. The man tilted his seat back and let Shakita do what she did best. When it was all over, the man had definitely gotten his money's worth. He told himself he would return for some of her sweet pussy when he got paid again.

Thirty minutes later, Shakita was back on the strip and looking for her next trick, and it wasn't long before she found one. A gray Lincoln Town Car pulled up a little way in front of her and she walked up to it.

"You tryna have some fun?" she asked the white man as she leaned in the window.

"How much?" he asked.

"Two hundred for pussy and fifty for head."

"Two hundred? Ain't that kind of steep for a piece of ass?"

"No, two hundred is cheap for this type of ass, baby. I should be charging you a thousand as good as this pussy is."

"I don't know, honey. Turn around so I could see that little tight ass of yours."

Shakita turned around, then lifted up her skirt and put her entire ass in the window, showing him her luscious back side. She then jiggled her ass cheeks in his face, giving the man more of a reason to want her.

"Not bad, sweetheart. Not bad," he said as she turned back around and lowered her skirt. "So do you want this pussy or not, daddy?"

"Do you do anal?" he asked in a creepy, whispering tone.

White men are such fucking disgusting pigs. They always wanna do some anal shit, she thought to herself.

"Yeah. But that's another two hundred."

"All right, get in. You better be worth it."

"Oh believe me, baby, I am," she said as she got in the car and shut the door.

"So do you want me to pay you now?"

"You know it. No money, no honey, baby." Shakita said as she held her hand out for payment.

The man quickly reached in his pocket and placed his badge in her hand.

"You're under arrest," he said before Shakita even knew what she was holding.

Another unmarked car pulled up beside them with the sirens blaring, backing up their fellow officer in case Shakita decided to run. She couldn't believe what the hell was happening to her and wanted to cry. The undercover officer cuffed her and placed her in the backseat. As the car pulled off, Shakita rode with her head down as the tears began to fall. She was about to go to jail for prostitution and she was scared as hell. She'd never been to jail and so far, this was the worst day of her life. Her mind was in a whirlwind as she headed off to jail. *What the fuck am I going to do now?*

As Cotton stood on the other side of the street watching all the action, she couldn't help but to find it amusing at how Shakita had gotten caught up. When the car that was transporting Shakita to jail was finally off the street, the other unmarked car came around to where Cotton was standing and stopped in front of her. She walked over to the car and lowered herself to the officer's window.

"Thanks for the tip, darling," the officer said to her.

Cotton smiled. "No problem. I owed you a favor, right? Favors are what we do for each other."

"Now I owe you one," he said as he waved a handful of money

at her. Cotton grabbed the money and then walked over to the passenger side and got in.

Cotton sat back in the seat as the car began to move. She was off to go show her cop friend a good time and had Shakita to thank for it. The money she received tonight for helping get Shakita busted was more than she would have made in a whole day. Shakita may have had a job at the spa that Cotton always wanted, but out in the streets, Cotton was the queen of the night. She didn't feel sorry for what she'd done to Shakita, and neither did the cops. Besides, it wasn't their fault that Shakita was born "black."

CHAPTER 19

"Turn to the left."

Snap!

"Now turn to the right."

Snap!

Shakita couldn't believe she was getting her mug shot taken and it was the most humiliating thing she'd ever had to do in her life, besides getting strip-searched. During the rest of her intake process, she was allowed to make phone calls before her hearing took place. There was no one she could call who would bail her out without asking why she was there in the first place. She thought about calling Eric, but she didn't want him knowing about her arrest. She still needed to work at the spa and didn't want Eric to lose his trust in her so soon. Since she couldn't call Eric, that meant her only other option was Latrice.

Latrice wouldn't understand why she was in jail either, but if Shakita had to count on someone, it would have to be her. She dialed Latrice's number and hoped she would pick up.

"Who the fuck is callin' me this early?" Latrice wondered. She looked at the clock to see that it was only 8 a.m. She hoped it was a telemarketer so she could cuss their ass out for calling her house so early in the morning.

"Hello," she answered, sounding halfway sleep.

The way the automated prompter came on, she knew it was a collect call from the D.C. Jail. "I actually talked to his ass yesterday," Latrice said, waiting to hear Bay's name.

"You have a collect call from... *Shakita Marshall*... Do you accept the charges?"

"What the fuck is she doing in there?" Latrice was so shocked that Shakita was calling her from jail that she almost forgot to accept the charges. She quickly sat up in bed and accepted the call. She couldn't wait to find out what was going on.

"Hello," Shakita spoke hesitantly.

"Girl! What the hell are you doing in there?"

Shakita didn't want to tell her what was going on yet, but she had to tell her something. "I can't explain everything right now, but I might need you to bail me out."

Latrice was momentarily speechless as she covered her face not believing what she was hearing. "Kita. I don't even know what to say to you right now."

Latrice didn't even like bailing Bay out of jail and now her best friend was asking her to do the same for her.

"I know you're mad at me, but I really need your help."

Latrice remained silent as Shakita continued to plea for her help until she gave in. "Aight. But you better tell me everything."

"I will. I need you to get me out of here first."

"When do I need to be down there?"

"My hearing isn't until ten-thirty, so you can come here around twelve."

"I knew this was going to happen to your ass one day," Latrice said, letting Shakita know how frustrated she was with her.

Shakita sucked her teeth. "What is that supposed to mean?"

"It means you always doing some grimy-ass shit. I wouldn't be surprised if you told me you were in there for credit card fraud or some shit like that."

"Could you just come down here, please?" Shakita asked not knowing what else to say to her.

"I'll be there as soon as I can." Latrice hung up the phone and not giving Shakita a chance to say anything else.

She was fully aware that Latrice was really pissed off with her and had every reason to be. If Latrice was mad about having to go pick Shakita up from jail, she was really going to have a problem when she found out about the money. Shakita hung up the phone and went to sit on a bench along with some other women in the holding cell. Shakita crossed her legs and then rubbed her goose-bump-covered arms, as she attempted to keep herself warm from the cool air that continued to travel through the bars. She looked leery at the other women in the holding cell. They were all in there for various crimes, and it finally resonated that jail was no where she wanted to be. She hoped 10:30 would come quickly.

Shakita was escorted into the courtroom in her jumpsuit while the judge had already been waiting for her. She noticed the judge was a black man and thought he might go easier on her, since she was a "sistah." Shakita wasn't worried about going to jail anyway. She was a first offender, and heard from other prostitutes that you only get hit with a small bail and a fine. She was expecting to be released by noon and still make it to work on time.

Judge Tomlin was a dark-skinned man with a small afro and wore thin-framed glasses. He had big eyes that immediately demanded your attention. Judge Tomlin had been on the bench for over fifteen years and had seen every type of individual walk through his courtroom. He hated it the most when black women were coming before him now at the same rate as black men. He didn't understand where so many of them went wrong.

"Miss Marshall. I see here that you have been picked up for soliciting. Is that correct?" Judge Tomlin asked as he looked over her file.

"Yes, Your Honor," Shakita answered meekly.

"I also see that this is your first offense, but you and I both know that this is the first time you've ever been caught." Shakita gave the judge a guilty look.

"How long have you been soliciting, Miss Marshall?"

"Only a few times," she answered, trying to sound believable.

"Only a few times? Is this what you want to be doing for the rest of your life?"

"No, Your Honor. I needed some fast money."

"I guess receiving a paycheck every two weeks isn't fast enough these days?" Judge Tomlin said sarcastically.

The situation Shakita was in would not allow a regular paycheck to fix her problem. She needed more money than the judge was able to understand.

"So, Miss Marshall, do you currently have a day job?"

"No, Your Honor."

"Why don't you have a job, Miss Marshall?"

"I've had a hard time trying to find one."

"That is funny you say that, Miss Marshall. I looked in the *Washington Post* this morning and saw pages and pages of them." Shakita didn't have anything to say. "You know what I think your problem is, Miss Marshall? You, along with most of young America, want instant gratification. You don't want to work hard for anything and want everything right now. Let me ask you this, Miss Marshall. Were you trying to get money to support a drug habit?"

"No, Your Honor. I don't use drugs."

"Are you homeless?"

"No, Your Honor. I have somewhere to live."

"So you are not on drugs, nor are you homeless. Do you like selling your body to men?"

"No, Your Honor."

"How old are you, Miss Marshall?

"I'm twenty-one, Your Honor."

"Is your father in your life?"

"No, Your Honor."

Judge Tomlin removed his glasses and rubbed his brow. He was a father and couldn't picture not being in his children's lives.

"Miss Marshall. I have two daughters that are around your age. One of them attends the University of Pittsburgh for law school and the other is a sophomore at Virginia State University. I understand how hard it is for a young girl to not have her father involved in her upbringing. I certainly didn't have my father in mine. Yet, I didn't use that as an excuse not to be able to succeed in life. Instead I found a few role models to help me get to where I am today. Just like my two girls, I also see promise in you, Miss Marshall." Shakita didn't ask for the motivational lecture, but she damn sure was listening.

"Now, Miss Marshall, normally what I do for women who come before me with soliciting charges is give them a minimum of thirty days in jail with a maximum of ninety."

Shakita's whole facial expression changed when the judge talked about how much jail time he could give her. She never thought that she would receive so much time for never being locked up, but she didn't ever think about what would happen if she ever got caught. Shakita was scared as hell.

"But since you are young, Miss Marshall, and still have a long life ahead of you, I'm not going to do that today. I'm going to offer you a chance to turn your life around. Will you accept my offer?"

"Yes, Your Honor." Shakita quickly nodded her head, willing to accept any form of punishment other than jail.

"What I am going to do for you is have you assigned to a counselor so they can seek job placement for you. You will meet with your counselor today between the hours of three and five p.m. Your counselor will then see to it that you get on the right track. Since you have never had any prior arrests, I am going to let you leave here today on your own recognizance, and conduct a follow-up on you in sixty days to see if you have made any progression. Also, I will be placing you under a strict curfew that will require you to be at your primary address by midnight. Your curfew hours will be set from twelve-oh-one a.m. to six a.m. each night of the week. Does any of what I have said to you sound unfair, Miss Marshall?"

Shakita wanted to tell him that his whole offer was bullshit and that he was severely interfering with her social life. That meant she couldn't work at the spa, she couldn't go to the casino, she couldn't do shit that made her life seem normal. Yet, if she went to jail, her problems would be way worse. She had no choice but to play along if she wanted to get out of there. She shook her head, letting Judge Tomlin know that what he was offering her was fair.

"Okay, Miss Marshall. I want you to know that if you violate your curfew, you will be sent to jail for ninety days. Is that agreed?"

"Yes, Your Honor."

"Now, if I ever see you in my courtroom again, I promise you I will not be as nice. Do you understand?"

"Yes, Your Honor."

"All right. Case adjourned," Judge Tomlin said as he banged his gavel. Shakita was escorted back out the courtroom on her way to getting processed out. Judge Tomlin watched Shakita leave the courtroom and thought heavily on his decision. He hoped he wasn't making a mistake.

CHAPTER 20

Shakita was processed and given back all her property except for the money she had in her purse. She couldn't get it back since it was considered trick money, so she didn't worry about it and made sure everything else was in her purse. She'd gotten all the information she needed to bring with her when she'd met her counselor and was hoping that Latrice hadn't shown up to come get her yet. It was only 11:15 and she wasn't expecting Latrice to be there for quite some time. Since she was released with no bail, she didn't need Latrice after all. Shakita hoped she could avoid Latrice a little while longer until she thought up another plan.

Shakita looked around for Latrice, and when she didn't see her, she proceeded to leave out through the doors, trying to make a smooth getaway.

"Did you forget you asked me to come down here?" Latrice asked, coming up from Shakita's blind side.

"Fuck!" Shakita said under her breath not wanting to turn around to face her. "No. I thought you might be waiting out in the car," Shakita said, turning around saying the first thing to come to mind.

"Yeah. Bullshit. You can't avoid me now." Latrice wanted some answers. Shakita was backed up against a wall now.

The car ride to Latrice's apartment was unbearably quiet for

Latrice as Shakita acted as if she was sleep to avoid being con-
fronted. There were so many things racing through her mind as
the thought of Shakita being arrested weighed heavy on her heart.
She looked over at Shakita, well aware that she was pretending,
but soon enough, her truths would be revealed.

Shakita sat down on the couch as Latrice stood over her waiting
for her to talk. Shakita had run out of ways to dodge Latrice or
bullshit her about what was going on. Latrice was not going to let
her leave without telling her everything.

"So what do you want to know?"

"What do you think, Shakita? I wanna know why you were out
there being a damn hoe."

"I had to make some money, that's all," Shakita said, not able to
look her in the eyes.

"Come on now, bitch. You were that pressed for some money,
you had to be a trick bitch? That's not even like you. Well, maybe
it is 'cause I feel like I don't even know you anymore. What the
fuck is wrong with you? Are you a whore? Are you on drugs?"

Shakita felt so bombarded with questions that she didn't know
which one to answer first. "No, I'm not on drugs," Shakita said,
answering the easiest one.

"Then what the fuck is your problem then? I know you ain't out
there lunching for nothing."

Shakita saw how angry Latrice was getting. She took a deep
breath and decided fuck it. It was time to be straight up with her.

"All right, Latrice. I'm gonna tell you everything. I love you and
you're my best friend. But once I tell you, I don't think we're going
to be friends anymore."

Latrice was confused. "What are you talking about?"

Shakita wiped her face with her hands before she revealed what was causing her and Latrice to become so distant.

"Latrice. I blew Bay's money."

Latrice gave her a puzzled look. "What money?"

"The money he had you hold for him until he got out," Shakita was embarrassed to say.

"Nah. You're lying," Latrice said, shaking her head in disbelief, as she went to go check where she'd hidden the money. Latrice ran into her closet and started throwing everything out of the way so she could get to the money. She opened up a mini door that led to a crawl space, and that's when she saw the large empty plastic bag that was once filled with money. Latrice broke down instantly.

"No! No! No! Fuck no!" Latrice cried out loud enough for Shakita to hear her in the other room. Shakita could then tell that Latrice was coming back to confront her. She could hear her footsteps and grunting getting louder. Shakita was ready for Latrice to explode as soon as she entered the room.

"What the fuck is wrong with you? I told you not to touch that fucking money! Bay's going to kill me over that shit! I feel like smacking your ass out right now! I can't believe you would do some dumb-ass shit like that!

"I'm sorry, Latrice. I tried everything I could to make it back."

"Yes, you are a sorry-ass bitch. What did you do gamble it all away?" Shakita didn't respond. "You did, didn't you? For that shit you're going to get us both killed. You know he's coming out this month, right? You really picked the best time to fuck up his money. He was going to use that shit to start up a record label with the artists I fucking got for him. Now I can't sign no fucking body!" Latrice was furious and couldn't believe her best friend had ruined everything she was working toward. Latrice began to pace the room thinking about what Bay was going to do to her while Shakita stayed quiet.

"You know what, bitch? Since you want to be on 'Wheel of Fortune' so fucking bad, then you're telling Bay your damn self."

"Okay, I will. I really didn't mean to get you into this shit. I know I fucked up."

"Bitch, you did more than fucked up. You just killed yourself. Bay merc niggas for stealing ten g's. So what the fuck you think he's going to do to us when he find out over two hundred thousand of his money he told me to fucking hold for him is gone? That nigga's going to go on a killing spree!"

"I'll tell him it was just me, and you had no involvement."

"You can tell him whatever the fuck you want. I know I got to get the fuck out of town," Latrice said as she headed back into her bedroom.

"No you don't, Latrice! I can fix this!" Shakita said, getting off the couch to follow her. Latrice started packing up everything she needed, not knowing when she would be able to return to her apartment.

"What are you doing?"

"I told you I'm getting the fuck out of here. I had dreams of making it big before you decided to turn my life into a fucking nightmare."

"Please stop and let me talk to you for a second," Shakita said as she sat in front of Latrice's suitcase. "Give me another chance to fix this shit. I owe it to you to at least do that. I've been doing some things that I'm really not proud of trying to get the money back, but kept coming up short. Please give me another chance to make this right and if I don't, we'll both leave together."

Latrice heard Shakita's sincerity but was still too emotional to acknowledge it. She told herself that she was going to give Shakita a chance to make things right before Bay got out. She didn't know how Shakita was going to pull it off, but she was praying for a miracle. Latrice had to accept that Shakita was now going to gamble with something she was never willing to do herself. Shakita was going to gamble with her life.

Shakita called Monique, the receptionist at The Black Emporium, and told her she wouldn't be coming in that day, and didn't know when she would be returning. She didn't tell Monique about her having a curfew since it wasn't any of her business but her own. Shakita wanted to tell Eric herself that she may not be back, but didn't want to hear his comforting voice over the phone. Eric wasn't willing to help her any more than he had, so there was no point in telling him more than he needed to know.

Shakita walked into the National Institute of Corrections building and went up to the fourth floor to the Office of Correctional Job and Training Placement. "I'm here to see Yolanda Graves," Shakita told the receptionist as she read the name off of her folder.

"And your name?" the secretary asked.

"Shakita Marshall."

"One second. Let me see if she is available," the secretary said as she got up and walked to the back of the office.

While she waited, Shakita looked at the other people in the office that were using computers or waiting to be seen, and couldn't believe she was there to actually get a real job. She hadn't been in the work force since she was a teenager and didn't want to deal with the minimum wage paying nine-to-five. She was used to chasing fast money at a high expense, but that was all about to change now.

The secretary walked back to her desk and right behind her was Yolanda Graves. Yolanda was a tall, brown-skinned woman and looked like she used to play in the WNBA a few years back.

"Miss Marshall. You can come with me," Yolanda informed her as she started to walk back to her office.

She could have at least shook my hand first, Shakita thought to herself as she followed behind Yolanda.

"You can have a seat right there," Yolanda said, signaling her as she stood outside her door waiting for Shakita to step into her office. Shakita sat down as Yolanda closed the door and sat behind her desk.

"So how are you?" Yolanda asked as she had her elbows on the table and bridged her hands under her chin.

"I'm fine," Shakita answered, wondering if Yolanda was trying to intimidate her by the way she was looking at her.

"So how long have you been soliciting yourself?" Yolanda asked smugly.

"Not long. Only a few times."

"Only a few times, huh? Let me ask you this, Miss Marshall. Do you respect yourself?"

"Yes, I respect myself."

"If you respect yourself, then why do you offer yourself to men? Your body should be your temple and not used as a doormat for men to walk on. You don't have to do sex work."

"Wait a minute. I thought I was here so you could get me a job? I didn't know you were gonna chastise me. I'm not some lil' whore who runs tricks 'cause she ain't got no self-esteem. I know who I am. I just made some bad decisions that required me to do what I had to do."

"I'm not trying to offend you," Yolanda said, taking the more subtle approach. "I wanted you to know that there are other ways you can earn money."

"Well, do you know how I can make over two hundred fifty thousand dollars in a month?"

"Now that amount would be unrealistic, don't you think?"

Shakita gave her a serious look. "Not to me. That's my reality right now. What's unrealistic is for me to still be alive if I don't get it."

Yolanda took concern. "Are you in some type of serious trouble? Do you think we should get the authorities involved?"

"The police already got involved. That's how I got arrested. They can't help me so don't even worry about it. I'll figure it out myself."

"Shakita, if someone is trying to harm you, I think you should let me know. I have people that can help you."

"Police don't help people like me. They only make the situation worse; they can't protect me every second of the day so I'm better off without them."

Yolanda saw that Shakita was being stern and wasn't going to force her to say anything she didn't want to. "Well, before you leave, what I'm going to do is give you a number of a good friend of mine. I believe he can help if you decide to change your mind, okay?" Shakita nodded her head yes.

Yolanda had misjudged who Shakita was in the beginning, and decided to give her a job that wasn't a sign of punishment for being a disgrace to her race. She was going to place her with a job that she could use as a career builder and at the same time displayed hard work. Yolanda felt Shakita needed another chance to show she had more to offer to society. Yolanda believed Shakita wouldn't like any job she gave her, but she placed her somewhere she would stay out of trouble.

"I'm going to place you as a custodial technician with BERK Transit System," Yolanda said. She then passed Shakita her paperwork. BERK was the name of the city's metro train system. The initials stood for Better Equipped Rail Kompany.

"I'm going to be a janitor?" Shakita asked confused.

"'Janitor' is the old term, Shakita. The pushing-the-mop stereotype is no longer associated with this position. You'll have plenty of duties and responsibilities. This position will give you an opportunity to move up in the company if you desire."

Shakita wasn't exactly sold on the whole idea of being a custodian, but there wasn't much she could do but play the game right now. Shakita's work hours were able to be set anywhere between the hours of 6 a.m. to 10 p.m., with two days off scheduled throughout the week that would be decided by her manager. This meant she wasn't able to find a way to get back to the spa to make some real money. She didn't know what she was going to do in order to come up with the money. She had to think fast. Bay's release date was rapidly approaching. Shakita walked out of Yolanda's office with a job, but still had no positive outlook on her future. She thought in the back of her mind, if push came to shove, that she might have to break the "street code," and get Bay caught up even more. He'd never see the light of day again.

CHAPTER 21

Shakita had been at her new job for a week now and still hadn't gotten used to being in a normal work environment. She hated all her job responsibilities except for punching off the clock on time. Other than that it was the worst job she'd ever had. She would rather be a waitress somewhere than change garbage cans and mop floors all damn day. She didn't know how much more she could take of it and needed to find another way to get Bay's money back. Time was ticking away and Shakita had three weeks to come up with something big.

Maybe I should rob a bank, Shakita thought to herself as she swept the sidewalk outside the Greenbelt BERK Station. *Nah, that shit's dumb as hell. That'll never work. What if I robbed some balling-ass nigga? That shit would take too long for the nigga to trust me though. If I knew how to get to Eric's shit, I would rob his ass.* Shakita began to laugh at her thoughts as she picked up her dustpan and broom, and went inside the station. *I can't think of shit. Damn, what am I going to do?* Shakita thought as she began to sweep around the subway passengers that were coming and going throughout the busy station.

Shakita continued to sweep until she heard a vibrant sound that sent shockwaves up her spine. It damn near gave her an orgasm. She immediately associated it with the same sound she heard at the casino when someone hit big on the slot machines. She quickly turned around and saw a BERK employee dumping hundreds of coins out of a fare machine and into a large metal canister. Shakita continued to watch the employee with hungry eyes as he went from machine to machine removing thousands of coins and bills. When he was done, she followed him outside and watched as he loaded the canister onto a long white Ford van with tinted windows and then left the station. Shakita stood there in total disbelief of what she had seen, and was soon able to think up a plan that would get her riches beyond her wildest dreams. She couldn't wait to tell Latrice her plan. She hoped this time she would be part of her scheme. She was definitely going to need her for this one.

"You wanna rob a train?" Latrice asked, totally astonished.

"No. We can't go on a train hitting people up. I want to rob the van."

"A van? What van?"

"The van that all the money leaves the station in."

"But won't the driver have a gun?"

"Yeah, but don't even worry about that. I got it all planned out to where he won't even be able to go for his shit. By the time he figures out what's going on, we'll already have the drop on 'em and have the whole van cleaned out."

"I don't know about that, Kita. It all sounds too risky. I think we should consider something else."

"Something else?" Shakita looked at Latrice like she was crazy. "Do you know how long it took me to think of this shit? There's no other plan better than this. We got three weeks to make this shit happen. You hear me? Three weeks. This is it. If we don't try it, we're good as dead anyway, right? So what the fuck do we have to lose? We got to get this money," Shakita said, desperately explaining their now-or-never opportunity.

Latrice was still unsure if Shakita's plan was going to work. Robbing an armed guard for the money he was transporting was as dangerous as running up into someone's drug spot and demanding their stash. The only difference was that the guard could legally kill them or have them convicted of a federal crime. Latrice didn't even want to begin to think about the years that the feds handed out for what they were thinking about doing. Even though Latrice was overreluctant about Shakita's heist idea, she still wasn't about to come up with a winning solution of her own.

She thought that Shakita's suggestion was naïve and perilous, but it could work. If the plan was carried out exactly right then, the payoff they'd get would be enormous. Bay would have his money back and they would have enough money left over to do whatever they wanted. She thought about Clarity and the rest of her artists that were at stake and wanted to hear more of Shakita's blueprint. Shakita pulled Latrice's attention closer and explained every part of her plan in full detail.

Shakita arrived at work a little earlier than usual hoping to find Reggie. Reggie was medium height, slightly overweight, and had patchy brown skin. Shakita knew him from high school, but he was never her type to pay much attention to. Reggie, on the other hand, always tried to get at Shakita back then and still did, which she planned to use to her advantage. Reggie was a Revenue Processing Technician who handled the money as it came in, and if anybody had any idea how the cash left the stations, it would be him.

Shakita spotted Reggie talking to another coworker when they were coming down the escalator. Reggie wore thick ugly glasses and she could spot him a mile away. Shakita had to find out what he knew.

"What's up, Reggie? Can I holler at you for a minute?" she asked as Reggie stepped off the escalator.

"Yeah, we can talk. All right, man. I'll get up with you later," Reggie said, ending his conversation with his coworker.

"Let's walk over here," Shakita said, leading him over by the elevator.

Reggie was surprised that Shakita wanted to ask him something and he was eager to find out what it was.

"So what's going on, Reggie?" Shakita asked, trying to make small talk.

"Nothing. About to clock in. What's up with you?" Reggie asked, wondering if she were going to ask him to borrow some lunch money. He figured since she'd just started working, that's what she wanted to talk about.

"Reggie, I need to ask you for a favor, but I need you to keep it between us," Shakita said in a low tone so no one else around could hear.

Reggie was assured then if she were trying to keep something low, that it had to be about borrowing some money.

"I got you. What's up?" Reggie said, trying to fuel his curiosity.

"You told me you work with the money that comes out of the fare machines, right?"

"Yeah. Why?" Reggie asked, confused.

"Do you know where it all goes once it leaves here?"

Reggie thought for a second before he answered. He needed to know why she was asking.

"If I did know, what would I get for telling you?"

"Hold up, Reggie. I thought we were better than that. Why it got to be about something?"

"Hey. You asked me for a favor, remember? I could see if we were all like that, but you know what it is."

"It wasn't like you were trying to be my best friend either," Shakita said in her defense.

"Girl, please. You know I was on your shit hard back in school. You weren't even paying my ass any attention."

"I used to talk to you all the time. You know I ain't do you like that," Shakita said, trying to get on his good side.

Reggie twisted his lips. "Yeah, whatever, girl."

"Well, if I did do that, then I'm sorry. But I'm older now so I don't think like a child anymore. I'm a grown woman now and I need a grown man favor from you."

"So you a grown woman, huh?" Reggie said, looking Shakita up and down.

"Yeah, I'm a grown-ass woman. Now if you tell me everything I need to know, I'll break you off a nice piece of change for helping out."

"You're trying to do some crazy shit, huh?"

"Ain't nothing crazy about anything as long as you plan right. You feel what I'm saying? Without you, this thing can't happen."

"So you need me, huh?"

"Let's just say you're the missing piece to the puzzle," Shakita said, not wanting Reggie to think he was going to be head of her operation.

Reggie thought for a second and then looked at Shakita with a sly eye. "If I'm going to be involved in whatever shit you got going on, then you got to do something special for me first."

"I'm already going to break bread with you. What else do you want?"

"Girl, you know what I want. I want that monkey," Reggie said as he licked his lips.

Shakita wasn't surprised at all by Reggie's request. She was well aware that he wanted to taste her ass back in high school, and judging by the way he was looking at her, the thought had been on his mind ever since. Reggie was not someone Shakita would ever fuck for fun, being that he was dog-face ugly and fat as hell.

Shakita was used to getting big tips for fucking someone like Reggie at the spa, and if having sex with Reggie would lead her to masterminding her plan, then that would be the biggest tip anyone could ever give her right now.

"I can make that happen if you can tell me where that money goes when it leaves here. I need an exact location. Can you do that?"

"As long as we can do our thing, I'll tell you whatever you want."

"Cool. When can you make that happen?"

"After I get what I want first. Then I'll talk."

Shakita didn't like putting out before she got what she wanted, but in this situation, she had no choice but to give in. "Okay. We'll fuck first. But you better not pull no bama-ass shit. 'Cause once you get this pussy, you're going to want it again."

"I hear what you're saying. So when are we going to do this?"

"The sooner the better. When can we meet?"

"Meet me tomorrow night at ten-thirty at the Fort Totten Station. I'll have my man working the booth cover us."

"You're trying to fuck at one of the stations? Why can't we go somewhere else?"

"You said the sooner the better, right? If we sneak in the bathroom there, we can be in and out. I'm trying to make it easier on you," Reggie said, not telling her that he really lived with his girlfriend, and couldn't take her back to his spot. He didn't want to pay for a room either since he didn't know if Shakita was worth it or not.

"All right then, ten-thirty. Remember what I said," Shakita warned.

"I got you. Don't worry about it, baby."

"I'm going to go clock in now. The next time I see you, make sure you're about business," Shakita said as she started to walk away.

Reggie gave her a nod and watched her walk on. *God must really love me. I finally get to tear that ass up*, Reggie said to himself.

Reggie got an instant hard-on thinking about what he was going to do to Shakita, and then quickly got on the phone to set up everything at the Fort Totten Station for tomorrow night. Shakita didn't even turn back around, not wanting to see Reggie's ugly-ass face until tomorrow night. Even that was too soon for her, but it had to be done. She couldn't wait for her business to be done with Reggie so she wouldn't have to deal with him ever again.

Shakita got off the train and was at the Fort Totten Station at 10:25. She didn't see Reggie yet and hoped he wasn't late since she needed to be home by midnight. She looked in the information booth and saw only one person. She figured he was the one who was going to watch out for them. She continued to wait for Reggie in the half-empty station, when she saw him waving at her as he peeked out the Fire Equipment Cabinet Room door. Shakita looked around to see if anyone were paying attention to her and then quickly went into the room with Reggie.

When Shakita was in the room, Reggie closed the door behind her and led her into the bathroom. Reggie locked the door so that they wouldn't be disturbed on accident.

"All right. We got to get this shit cracking. I got to get back over my way by twelve," Shakita said as she undid her pants.

Reggie hurried and kicked off his boots, not wanting to waste any time either. He was standing in only his wife beater and socks, as he wondered why Shakita hadn't taken her pants off yet. "Are you going to take 'em off or do you want me to do it?" Reggie asked with lust in his eyes.

"No, I'll do it. I'm only taking one pants leg off," Shakita said as she kicked off her shoe.

"So how you want to do this?"

Reggie walked toward her. "I want to hit that shit from the back."

Shakita turned around and leaned up against the sink. "Hold up. I want to suck those titties first," Reggie said, turning her around and lifting up her shirt. He pulled up her bra and began to lick all over her soft breasts. After a few unpleasant minutes of her nipples getting bit and tugged on, she was ready for him to get to it.

"All right. Are you ready yet?" she asked with irritation.

"Are you?" he said, moving his fingers down her stomach to feel how wet she was.

"I'm always wet," Shakita said after Reggie pulled his slick fingers out of her opening.

"Yeah, you wet than a mothafucka. I still want to add my own lubricant to it, though."

Reggie bent down and started licking her pussy. Her juices dripped off of his tongue and gathered onto the bathroom floor.

Damn! This nigga's eating my pussy like he's trying to bite the shit off! Shakita thought as Reggie moved his head viciously back and forth. She hoped that he would stop soon. The shit didn't feeling good at all. Reggie continued to devour on her until his jaws started hurting.

"All right, turn back around now," he said, wiping his mouth off and getting back on his feet. Shakita turned back around and then lifted up her shirt so Reggie could easily find his way into her pussy.

Damn! Her ass wasn't fat like this in high school. She got to be on the shot, Reggie thought, admiring her plump ass. Reggie wiped the precum off his dick and was about to put it in, until Shakita turned around and looked at him crazily.

"Boy. If you don't put on a damn condom and stop playing with me. I don't even get down like that."

"My bad, boo," Reggie said as he disappointedly reached into his pants pocket and pulled out a condom. Reggie wanted to hit Shakita raw dog bad as hell but didn't put it in fast enough. After she watched him slip on the condom, and then put himself inside her, she turned around and faced the mirror. She couldn't help but laugh on the inside at how small his dick was. She started cracking jokes to herself. *Damn. Baby dick tried to pull a fast one on me. I hope that condom don't come off with his lil'-dick self*, Shakita thought, putting her head down so Reggie couldn't see her laughing at him.

Reggie was inside her and felt like suddenly, he was in heaven. He was really enjoying how good her pussy felt. *Damn, this pussy's bomb as shit. I can't believe I'm hitting this shit*, Reggie thought as he danced inside her doing all types of tricks.

What the fuck is he doing? Shakita wondered, as she looked at him through the mirror while he danced behind her.

Shakita sucked her teeth. "Aye, nigga. Stop doing the fucking two-step in my pussy and fuck me, all right? You're wasting time."

Reggie stopped playing around and began to focus on what he was doing. He started to pump hard as Shakita looked at him through the mirror watching him make ugly-ass faces while he tried to concentrate. Shakita was not fazed by his weak penetration and wanted him to hurry up and finish. Reggie continued to pump fast and then really got into it when he felt he was about to bust. It felt so good to him when he let off in her warm pouch that he got chills through his entire body. Reggie pulled out and leaned up against the stall unable to stand up straight. He was breathing heavy from exhaustion and had sweat beads all across his forehead.

Shakita was so glad that it was over; she hurried to put her pants back on.

"Hold up, baby. I'm trying to do it again. Give me a minute or two," Reggie said, sounding winded.

"Nah, mothafucka. I need you to tell me what I want to know first."

"What you want to know?" Reggie asked, still trying to suck in as much air as possible.

"Reggie, get your tired ass together and tell me where the damn money goes."

"I don't know that shit," Reggie said with a smirk on his face.

Shakita got even more pissed off as she got up in his face. "Reggie, you better be fucking with me. You already told me you knew where the fucking money goes! Now tell me where the fuck it goes, nigga, and stop bullshiting!"

Reggie started to laugh. "Girl, I was faking like shit. I don't know where that money be going. I only process the shit. Now I bet if you fuck the driver, he might tell you. Now come here, girl, and give me some more of that good pussy," Reggie said as he tried to pull Shakita closer to him.

Shakita was so fucking mad she got played that she pushed Reggie back into the stall, and then kicked him hard in his balls, sending him down to the floor in pain.

"I'm going to get somebody to fuck you up real good! You going to fucking lie to me so you could get some pussy, you fat motha-fucka!" Shakita started kicking him in his chest. She repeatedly kicked him until her shoe almost came off.

Reggie cried in pain as he continued to hold his throbbing nut sac. "I don't know what pain you're feeling, you lil'-dick motha-fucka!" Shakita clawed his glasses off him and then spat in his face. "If you tell anybody about what I'm trying to do! Whoever I send after your ass I'll make sure they cut that lil'-ass dick off too, bitch!" Shakita took his glasses and threw them at the wall, causing the lenses to shatter while crippling the frame. She then stormed out of the bathroom leaving him almost ass-naked on the floor.

Shakita ran up the steps hoping to catch the waiting train. The train doors were about to close as she ran and made it on. She sat down and started to bang on the window out of frustration as tears filled her eyes. She felt so nasty and degraded and couldn't believe that she'd let fat-ass Reggie take advantage of her. She became so distraught that she didn't know what she was going to do next. Shakita never had pictured it going down the way it had and wasn't prepared to use her back-up plan. Following the money herself would be hard as hell to do with the way her work schedule was set up, and she needed some special help to get the job done in time. She only had a few weeks to make it all happen, so she would have to get Latrice to be the mole and follow the van.

CHAPTER 22

Latrice was staked out in the Greenbelt BERK parking lot waiting for the long white van to appear. Latrice's job was easy, but she still felt scared knowing she had to be the one to follow the van. She'd never done anything like this in her whole life and didn't know if anything could backfire on her. She checked her rearview mirror and was suddenly distressed by the sight of the van. She quickly turned around and saw the van heading for the station to make a pickup. Her heart started to beat uncontrollably as the time to follow the van had now arrived. She folded her hands and started to pray knowing that she was wrong for asking God to help her through this situation, but she couldn't think of anything else that would help calm her nerves.

Latrice noticed the white van making its way back out of the station so she started her car up and waited for the right moment to follow it. The van made a right turn out of the parking lot and Latrice followed slowly behind. It made another right turn onto Greenbelt Road and then proceeded down River Road on its way to the College Park Station. Latrice took out her pen and wrote down the exact time the van made it to the station. Latrice saw that there was only one officer in the van and jotted it down to let Shakita know everything that was going on. Latrice thought that it was a good idea to take a photo of the driver. Shakita may have wanted to see what he looked like also.

The van veered off of the main road and then after a few turns, it ended up on Barton Road. The van then pulled into a lot that led to what seemed to be a large depository center. Latrice's suspicion was confirmed when the driver got out and started unloading the canisters while two other men helped him bring them into the building. Latrice snapped more pictures of what she was observing to give Shakita a better perspective of what they were up against. She took down a few more notes and then drove away without being seen. She felt she'd gotten a lot accomplished and would be able to give Shakita a thorough report on her findings. Even though Latrice had all the information she needed, she still didn't know what Shakita was going to do on her end. She couldn't visualize how she was going to make it happen. She hoped Shakita's outlook was a hell of a lot better than hers.

Shakita got off work and met up with Latrice shortly after.

"So whatchu find out?" Shakita asked intensely, taking a seat on Latrice's couch.

"Let me go back to the beginning of my notes," Latrice said, flipping through her notebook until she was on the right page. "The van came to the Greenbelt Station at two forty-three. Right around the time you said it would. I followed the van down to the College Park Station and then down to the end of the line at Branch Avenue. After that I thought it was going to the Blue Line to start collecting there too, but then it changed direction, and went to drop the money off. The van went to this big warehouse-looking place off of Barton Road. When the driver got out unloading the canisters, two other men helped him." Shakita was taking it all in as quickly as Latrice was able to spit it out.

"These are the pictures I took to give you a better idea what everything looked like," Latrice said as she sat down beside Shakita, and explained each picture she had in her digital camera. "This is the driver."

"That mothafucka cute too, oh well. He still going to catch hell if he fucks up and make the wrong move," Shakita implied.

"This is the kind of gun he have. Do you know what kind that is?"

"I don't know. It could be a nine or a forty-five; we got to ask Cap Cap. We got to go see him anyway about supplying us with some guns."

"And these are the pictures I took of the building where the money went. You can see right here and over there they have guards surrounding the whole shit."

"Yeah, I knew they were going to have that money guarded like shit. We're going to have to cut the driver off before they even get near there," Shakita said as she rubbed her hands together.

"How many canisters did they pull out the van?"

"Twenty-five of them. That's almost two per every stop."

"That's a lot of fucking money," Shakita said after lighting her cigarette and taking a pull from it.

They both sat and shook their heads thinking about all the money that would be on the van when they robbed it. If everything went smooth to the plan, they would be sitting on a lot of fucking money. This was going to be their ultimate come up.

Latrice and Shakita walked into Cap Cap's corner store that was right off of New York Avenue. Cap Cap was sitting on a stool behind the counter watching television as usual, waiting for the day to pass. He was a skinny, dark-skinned man in his late forties with not a single strand of gray hair. The streets had given him the name, Cap Cap. They used to say that he was so black that the only reason it got dark outside was because he captured all the sunlight when he came outside. Cap Cap saw the girls walk into his store, but he didn't even acknowledge them and kept watching TV. Cap Cap never smiled so you never could tell what kind of mood he was in. He could have been having the best day of his life and still kept a straight face. Cap Cap was the type of person who wouldn't speak to anyone unless you spoke to him first. That was how he'd always been, and no one ever took offense to that demeanor.

"Hey, Cap Cap. What's going on?" Shakita and Latrice both asked, laughing after standing in front of him without saying anything for over a minute, trying to test his will not to speak to them.

"I thought y'all were only going to stand there and watch my ass all fucking day," Cap Cap said, rolling his eyes at them. "What can I do for you two?" he said, giving them his full attention.

"Could you tell us what type of gun this is?" Shakita asked, handing him the camera. "And I know you took that pack of gum off the counter, you lil' slick bitch. I ain't got to be looking at you to know if you did some funny shit. You're paying for that before you leave," Cap Cap said, letting Shakita know that she had gotten caught.

"Come on, Cap. You've known me long enough to know I would never steal from you."

"Yeah, right. As many schemes as you be pulling, it wouldn't surprise me not one fucking bit. Now let me see that camera," Cap Cap said, reaching for it out of Shakita's hand. "That's a forty-five-caliber right there. A lot of pigs are using them now."

"Can you get us a couple?" Shakita asked curiously.

Cap Cap looked at her sideways. "Now why in the hell would I do that?"

"We need them."

"Oh you need them, huh? Those guns you want ain't got nothing to do with this picture, do it?" Cap Cap asked, eyeing them both as they remained silent. "I'm going to take a wild guess. This is either a cop of some kind or the fucking milk man in a white-ass milk truck, which I thought didn't exist anymore. So ladies, please tell me I'm wrong."

Shakita and Latrice didn't say anything at first, knowing that he was on to their plan.

"I'm waiting, ladies." Cap Cap demanded an answer.

Shakita looked over at Latrice and then back at Cap Cap before she answered. "We're trying to rob a BERK van."

"So y'all wanna be some *crooked girls*, huh?" Cap Cap said, nodding his head and looking at both of them. "Robbin' the BERK ain't never been done before or attempted. I hope y'all know that's some heavy shit right there. See that gun on his waist?" Cap Cap said, pointing at the photo. "Well, ladies, that ain't filled with no damn water. That officer by law is allowed to fill lead in anybody's ass who he even suspects is tryna flatten one of his tires. The level of difficulty is high than a mothafucka. You really gotta have a plan to pull off that shit."

"Latrice has routed out the van's every move. All we got to do is set up an ambush. We got the perfect plan. Once we trap 'em, that's it."

"I hope y'all do 'cause if not, that shit's gonna end horribly. If y'all really tryna be *crooked*, then I gotta hook you up with some gangsta shit. Wait right here." Cap Cap went behind a curtain that led to the back of his store.

Cap Cap loved money chasers and was more than willing to help them out. After the girls were waiting for a few minutes, Cap Cap returned with a box full of supplies. He set the box on the counter. "Inside this box," Cap Cap said as he tapped on the lid.

"There are forty boxes of bullets, two silencers, and two baby nine-millies."

"Nines? Shouldn't we have forty-fives like the driver's gonna have?" Latrice asked, confused.

"Y'all girls ain't gonna be able to handle that type of fire power. Besides, nines fire quicker and will never jam up on you. It don't matter what you shooting at 'em wit' as long as you hit bone, you're successful. The type of gun you got don't mean shit if you can't aim the mothafucka right. You can kill a bear with a pellet gun if you hit his ass in the right spot. Make sure you use them silencers. If it comes down to you having to bust ya gun, then end that shit before they start firing back. You don't need any more attention than you already have."

"Thanks, Cap. How much do you want us to give you for all this shit?" Shakita asked.

He gave them a real stern look—one that would let them know that what he was about to say required their full understanding. "Ladies, before you take this box, I want y'all to really consider what I'm handing over to you. Everything in here could get you ten years to life in prison. Are y'all ready for all that?"

"Yeah, Cap. We know what we facing," Shakita said, sounding more serious than she'd ever sounded in her entire life. "We gotta do a power move and we can't think of anything better than this. We can do it," Shakita said with conviction.

"All right, *crooked girls.* I tried to talk you out of it, but since I can't, I'm going to need two grand for all the shit I gave you. If you ain't got the money right now, then you can pay me after the hit. If y'all get scared and go chicken shit, then bring all my shit back. We gotta understanding on that?"

"We got you, Cap. We'll bring you the money afterwards. Thanks for everything," Shakita said as she picked up the heavy box off the counter.

"Don't thank me for shit yet. Wait until after the job's done. 'Cause all it looks like I did right now was help prepare you for a casket. Make sure y'all practice hitting some cans or some shit like that before playing Thelma and Louise. There ain't going to be no time to practice when the shit gets thick. And believe me, the shit will get fuckin' thick."

Both of them nodded their heads understanding exactly what he was saying, and then walked away with him on their minds as they were about to leave the store.

"Oh, and another thing, ladies," Cap Cap called out to them before they left. "Ya'll ain't get that shit from me. Ya dig?" He lowered his brow.

They both nodded again and walked out the door holding on to his words. Cap Cap watched as they left the store and could only shake his head at what he was thinking. *Those damn girls gonna get themselves killed.*

CHAPTER 23

TWO WEEKS UNTIL BAY GETS OUT

The time had come for Shakita and Latrice to handle their business and they were both scared as hell. Shakita couldn't stop chain smoking and Latrice couldn't stop shaking. They were both in two different locations and had been communicating with each other through walkie-talkies. The time was 4:20 p.m., and the van would be passing by Shakita on its way to the depository center any minute.

"Latrice, are you okay?" Shakita asked as she paced back and forth outside the car she was driving. Shakita was wearing a long blonde wig and some thick nonprescription glasses that made her look like a ditzy nerd. She had on some black leather gloves and a short orange dress with black leather boots.

"I'm nervous as shit. I can't stop shaking," Latrice informed her as she sat in a car.

"Me too, but we got to do this. It's now or never and I can't wait for never. You can do this. I trust you." Shakita lifted up the hood of the car to make it look like she was having car trouble when the van passed by.

"Whatever happens, Kita. I want you to know that you're my best friend and I love you."

"I love you too. I know what you're thinking about and don't worry. Everything will be fine. We're both going to be laughing about this shit when it's all over."

Latrice wasn't too sure about that, but she still put her faith in Shakita that she knew what she was talking about. "I hear you, girl," Latrice said as she fixed one side of her long blonde wig in the overhead mirror. Latrice was wearing the exact same disguise as Shakita, except that she had on a longer orange dress, and had been sitting in back of an industrial building waiting for the mission to begin.

"Here it comes, girl," Shakita said, breathing heavy with her eyes wide, informing Latrice that the van was now turning onto the street. "I'll see you in a minute."

"Okay. I'll be here."

Shakita threw her walkie-talkie under the front seat and started to flag down the van to get it to stop. The driver noticed the damsel in distress and thought she could use some help, but he didn't know whether it should be him to help her, since he was so close to the depot station. He thought about his sister and would want someone to help her if she were having car trouble. The Good Samaritan in him decided to pull over and help the poor girl out.

Shakita continued to wave her arms around until the van pulled up in front of her. She took a deep breath and was ready to become an actress.

"Thank you, mister, for stopping! Oh, thank you, thank you, thank you!" Shakita said, running up to the driver's side of the van.

"No problem. It looks like you're having some car trouble?"

"Yes I am. My engine won't start and I have to get to the hospital," Shakita said frantically. "My sister is having a baby and her no-good-ass boyfriend won't be there 'cause he left her for another woman, and I have to be there for her! I just have to!"

"Okay. Calm down. I'll help you the best way I can."

"Thank you so much, mister. Can I please use your cell phone to call for a ride? I really need to get there."

"What hospital is your sister at?"

"She's at Southern."

"Here, hop in. I'll take you. I got to stop at the station first to drop my van off. The station's right down the street here. I'll be in and out. Put your hazard lights on and we'll come back to it later."

"Thank you so much, mister. Hold on one second." Shakita ran to the car and turned on her hazards. *This shit was easier than I thought*, she said to herself as she ran back to the van and got in on the passenger side.

The van started to move and Shakita had to continue to put her plan into action. The driver glanced over at Shakita a couple of times and thought she was a pretty girl and would be even prettier without her glasses on. He was going to ask her out to dinner as soon as her situation was resolved.

"Thank you once again, mister. You're such a nice man. I wish more men could be like you."

The driver smiled. "It's the least I could do for such a pretty girl."

Shakita smiled back. "I have to give you something for helping me out," Shakita said as she bent down so she could get to her boot.

"No, that's all right. I'm doing this out of the kindness of my heart," the driver said, trying to stop her from giving him an incentive. He wanted his reward to come later in the form of a date.

"No, please. I insist," Shakita said as she pulled out her baby nine-millimeter with the silencer already attached, released the safety and pointed it at the driver. He was so scared he almost shit on himself when he saw the gun aimed at his chest.

"What the fuck are you doing?"

"What the fuck do it look like? I'm robbing this mothafucka! Now drive!"

"Look. You don't want to do this. It will never work."

"It'll work as long as ya ass stay cool. Now turn left."

The driver did what she said, but tried to press the panic button on his dashboard, so he could have a response team track where he was going. Shakita noticed his movement and responded to his foolish move.

Shakita aimed the gun at his head. "Get both of your fucking hands on the steering wheel now! This is not your fucking money so don't die for it!" The driver put both of his hands on the wheel and continued to drive. "Keep those hands on that wheel and you'll be able to live another day."

The driver didn't speak another word, not wanting to increase his chances at getting shot. He had a young boy at home to look after and didn't want the mother of his child to have full custody of him. He decided not to give Shakita any problems so she would let him live. It wasn't his money to die over.

Latrice looked in the rearview mirror and saw the white van approaching. She wanted to wait to get out of the car until she made sure that Shakita had everything under control. She watched the van pull up beside her and waited for Shakita's command. Shakita gave Latrice the signal to come over to the van so she could help her secure the driver. Latrice quickly ran over to the driver's side door and opened it.

"Give her your hands," Shakita commanded.

The driver did what he was told and Latrice handcuffed his hands to the driver-side armrest. Latrice turned the van off and took the keys out of the ignition. Shakita ran to unlock the back door of the van while Latrice held the driver at gunpoint.

Shakita opened the doors and saw that there were only fourteen canisters on the floor. She expected there to be over twenty of them. "He must not have done a full route," she whispered. She had no time to think about it too hard and wanted to concentrate on the money. She started loading all the heavy canisters in the back of the truck that Latrice was driving, and really had to move quickly to make sure they didn't get caught.

"All right! Let's go!" Shakita yelled.

"Later, baby," Latrice said, winking at the driver and then ran to the Expedition. She hopped in the driver side and floored the gas, taking off as fast as she could down the street. The driver waited a few minutes to make sure the girls were out of sight before he used his face to press up against the panic button. He was relieved after he pressed the button knowing someone would be there for him soon. He was so happy that he was not harmed and all he could think about was getting to see his son again. *Damn, those young bitches were crazy*, he thought.

Shakita slammed the hood down on the car she was originally driving, and followed Latrice to a motel to count up all the money. Before they counted, they had to ditch both vehicles and their disguises and transfer the canisters to Shakita's truck. They didn't want the police looking for two blonde-haired girls with glasses in a car that was used in a robbery, so they had to move as fast as possible without looking suspicious.

"I counted forty thousand dollars already, and I'm only done with the first canister!" Latrice shouted overjoyed as she sat on the floor and marveled about their big come up.

"There should be a hundred thousand in them as heavy as these bitches were," Shakita said, rubbing her shoulder. "The ones with the coins in them were even heavier."

"I wish you could've seen the way you was carrying these big-ass things from the van, girl. You were walking like a damn midget with no neck trying to carry them things," Latrice said, unable to control her laughter.

"Them mothafuckas was heavy as shit, yo. I was about to leave them damn things there and only take the light ones. But then I said fuck that. I'm getting all this money. I was pressed as shit, wasn't I?"

Latrice was laughing so damn hard that she wasn't even able to respond. Shakita and Latrice continued to laugh and talk about their unbelievable experience as they counted the money.

It was 10 p.m. and they were still at the motel counting the money. They had counted over two hundred thousand dollars so far and still had three more canisters with bills left in them to go. They were concentrating on their count when the news came on. They had been waiting to see if they had made the nightly news and now they were all ears as the Afro American female newscaster began to speak.

"Good evening. This is Amanda Coster with Fox 5 News. The top story tonight is the armed robbery of a BERK metro van. Two women, both believed to be Afro American, ambushed the driver of the van, where he was later handcuffed. The women stole fourteen metal canisters which may have held up to five hundred thousand dollars in them altogether."

"Damn! We some rich bitches," Shakita said when she heard how much money they could have, as the news lady continued.

"This is what the driver of the van had to say," the news lady said, before the driver they robbed appeared on the screen.

"The one girl was acting like she was having car trouble, so I stopped to help her, thinking that she really needed some help," the driver said emotionally as he continued. *"She gets in the van and before I know it, she pulls out a gun and has me drive to where another girl was waiting*

for her. That's where I was then handcuffed to the armrest and held at
gunpoint until they took all the money. Thank God that I'm still alive.
I have a son that needs me."

"He's such a bitch. The nigga's about to cry and shit," Shakita
remarked.

The screen then switched back to the anchorwoman.

"The two women are both said to be about five feet six in height, between
the ages of twenty to twenty-four, and both women had blonde hair and
glasses and were wearing orange dresses, which authorities allege were
all part of their disguises. These women are said to be armed and danger-
ous. There will be up to a twenty-five thousand-dollar reward to anyone
who has any information that can be provided for their capture. Please
call 1-888-CRMSTOP if you have anything you want to offer the
authorities about these two women. Right now there are no further leads.
Now in other news..."

"Bitch, we done made the mothafucking news," Shakita said
happily after she turned off the television.

"What the fuck are you so happy for? Mothafuckas are looking
for us."

"No they're not. They're looking for two nerdy-looking bitches
with blonde wigs and some ugly-ass orange dresses. They don't
know shit about what we really look like. You heard what they
said, right?" Shakita stood up and then continued. "They ain't got
no further leads. They don't know shit, girl. We done got away
with like a half a million dollars."

Latrice didn't look enthused about what Shakita was saying and
gave her a troubled look. "Ya ass could at least smile," Shakita
said, putting her hand on her hip. "We did get Bay's money back.
I thought you would be happy, shit. I know I am. I thought I was
gonna get killed over that shit."

"But what if the driver sees us again and recognizes us?"

"That driver doesn't know what the hell we really look like. We could bump into his ass tomorrow and he wouldn't know who the hell we were. I'm telling you, girl. You need to cool ya heels and enjoy some of this money like me. I make it rain. Watch me make it rain with it," Shakita sang as she picked up a pile of uncounted bills, and started to flick them into the air with her hand as she moved her hips.

Latrice started to laugh at Shakita acting silly as some of the bills landed on her lap and on top of her head.

"Get up here, girl, and make it rain with me. Come on up here; you know you want to," Shakita said, trying to get Latrice to have some fun with her as she danced on the bed. Latrice couldn't resist the temptation. She grabbed a hand full of bills and started dancing with Shakita, as they both brushed money off their hands into the air. They laughed together so hard, remembering what it felt like to be happy around each other again.

CHAPTER 24

"Hello, Shakita. How have you been? Haven't seen you here in a while," Monique said as Shakita walked into The Black Emporium.

Shakita smiled. "Hey, Mo. How are you?"

"I'm fine. Carrying out the daily usual. Are you coming back to work today?"

"No, unfortunately. I just came here to talk to Eric. Is he here?"

"Yep. Let me give him a buzz for you," Monique said as she dialed up

Eric's extension. "Hello, Eric. Shakita is here to see you. Okay." Monique hung up the phone and handed Shakita a silver card.

"Thanks, girl. See you when I come back." Shakita walked to the elevator.

Shakita checked the time on her cell phone and saw that it was almost noon. She didn't have to be at work until 1:30, and seriously needed to talk to Eric about some business real quick. She stepped off the elevator and saw Eric instantly. He looked so damn fine to her in his JoS. A. Bank black dress shirt and colorful silk tie as he paced around the room.

I did not come here to fuck him, but damn, this man look good! Just stick to the business, bitch, and you'll still have your panties on when you leave here, she said to herself, getting bothered by his sexy appearance. Shakita walked over to him and tried to get all her dirty little thoughts out of her mind before she spoke. "Hey, Eric. How are you?" she said hesitantly.

Eric stopped pacing and gave her his full attention. "Hello, Shakita. It's nice to see you again. It's been awhile."

"It has. I've been going through a lot lately, which is why I haven't been to work."

Eric stared into her troubled eyes trying to see if he could figure out what she'd been up to.

"Only a man could keep you away from making the money you said you needed," Eric inquired with a hint of jealousy.

"I wish it was that simple. What I'm dealing with is way greater than that. But if that was the case, the man that would be holding me back is standing right in front of me."

Eric's eyes twitched in regards to Shakita's sarcastic remark.

"Well. Since that's not the case," Eric said, shunning off her notion as he continued. "Why are you here? If your problems can't bring you to work, how can I help you?"

"I need to ask you a favor. Better yet, I need you to help me with something. You're the only one I trust."

"Before I agree to it, I need to know what it is first."

"I have a lot of coins that I need you to change into bills for me."

"Why don't you go to the bank and do it yourself?"

"I would but there's too many of them."

"How many coins are we talking about?"

"About a hundred thousand dollars' worth."

"How did you happen to run across that much money, Shakita?"

Shakita took a deep breath. "I don't know if you've been watching the news lately but—"

"You robbed that BERK van? That was you?" Eric asked, cutting her off and aware of what she was about to tell him.

"Yeah, that was me."

"What the hell were you thinking, Shakita? If they catch you, do you know how much time you could get?"

"I knew the risk before I did it. When my back was up against the wall, I did what I had to do."

"But you didn't have to rob a BERK van. The driver could have killed you. You're lucky to be alive, you know that?"

"The driver didn't have nothing to do with me still being alive. The money does. I already told you my life was on the line."

"You're crazy," Eric said as he stared into her overwrought eyes. He believed she was in trouble, but didn't think she would go to that extent of taking matters into her own hands.

"So can you help me?" Shakita asked him as he started to pace the room again.

"Do you know what you're asking me to do? You're asking me do be an accomplice to armed robbery. That's a serious, serious offense, Shakita. If I get caught, that'll jeopardize my business."

Shakita looked at him audaciously after his foolish words escaped his mouth. "Jeopardize your business? Are you serious? You know what, Eric. You ain't no different from me. You might dress more professional and know how to put your words together a lot better than me, but other than that, we're the same. I might have to rob or steal to get mine, but that ain't no different from the whoring we do for you to take money from all these high-powered lawyers, and government officials that be up in here every day. Your whole business ain't nothing but a damn well-polished hoe house that sells pussy that ain't meant to be paid for. See, Eric, we are both *crooks*. I'm just not afraid to admit it."

Eric couldn't believe that she'd called him out like that, yet there was no need in him denying the truth.

"You know what?" Eric said as he walked back over to her with tension in his eyes. "We might be the same in some ways, but I wouldn't put myself in a position where I might have to kill somebody over someone else's money. Now that's where your vision and my vision go astray."

Shakita could tell by the way his nose flared that he was getting offended, which wasn't her intention. "Look, Eric. I didn't come here to bad-mouth what you do. I love working here. I only came by to ask for your help. If you can't help me, I understand. I'll find another way to get it done."

Eric paced around the room again with his hands on his waist as he sighed deeply. Shakita always found a way to breach his strong exterior until she was able to eat away at his delicate heart. She was truly his Achilles' heel. Once again he was powerless against her.

"Okay. I'll do it but only this once. After this I won't adhere myself to another criminal act. Is that understood?"

"I got you. I will never ask you for something like this ever again. You have my word."

"How soon do you want this to happen?"

"I'll give you my girl Latrice's number so you'll know whose number it is when she calls." Shakita reached in her pocket and pulled out a piece of paper with Latrice's number on it. "I'll have her call you to tell you where y'all can meet."

"I guess this is the girl who pulled off the robbery with you?"

"Yeah, that's her. Be expecting a call from her tonight."

"Will do."

Shakita started to walk to the door and then stopped and looked at Eric. "Thanks again, Eric. What would I do without you?" she asked sincerely.

"That's a billion-dollar question," Eric said, raising his eyebrows at her. Shakita smiled as her eyes became misty and hurried to turn away, so Eric wouldn't see her cry. Eric was the only one who never let her needs go unrequited no matter how severe or unvarying they became. No matter what course both of their lives went, he would forever be her only love. Even the love she had for Kam would never compare to how she felt for Eric.

Eric waited until Shakita got on the elevator before he walked over to the window. He was bothered at what he'd let happen and wish he would've handled the situation a different way. He put his hands over his face wondering what the hell he was about to get himself into. He continued to dwell on his current situation as his older brother, Danny, entered the room.

"Wow, I heard the whole conversation. You really got yourself in some shit with her now. Huh, bro?" Danny said, walking over to Eric as he turned around.

"What's new?" Eric said as he placed his hands in his pockets while shrugging his shoulders.

Danny shook his head. "You really got it bad for this girl. You weren't lying."

"Dan, I don't understand what it is about her, man. I think about her all the time and when she comes around, I always give in to her. She's the only one that I let get the best of me and I don't know why."

"Eric. I got to ask you, bro. If this girl makes you feel like no other, then why did you arrange for me to have sex with her? If she's the one that you spend most of your time thinking about, then why is she even part of your business here?"

Eric truly felt in his heart that Shakita would be the perfect woman for him, except she had too much of a fallen past. He wanted an angel in his life and Shakita was everything but that. He loved her dearly, but was unable to secure a relationship between the two of them, that would stand the test of time without collapsing. He wished he could meet someone who closely resembled her in appearance, but was the exact opposite in nature. Eric looked at his brother and gave him the only answer that made sense to him. "I thought it would make me let go of her."

CHAPTER 25

Shakita arrived at work and all the other employees talked about was the BERK van robbery. Shakita sat in the lounge while everybody gave their version of what really happened. Shakita heard one male coworker say that the robbers were really men dressed up like women and his cousin knew who they were. She heard a female coworker say that there were three women and not two, and one of them pistol-whipped the driver. She then heard another man say that the driver was in on it the whole time and had his two sisters help him steal the money. That's what he said everyone was saying in his neighborhood. Shakita thought that it was so funny to hear all these different stories and none of them were true. That only proved to Shakita even more that you couldn't believe everything you heard. Ninety percent of the time it's all bullshit.

Shakita had enough of hearing the foolish gossip and left the lounge, so she could start her shift. She ended up running into Reggie out in the hallway. This was the first time she'd seen him since their last interaction. Shakita noticed that Reggie didn't have on the smashed-up glasses like she thought he would, but instead, he was wearing contacts. He still looked ugly as hell and Shakita had to go fuck with him.

"What up, Reggie? I don't know what it is, but there's something that seems different about you. Did you get a haircut?"

Shakita asked sarcastically as she held her chin. Reggie gave her a stupid look. "No, that's not it. Did you get your braces taken out? No, you didn't have braces, did you? Oh! You're not wearing any glasses. I should have known."

Reggie scowled showing Shakita he was irritated by her smart-ass comments but she didn't care and kept on going. "I'm so glad you decided to get contacts. Those dorky-ass frames did nothing for your face. You look a hell of a lot better."

Reggie still declined not to respond knowing that she was the one that pulled off the robbery. He was convinced she was really crazy now and didn't want to say anything to piss her off again.

"Reggie. I just gave you a compliment. Aren't you gonna say thank you?" Shakita asked, grinning.

"Thanks," he said meekly.

"I know you ain't got shit to say to me right now and I couldn't care less. And I'm not sorry for kicking you in your dick area and maybe fucking up your future kids. Your bitch ass had it coming." Reggie didn't respond.

Shakita wasn't that mad at Reggie anymore for doing what he'd done to her now that she'd gotten the money on her own. She still needed to make sure he kept quiet about what he knew.

"You know I did that shit without you, right? If you know how to keep quiet, I'll give you something to keep your pockets full, ya dig?" Reggie slowly nodded his head, agreeing to her terms.

"Now don't do no snake shit 'cause you already know I'm a crazy bitch, and there's another one still out there just like me that you don't know about. So before you do something you'll regret, remember she knows what you look like. I'll see you when I see you, Reggie," she said, walking off with a smile on her face after threatening him.

When Shakita walked away from him, Reggie looked confused

as hell as to how her collaborator had a photo of him. He then remembered the yearbook picture he'd taken three years ago. He had no choice now but to stick to his word.

Latrice drove Shakita's Explorer into Eric's oversized five-car garage, which was part of the guesthouse that sat behind his mansion in Fort Washington, Maryland. Latrice had only been to this wealthy Tantallon neighborhood once but dreamed of owning a mansion there one day. The garage door came down and Latrice turned the car off. Latrice was going to wait inside the car until Eric appeared. She'd never seen him, but Shakita assured her that she would definitely know him when she saw him. She told her that his overbearing good looks were too rare to go mistakenly unnoticed. This was something she had to see for herself.

Latrice saw two big men enter the garage from the guesthouse and walked toward her. She didn't think that neither one of them were that attractive and was hoping that one of them wasn't Eric. Latrice then looked back at the door, and saw the most gorgeous man she had ever laid eyes on. The way Latrice was gawking at him, she felt like she had her face pressed up against the window, trying to get the best view possible. Eric was too good to be true and she wanted to touch him to see if he were real. She didn't want to go after what was Shakita's, and wished there were two of them. Eric walked up to her window and waited for her to open the door.

"Hey, Latrice. I see you didn't have a problem finding me?" Eric said to the still dazed Latrice.

She blushed. "Yeah. It was pretty easy."

"Good. So the coins are in the back?"

"Yeah. They're in big metal canisters."

"No problem. Pop the trunk and we'll get them."

Latrice unlocked the cargo area, so the two bulky men could

get the canisters out. The men cracked open each canister and dumped all the money into large rucksacks, and put them in the back of an Escalade. The two guys put the busted-up canisters back in Latrice's truck and closed the door. The garage door opened up and the two men rolled out in the Escalade.

"Are you in a hurry?" Eric asked her.

"No why?"

"Would you like to come in for a minute so we can talk?"

"Sure. Why not," Latrice said, not wanting to pass up the opportunity to see what he was really like. As she got out the truck, and followed Eric's fine ass into his house, she made certain to keep her best friend in mind.

"Have a seat," Eric said, directing her to a small black couch in the living room. Latrice took a seat and immediately got comfortable in her surroundings. "Would you care for something to drink?"

"Sure."

"What would you like?"

"I'll drink anything. You can surprise me."

"All right, I'll be right back." Eric went into the kitchen while Latrice's eyes couldn't stop watching him. Shakita had told her she'd only seen him in suits, but today Eric was wearing a pair of light denim jeans, a white Ralph Lauren Purple Label polo shirt, and a pair of Louis Vuitton sneakers. Latrice loved the way his muscles bulged out of his chest and thought about rubbing her hands across his washboard stomach. Eric came back with her drink and she snapped out of her daze.

"I brought you some grape juice. Everybody loves that." He smiled.

"You're right. Grape juice is one of my favorites," she said, smiling back.

Eric took a seat on a black sofa that was across from her, while

Latrice wondered what he was drinking. "I see what you have in your glass is clear. What is it?"

"Some Cîroc," he said as he took a sip.

"I guess you thought I wasn't a drinker, huh?"

"Oh, I'm sorry. I think it's unattractive to offer a lady alcohol the first time she's in your home. Unless she wants some, of course."

"If you don't mind, I do."

He then stood. "Okay. I have a full bar, so do you have any special request?"

"I would like some p.i.n.k. vodka, if you have it. If not, I'll take some Cîroc."

"What you know about p.i.n.k. vodka?" Eric asked, surprised.

"I was invited to a p.i.n.k. vodka launch party in Miami a few summers ago."

"You must have friends in high places to get invited to one of those types of parties."

"No. I was lucky, that's all."

"I do have a bottle of p.i.n.k., so I guess I'll be getting that for you, high-roller. I'll be right back," he said before leaving the room again.

I'm about to get fucked up! Latrice said to herself. *I should have gotten some Cîroc. But then again the last time I drank that shit, Clarity ended up fucking me. But I'm with Eric now. This time would be way different. I wouldn't mind waking up to his sexy ass in the morning. What am I saying? This is Kita's nigga. I can't fuck him. Damn, that bitch is lucky I'm her friend.*

Eric came in the room with her drink and set it down on the glass table in front of her. "Can I get you something else?" Eric asked while he was still standing.

Some dick. Girl, if you don't leave this man alone. "No, I'm fine for now."

"Okay." Eric sat down and took another sip of his vodka. He had a few things on his mind and thought now was the best time to talk about them.

"So you and Shakita robbed a BERK van? That's pretty brave of you all, don't you think?"

"It was. And it was a one-time thing, too. I'll never do that again."

"I don't know about that. I've been told that crime is addictive. The rush that you get from not getting caught keeps you going to commit more crimes. Do you still feel that rush?"

"No. I didn't feel anything but scared. I don't know what rush you're talking about. I only felt relief that I got the money I needed."

"The money you needed? Wait, I'm confused. I thought Shakita needed the money?"

"She did. It's a long story, but the money was really for me. She was helping me get it back."

"I feel like I'm being duped. Would you mind telling me what's really going on? Since I'm involved now."

"Honestly, I could tell you my part, but the rest of it is all Shakita's business and I don't know if I should be telling it."

"I understand your loyalty to her, but what would you be losing if you did tell?"

"Don't you mean is there something I could gain by telling you?" Latrice asked, thinking business-minded.

"That's exactly what I mean."

"What are you willing to give up for the info?"

"It all depends on how valuable the information is to me. The only way I'll know that is if you tell me everything."

"How do I know you won't go back and tell her what I said? I don't know you like that to say I really trust you."

"True, but we all have to take risks at some point. Do you feel like this is that time?"

Latrice thought about what Eric was suggesting. She never was a chatterbox and didn't want to throw her friend under the bus, but then she thought that Shakita's business was also her business, since Shakita got her involved by taking Bay's money in the first place. As long as Latrice's name was a part of it, she could tell anybody whatever she wanted. If it was anything about Shakita, it was probably something he might have already heard.

"Okay. I'm going to tell you everything that I know and whatever Shakita has told me," Latrice said, ready to tell all, as Eric listened attentively.

"My ex-boyfriend gave me some money to hold before he went to jail, and Shakita took it without my knowledge and blew it all on gamblin'."

"How much did she take?" Eric asked, cutting her off.

"It was two hundred fifty grand."

"She took that much from you? How did you find out she took it?"

"I found out when she called me to bail her out of jail for prostitution."

Eric couldn't believe what he was hearing. "How long ago was this?"

"This was about a week or so ago."

"So that's why she hasn't been coming to work lately."

"Work where? Shakita never had a damn job. What are you talking about?"

"Well, since you're telling me stuff I didn't know, I guess I can tell you some things as well. Shakita has worked in my spa off and on for the last two years."

"What spa are you talking about?"

"The Black Emporium. Have you heard of it?"

"You own The Black Emporium?" Latrice said with her mouth open wide.

"Yes. I guess you have heard of the place?"

"Yeah, but what I heard was that it wasn't just no damn spa. I heard you could get any sexual favor imaginable there as long as you were a man. Is that true?"

"I'm afraid so," Eric said, watching closely to see how Latrice would react to hearing how her friend was doing everything conceivable at his spa.

"I had no idea that Shakita was even into no shit like that. But what I wanna know is how come you don't have a place like that for women? You know there are a lot of us girls who wouldn't mind going to a place like that. There are a lot of men out here who can't work it right. Everybody can't get their fantasy fulfilled at home."

"I'm glad you say that. I will be opening up one that only caters to females in L.A."

"L.A.? Why not here?"

"I do plan on opening one in the District, but the laws are a little bit stricter here about an all-male spa than they are in other parts of the country."

"Why is that?"

"Because some lobbyists and politicians are gay, and the ones who aren't, tend to be homophobic, wanting to ward any scandals with government officials that could arise. It wouldn't make good press."

Latrice looked like she understood, so Eric wanted her to continue with her story. Latrice continued to tell Eric about Bay, and how Shakita almost cost them their lives. The more she drank, the more she let Eric in on Shakita's grisly ways and her own plans to get into the music industry. Eric now looked at Shakita in a whole new light, thanks to her best friend, Latrice.

CHAPTER 26

"Why isn't she answering her phone? Shit!" Shakita hung up her phone after trying to contact Latrice for the third straight time. She wanted to find out how everything went last night with the money exchange. It was only 8:20 a.m., which gave Latrice valid reason to still be asleep. Shakita trusted Latrice and had no reason to worry. Even though Eric was immensely attractive, Latrice only had interest in entertainers. Eric wasn't her man, but the way her and Latrice rolled, they never rode the same dick to avoid any male conflicts between them. Shakita put her mind back on her job and wouldn't try to call Latrice again until lunchtime.

Latrice woke up in a bedroom not knowing where she was. She looked around to find that she was alone. She was completely naked with her clothes scattered across the floor. *What the hell did I do?* She sat up trying to figure out whose bed she was in. She thought back at what she'd done last night and remembered she had gone to see Eric. There was a knock on the door and moments later, Eric appeared in the room with her. She quickly pulled the sheets up under her arms to keep herself from being exposed.

"It's okay. I didn't see anything," Eric said, trying to make her feel comfortable.

"You probably already did. Did we have sex?" Latrice asked, feeling embarrassed.

"No. If we had sex, I would hope you would remember. Even if your mind didn't, I know your body would," Eric said, giving her a wink.

Damn, I feel like jumping in this nigga's arms right now and fucking the shit out of him! Big sexy going to say some slick shit to me like that and I can't say nothing back. This man is so lucky. "If we didn't have sex, then how did my clothes get off?"

"You took them off yourself. You said you can't sleep with them on. When you started to do that, I left the room."

"Damn. That p.i.n.k. had me smacked last night. Thanks for letting me stay over until I got myself together."

"Ain't no problem. Are you hungry? I can make some breakfast."

"Yeah. That would be fine."

"Okay. I'm going to start everything while you get dressed. Just come out when you're ready."

"Okay."

Eric smiled and closed the door. Latrice rubbed the back of her neck as she stretched, She wanted to know the time and how long she'd been sleeping. She opened her purse to get her phone.

Latrice saw the missed calls from Shakita and wondered if she really wanted something or was she being nosy. Whatever the situation, it would have to wait. Latrice didn't feel comfortable calling her back from Eric's house. Even though nothing had happened between them, Latrice still felt guilty for even staying the night. She immediately put on her clothes hoping she wouldn't feel shameful anymore. Then she thought that if it wasn't for Shakita, she would have never gotten mixed up with Eric in the first place. Eric was now her friend also, and whatever the reason that brought them together, Latrice simply justified it as fate. She was convinced that maybe her and Eric's encounter was meant to happen. For what intention, she still didn't know.

"I can't believe it's almost one o'clock," Latrice said as she walked into the kitchen where Eric was and sat on a stool at the counter.

"You slept good, huh?" Eric asked, looking at her over his shoulder as he stood in front of the stove with three burners going.

"Yeah. I slept too good."

"Do you have somewhere you have to be today?"

"No. I don't think so, why?"

"Because your money should be back here by three o'clock. Four thirty at the latest. Do you want to stick around and wait for it?"

"Sure, why not."

"Okay, cool. Hey, how do you like your eggs?"

"It doesn't matter. I'll eat them any way you make 'em."

"Do you want cheese in them?"

"Yeah, that's cool," Latrice said, pouring her some orange juice from a pitcher that was sitting on the counter. "Everything smells so good. Did your mama teach you how to cook?"

"No. Actually, I learned from my cousin while I was in college. My cousin Jay and my father have their own restaurant in Pittsburgh. I had a job being a cook while I was out of school over the summer."

"What kind of restaurant do they have?"

"It's Italian," Eric said as he dumped the fried potatoes into a plastic bowl.

"Black people making Italian food, that's so unique. Usually when you find out black people own a restaurant, you assume that they're going to be serving up soul food. I would love to go to that restaurant to see how ya peoples get down."

"That can be done. Maybe I can take you and Shakita there when I visit my family for Memorial Day weekend," Eric suggested as he placed cheese eggs in another bowl and some turkey sausage on a plate.

"I'm with it. But I don't know if Shakita's going to be able to go since she's got curfew."

"Well. Maybe it'll only be you then." Eric smiled.

"Maybe," she said, smiling flirtatiously.

Latrice felt some sort of chemistry between them but wasn't sure how genuine it was.

She was clueless if Eric had been overly alluring with her, or if he was a manipulating charmer with subliminal motives. Whatever his intentions were, she would find out in due time. She hoped her feelings weren't involved when she did.

Latrice sat in her car as Eric's men loaded it with bags of money. Eric soon appeared and spoke with the men briefly. He then walked up to the front of her car.

"Okay. The money's in the trunk. This is how much you got back in cash," Eric said as he handed Latrice a piece of paper through the driver-side window.

"Damn. That was a lot of change," Latrice said happy with the amount she saw on the paper.

"Yes, it is a big sum when you're talking about a bunch of dimes and nickels."

"Thank you so much for doing this for us. We really appreciate it."

"No need to thank me. As long as I don't have to do this again, that's all the thanks I need."

"You won't. At least I won't ask you. I don't know about Shakita, though."

"Well, for Shakita's sake, I hope this is her last time doing something like this, and I also pray she gets her life together."

"Me too," Latrice said tenderly, knowing it was a lot to ask for.

"Be safe riding around with all that money."

"I will. I'll call you to let you know that I got home all right."

"Make sure you do that," he said as he reached for the garage door opener. The garage door lifted up and Latrice backed the truck out and made her way down the street. Eric watched Latrice leave and shook his head as he stared at her taillights. He couldn't understand how it was possible for two people that seem to be nothing alike end up being the best of friends. He guessed it was true when they say opposites attract. In his eyes Shakita and Latrice were without a doubt like north and south.

Latrice continued to think about Eric as she cruised down Indian Head Highway on her way back to her apartment. Eric was irresistibly mystifying to her, being why she couldn't keep her focus off him. Eric wasn't like the typical rapper or producer Latrice was usually into. He was the most attractive man she'd seen in a long time, and the fact that he was off-limits made him even more desirable. It was either she had to have him or not deal with him at all. There was no in between with her when it came down to someone she simply wanted to fuck. Latrice needed to see how Shakita really felt about Eric, hoping not to put a bug in her ear instead. If Shakita gave her the slightest indication that she didn't care about Eric, Latrice was going to make her move. She was trying to think of the best time to indirectly ask Shakita about Eric when her phone rang. It was Shakita.

"Hello," Latrice answered.

"Girl, what is going on? I've been trying to call you all morning."

"Girl, I was sleep like shit. I had seen that you called, though."

"Yeah, I did. I was trying to see if you saw Eric about that thing?"

"Yeah. I got it back about fifteen minutes ago."

"Damn. You got the shit back that quick?"

"Yep. I got it with me right now."

"Damn, I can't wait to see what that shit looks like. I'll be over after I get off at eight."

"All right, Kita. I'll be there. I ain't doing shit."

"Cool. So what's up witchu doe?"

"I'm driving slow as shit right now. I'm trying not to get fucked with. The police out here are serious."

"All right. I feel that. I'll let you go, so you can handle that shit."

"All right, girl."

"Okay, bye." They both hung up.

Latrice had frozen up when she had the chance to ask Shakita about Eric. She thought that tonight might be a better time to play detective when they were face-to-face. That way she could look into Shakita's eyes and see what she was really feeling.

Shakita walked into Latrice's apartment and froze right before she reached the kitchen. "Damn. How much is this?" Shakita asked as she looked at the piles of money on Latrice's kitchen table.

"Sixty g's. White folks be stuffing the shit out of those canisters, don't they?" Latrice implied.

"Nah. That's some nigga shit right there. White people be using credit cards and debit cards n'shit. We the broke mothafuckas that be nickel-and-diming shit all the time. We're the ones that be putting enough on a card to make it home n' shit."

"I guess that's a sign of how much we be depending on the train to get around."

"You damn right, it's a sign. And this right here is evidence of that shit," Shakita said, waving a stack of money in the air.

Latrice shook her head in disbelief. "I can't believe we got a total of four hundred seventy grand in one day?"

"Damn. How much is that when we split it?"

"Well, if I take out Bay's money and then divide the rest in half between the two of us, we got one hundred ten each."

"Get the fuck out of here! Are you serious?"

"Yep. I already did the math."

"Damn, girl! We got to celebrate! We got to do something real big for this shit! We got to go out of town or something!"

"Calm down, girl. We can't do nothing like that yet. You still got to catch calls."

"Damn. I forgot about that shit. Well, fuck it then; we are going at least have a girls' night on the town. After I catch that call, I'm out."

"I don't know about that, Shakita. Ain't that a little risky? Why don't we try to have a party at your house?"

Shakita looked at her sideways. "A party? Bitch, who the fuck are we going to invite? You don't have any friends, and I damn sure don't have any friends, so it's going to be two lonely bitches gettin' drunk and blowin' out cupcakes n' shit. I'd rather go to Chuck E. Cheese's than to deal with that depressing shit."

"Girl, it ain't even like that. We have friends and you know it," Latrice said, laughing. "Whatever. Name one friend I got."

"You can invite Eric. I know he'll come through for you. Y'all are real cool."

"True. But our relationship doesn't work like that. I only go to him in my time of need."

"Why only then? Y'all seem so right for each other."

"As much as I wanted to, Eric could never be my man."

"Why you say that?"

"For one, the mothafucka's fine as hell and every bitch in the world wants his ass. I ain't got time to be pulling bitches off my man every five minutes. And for real for real, he's too good for me anyway."

"Why you putting yourself down like that?"

"I'm not. I'm just being real. Eric got everything going for him and I'm still trying to get my shit together. I'm always fucking something up and I would only be a burden in his life. I already know I'm one now, so I can only imagine what it would be like if I was his girl. I can't mess up that man's life like that. I respect him too much."

"But what if he gets in a serious relationship and end up getting married? Wouldn't you wish it could've been you instead of some other chick?"

Shakita sighed. "That's an old dream of mine. So much has happened since we met that there's no way we would work out. I wouldn't even be mad if he found Mrs. Right. I know they'll make him happier than I could."

"I think if it's meant for y'all to be together, it will happen. You should give it a try and see what's up."

"Nah. The only thing we can do is fuck and be friends. That's it. Other than that, it's a wrap for us. Ya dig?"

Latrice didn't say anything. She thought whatever could have happened between the two of them was a lost cause, and that meant Eric was fair game for anyone who was interested. Latrice's eyes were definitely interested.

CHAPTER 27

One Week Until Bay Gets Out

As the days moved on, all the talk about the BERK van robbery had slowly come to a halt, but all the heightened surveillance and security around the stations were still unchanged. The BERK police were waiting for the robbers to strike again, so they stayed alert on all the BERK lines, ready to take down anyone who looked suspicious. Shakita thought it was funny how everyone at the station was either acting scared and uptight or taking their jobs way too serious. Passengers were getting harassed for even running through the station trying to catch their train. Some even got arrested for not having proper ID. Everyone at BERK was turning the stations upside down trying to make an example of anyone who crossed the line. If only they knew it was Shakita they needed to worry about the whole time.

Shakita saw Reggie for the first time in a week and wanted to give him the money she'd been holding in her locker for three days. Once she did, she didn't need to speak to his ass ever again in life. "What up, Reggie Reg!" she yelled out like they were friends.

"What's up?" Reggie said, giving her a little fake nod.

"You got a minute?"

"Yeah, why?" he asked suspiciously.

"Come with me real fast." Reggie didn't know what she was up to, but he still followed her with precaution.

Shakita quickly looked around before she opened her locker. When she saw that everything was cool, she pulled out a thick envelope and handed it to Reggie.

"How much is this?" he asked as he skimmed his hand over the money.

"It's ten g's."

Reggie turned up his nose. "Ten g's? Y'all took like a half a mil and all you're gonna give a nigga is ten g's?"

"Hell yeah. What the fuck you think, I'm going to hook ya ass up for not doing shit? This is hush money, nigga."

"You think this lil' bit of money supposed to keep my ass quiet?"

"It's either that will or one in the scalp, nigga. Now you tell me which one will make you shut the fuck up."

Reggie gave Shakita a long stare, rolled his eyes, and then stuffed the envelope in his jacket. Shakita smiled seeing that he'd made the right choice.

"I knew you were a smart nigga. I thought you had lost ya mind along with your ugly-ass glasses for asking me some stupid shit like dat." Reggie was speechless.

Shakita walked away when her business with Reggie had concluded. She could've offered him more money but didn't. Reggie was going to have to take what he got and live with it, or she was going to have somebody pay him a special visit. As unpredictable as Shakita had been lately, she would probably kill Reggie herself if she thought for once that he would turn her in. She considered herself an outlaw after committing the robbery, and would stop at nothing to make sure she stayed above the law. Shakita would rather die first before she went to prison.

Latrice walked into the small city building, which served as a premier recording hub for some of the best artists and producers on the East Coast. "Hello. Could you tell me what studio the group N.A.R.C. is in?" Latrice asked the male guard at the help desk.

"They're in Studio G. You go down this hall and it's the fourth door on the left."

She gladly thanked him and then started down the hallway. As Latrice walked past all the studios, she heard all the different sounds that were being created and started to get excited about what was about to go down when Bay got out. Bangspot Records was the future of the industry and she couldn't wait to help spearhead the company to its success. Latrice couldn't wait to hear what Killa D and Piff were cooking up.

Latrice walked into Studio G and saw Killa D and Piff bobbing their heads to a monstrous bass track. "What up, fellas?" Latrice said, entering and feeling the beat.

"What up, Missy? I guess you found us okay?" Killa D asked.

"Yeah. What y'all listening to?"

"It's a beat Piff made. It crank, don't it?"

"Yeah, that shit's hot. So you trying to produce now, huh, Piff?"

"Yeah. Ever since I found out we were signing with your team, I became motivated."

"Good. Keep that motivation up, baby. We are going to definitely need it to keep these haters off us. Ya dig?"

"No doubt. We on some takeover shit right now. We're going to stay focused," Piff assured her.

"I feel that. I'm also feeling the group name you picked out. What does N.A.R.C. stand for anyway?"

"It stands for Niggas Against RICO Convictions," Piff said proudly.

"Oh that shit is serious! Bay's going to love it!"

"So when are we gonna actually be signed?" Killa D wondered.

"Bay gets out next week. So once he gets settled, we'll all sit down and go over business. I know y'all hungry, but can y'all hang in there until then?"

"Yeah. I guess it'll be another week of hustling for us then," Killa D said, hinting around that they were going to still be selling drugs until they got an advance, while Piff nodded his head in agreement.

Latrice looked at them like they were both full of shit. "Y'all are going to sell drugs regardless. A little advance money ain't going to change that. Do what you do, fellas. Just make sure you don't fuck up before next week. Ya dig?"

Killa D and Piff understood what she was talking about and didn't plan on getting locked up for drug trafficking. They were convinced their operation was run thoroughly. They had been selling drugs all their lives without ever getting convicted, and Latrice learned firsthand from Bay's experience, that if they kept up what they were doing, it wouldn't always be easy to stay out of the system.

Shakita was back in the casino now that she had some money to gamble with, but soon found out that nothing about her luck had changed.

"What the fuck is wrong with this fucking machine!" Shakita yelled, as she banged on the slot machine for not giving her any type of return after playing it for over two hours. Shakita thought by going to Dover Downs casino, her outcome would be different than it was at Charles Town or in Atlantic City, but it wasn't. She was performing terribly and didn't understand how it had gotten so bad for her. She was chain smoking and drinking as she got more and more upset by the minute for not being able to win anything. Shakita had only $45,000 left from the $100,000 she once had. She grumbled knowing she was bound to blow that eventually as well. She was upset with herself and had to find a way to feel better about losing all her money again. She only had one guaranteed way to make up for the money she'd lost, and her eyes turned green as she thought about new money that could run through her voracious fingers. Her decision had been finalized. She needed to rob another van.

Latrice heard the buzzer and walked over to her door and opened it.

"Come on in. I'm glad you could make it," Latrice said as she greeted Teyron into her apartment.

"I'm glad I could make it too," Teyron said, admiring Latrice in her ivory BeBe stretch wrapped dress. Latrice was looking extra sexy and Teyron couldn't help but to lick his lips as he stared at her with lust in his eyes. Latrice invited all her soon-to-be artists over to her house for a little meet-and-greet, so they all could get comfortable with each other. Killa D and Piff were already there and now she was waiting for Clarity to arrive.

"Teyron, this is Killa D and Piff. They are the group N.A.R.C." Teyron dapped them both up and sat down across from them as they were rolling up weed while drinking p.i.n.k. vodka. Teyron sat with the two rappers and could tell by talking to them that they were straight hood, and he admired that about them. He could also predict that they were going to be big stars just like him.

Before Latrice could take a seat from making more drinks for her guests, her buzzer rang again. She walked to the door expecting to see Clarity. "What up, Ma?" Latrice said as Clarity came through the door with Dull right behind her.

"Ain't nothing, I see you lookin' good like I expected," Clarity said, checking Latrice out in her tight-fitting dress.

"Don't give me a compliment you should be giving yourself." She gave Clarity a wink and then got everyone's attention.

"Hey, you guys. I want you to meet Clarity and Dull. This is Teyron, Piff and Killa D."

Clarity had on a green, white, and black floral strapless Alfani dress, and held the attention from the rest of the men in the room. Killa D and Piff started to plot immediately with themselves on who would get Clarity first. Even though Teyron thought Clarity was sexy as hell, he still wanted Latrice. He respected that they'd already established a connection, and he didn't want to lose that over trying to have sex with one of his label mates.

A few hours into the modest mixer, Killa D and Piff decided to roll out since they didn't get any sexual vibes from Clarity. She was playing her high-profile position and the fellas didn't have the patience to try and get inside her head. They never noticed she had been eyeing Latrice the whole night. With Clarity seeking Latrice, they really didn't have a chance in hell anyway. As time went on, Dull decided to make an exit his damn self. He wanted to hit the club up where he could be around more eligible women and let Clarity do her thing with Latrice. Teyron was drunk as hell off the p.i.n.k. vodka he was punishing, but the infused caffeine kept him wide awake. He wanted to use all his energy on Latrice, but for some reason, he couldn't get Clarity to leave. Clarity was drunk and feeling the same way Teyron was and couldn't find a way to get his ass to leave either.

"Who wants to hit a hookah stick with me?" Clarity asked as she smashed out the blunt in the ashtray. They smoked and talked about music for hours with no sign of the hot topic coming to an end.

Teyron checked the time on his cell phone and sighed deeply. It had gotten too late to be waiting around for Clarity to budge, and he was going to catch Latrice at another time. He didn't want to seem so obvious that he was trying to get at Latrice in front of Clarity, so he decided to wait until the time was right again. Teyron figured that Clarity may have wanted to stick around to have girl talk. It never dawned on him that she was there to fuck Latrice herself. Now that Teyron was on his way out, Clarity was now able to take full advantage of poor little drunken Latrice. Teyron said his goodbyes to them both, then walked down the stairwell. He lamented what could have happened if he would have stayed a little bit longer kept playing in his mind. He never looked back but wanted to knock on Latrice's door again to give it another try. He felt that their parting tonight probably happened for a reason, and didn't want to rush anything that was meant to be taken slow. He walked to his car as Latrice commanded his every thought.

"Everybody's gone." Latrice smiled, thinking back on the night that passed. She then lay back on the couch and closed her eyes. "Damn, it was so fun having everybody together. Didn't you have fun?"

"Yeah. But not as much fun as we 'bout to have right now." She then kicked off her Coach heels and moved in closer to Latrice.

"What are you talking about?" Latrice asked, unable to comprehend what was going on. Before Latrice could react, she felt Clarity's cold lips kiss her left knee.

"Nooo. This can't happen again." Latrice leaned up and tried to keep Clarity away from her.

"Come on, mommi. Don't fight me." Clarity still tried to rub and kiss on her. "Let me get my way."

"I already told you that what we did was a one-time thing, so please stop playing and get off me."

Latrice tried to push Clarity away but she kept coming at her.

"I haven't signed any deal yet, so I guess we got time to do it again."

"You're gonna get signed next week. I already told you that, so stop touching me."

"Yeah, that's what you say, but anything can happen from now to then. Ya dig? You might not want to sign me anymore."

"Why wouldn't I want to sign you? You're already in with me. You got my promise."

"Sorry, baby. I need a lil' bit more assurance than that. This is the only way I understand that you're going to stay true to your word," Clarity said as she slid her fingers under Latrice's thong and began to tug on it.

Latrice suddenly found herself caught up again in Clarity's lure of entrapment and didn't see an easy way out. Latrice was pinned up against the sofa. She didn't have a way of clinching Clarity's trust without her doubts of getting backstabbed. Latrice was running the same game on Clarity but didn't expect her to counteract. Latrice acknowledged to herself that Clarity was a slick-ass bitch, and neither one of them would win unless she decided to become submissive. Latrice stopped being difficult and took a deep breath. She then arched her back so that Clarity could remove her thong. Clarity then pulled Latrice's dress over her head and tossed it behind the couch. Clarity did the same with her dress and grabbed

Latrice's face and gave her a nice wet kiss. Latrice closed her eyes and hoped she would not enjoy anything that was about to happen—again.

Bang! Bang! Bang! Bang! Bang!

Latrice thought she heard something so she quickly opened up her eyes.

Bang! Bang! Bang! Bang! Bang! There it is again, she said to herself, thinking that the loud noises were a result of her hangover that may have given her a headache. But then Latrice realized that she didn't have a headache and the noises were coming from her front door.

Bang! Bang! Bang! Bang! Bang!

"Who is it?" she yelled.

"It's Kita!" Latrice's eyes widened. She started to panic as Clarity lay on top of her naked.

Latrice didn't know what she was going to do as her adrenaline rushed to the max. She was stuck like a frightened deer caught in the headlights.

Bang! Bang!

"Come on, bitch. Open up!"

"All right! Hold on!" *What the fuck am I gonna do?* Latrice thought nervously as she sprang into action. *I got to get this bitch out of here. Kita would never fucking understand this shit.* "Clarity, Clarity, wake up. Wake up, Clarity," Latrice whispered as she pushed Clarity off of her.

"What's wrong, babe?" Clarity asked as she awoke sounding groggy and confused.

"Listen. My best friend is at my door right now and I can't let her see me like this. Go in my room until she's gone," Latrice commanded as she quickly tossed Clarity her clothes. Clarity understood the position Latrice was in and willingly made her way into the bedroom. Latrice quickly got dressed, praying that Shakita wouldn't be too suspicious of her, and would hurry up and leave without asking a lot of questions.

Latrice opened her door. "What the hell, girl. You're knocking on my damn door like someone's after your ass."

"I'm sorry to come over this early, but I gotta talk to you." Shakita sounded on edge.

Latrice rubbed her eyes. "What time is it anyway?"

"It's almost eight o'clock."

"All hell nah," Latrice said as she placed her hands on her hips. "Girl, it is too early for this. Hurry up and tell me what's going on, so I can take my ass back to sleep."

"My bad, girl. After I tell you what's up, I'll be on my way," Shakita tensely assured. Shakita swallowed hard as pressure mounted in her chest. "We got to do it again," Shakita said meekly.

Latrice didn't even have to ask what she was talking about. Shakita's trembling face gave it all away. Latrice turned her volume up on her television so that it would be harder for Clarity to eavesdrop. Latrice played it off by changing to an audio channel, acting as if she needed to hear some music to calm her nerves down.

"I cannot do that again. We both agreed that we were done with that shit."

"I know, but we got to do it."

"No. You gotta do it. I got the money I needed to get us out the shit you started. You got over a hundred thousand already. Ain't that enough?" Shakita didn't answer. Latrice's eyes broadened as she looked at her best friend in disappointment. "You fucking gambled it away, didn't you?" Shakita was still speechless. "Why, Kita? Why you got to be such a fuck-up? You could've done anything you wanted with that money, but you blew it all at some fucking casino. You have a serious fucking problem and you need to get some professional help, bitch," Latrice scolded, as she pointed her finger in Shakita's face. "You can't keep dragging me down in your bullshit. I won't let you."

Tears filled Shakita's eyes. "I'm sorry, Latrice. I promise this will be the last time. I swear it will. I'll go to therapy if I need to, but this will be my last time. I promise you this will truly be my last time...our last time." Shakita poured her heart out trying to convince Latrice to come with her on one more robbery. Latrice was furious that she couldn't say no. The only reason she was going to agree to do the robbery again, Shakita would never leave until she said yes. Clarity was still in her house and Latrice had to get Shakita out of there before it was too late.

"All right, bitch. I'm going to do it, but you best believe, this is the last time. I'm not doing any shit like this ever again. You got that?" Latrice said as her lips quivered. Her body raged with unwanted emotion.

"Yeah. I got it. After this move, I'll get straight and get my ass in therapy...I promise." Shakita sounded convincing, but Latrice wasn't completely sold on her promise. She first had to make a vow of her own, one that could never be broken once it was agreed upon.

"All right, Shakita. I got your promise, but I'm going to tell you this. The day you ask me to do another fucking thing that got shit to do with stealing some mothafucking money, that's the day we're no longer friends. You understand?" Latrice said with heated conviction.

Shakita couldn't believe that Latrice had given her such a brash ultimatum, but she undoubtedly understood why. Shakita had been involving Latrice in her shit for years, and now she had finally had enough. If Shakita was any type of friend, she would respect Latrice's decision and keep her promise.

Shakita sighed deeply. "I understand."

"So when do you want to do this?" Latrice asked halfheartedly.

"In two days. We're going to hit the same van again."

Latrice was shocked. "Bitch, is you crazy? Why the fuck can't we rob the van on the Red Line? We can't rob the same van twice."

"Yes we can. See that's the thing. Ain't nobody going to suspect the same van to get robbed, so all the focus is gonna be on the other lines. They ain't thinking we're going to strike the same place twice, and that's what makes the whole thing more beautiful. Ya dig? That bitch is going to be wide open for the taking. You can believe that."

"Even if the security is relaxed on the Green Line, don't you think as soon as somebody sees two bitches with blonde wigs, that our whole shit is going to be blown?"

"I already thought about that and I have an idea." Latrice was interested in hearing what Shakita had to say. "We're gonna dress up as men."

Latrice was confused. "Why the fuck we goin' do that?"

"Because they already looking for two women. If we go as men, nobody will see the shit coming. Before they know it, those mothafuckas is got. Think about it, girl. That's the only way we're going to get close. After they think two men robbed 'em, this time they won't know what the fuck to believe anymore. They're going to stop looking for black girls and center their case on some white masterminds. Now who would believe that two bitches would be able to do that? I'm telling you, it's foolproof."

Latrice was okay with Shakita's idea and hoped it worked out as easy as she said it would. She still couldn't help but think that this shit was getting way too crazy.

Clarity had her ear to the door trying to hear over the loud music what was happening on the other side of the door. She could only hear bits and pieces of their conversation, but it still wasn't enough to make any sense out of it. All she could presume was that Latrice and her friend were up to something big. Shakita left Latrice's house with another chance to pull off a big hit. She tried to promise herself that this really was the last time, and she would never gamble again. Latrice couldn't believe she'd let Shakita talk her into doing some crazy shit again and would really hate herself if they got caught. She would undeniably jeopardize everything she had going on with the label. She only needed to make it one more week, and hopefully, she wouldn't be going to jail the same time Bay was coming out.

CHAPTER 28

FIVE DAYS UNTIL BAY GETS OUT

Latrice sat in the car nervous as hell hoping that everything was going to go as planned. A million butterflies fluttered around in her stomach. Her heart raced at an excessive pace. She had never felt anxiety like this in her life, and she couldn't stop thinking about what she was about to do. Latrice had on a black-haired men's wig and was wearing a fake mustache. Latrice could easily have passed for a man with her disguise. Her delusion was all together except for one side of her mustache wouldn't stay on. She'd used all the adhesive that came in the mustache kit, but it still wasn't enough to hold it in place. Latrice looked in the mirror and realized the mustache wasn't going to work. She was beginning to get second thoughts about what she was doing. Her eyes started to mist.

Shakita was getting in position and felt the adrenaline running through her body. She was charged up and couldn't wait to get this job done and over with. Shakita had their whole line of attack planned out, and it was only a matter of minutes before everything went down exactly the way she wanted it to. "Shakita! Can you hear me!" Latrice said over the walkie-talkie.

"I'm here, Latrice, what's up?"

"My mustache won't stay on. I need you to help me fix it."

"Just put it on the best way you can. It only needs to hold for a few minutes."

"It won't hold at all. I need some more glue. I need you to meet me. I got to have this mustache on," Latrice cried.

Shakita could hear the nervousness in her voice and didn't want Latrice to panic. "All right, Latrice. Meet me at the recreation center on the Warner Ave side."

"Okay. I'll be right there." Shakita didn't want to leave her post, but she had to get Latrice back on point before she ruined the whole operation.

When Shakita pulled up by the rec center, she saw Latrice outside leaning up against the car. Shakita rushed over to her so they could hurry up and get back in place. "Okay. Where's your mustache at? We ain't got that much time," Shakita said, looking around in the car for the mustache.

"I'm not going."

"What did you say?" Shakita asked, wondering if she'd heard her correctly.

"I said I'm not going."

"You're fucking with me, right?" Latrice remained silent. "Tell me you're just fucking with me, Latrice!"

"No, Kita. I'm not. I can't do this anymore."

Shakita couldn't believe what she was hearing and started to lose her mind. "We're minutes away from hitting this fucking van and you're backing out on me! You can't do this shit to me! You promised me you would do it!" Shakita yelled.

"Well, I changed my mind. I got dreams, Kita. Big dreams and I can't fuck up what I got going on to follow your ass on some fucking wild-ass robbery shit. You can gamble with your life, but I'm not gambling with mine no more. You're going to have to do this on your own. I'm out." She pulled her gun out of her waistband and tried to hand it over to Shakita. Shakita looked at the gun and then coldly back up at Latrice.

"Remember when you said that if I ask you to do anything else after this, that we wouldn't be friends anymore?"

"Yeah, I remember."

"So I'm giving you the same option. If I take that gun from you and we don't do this job, then that's going to be it for us." Shakita stared at Latrice, meaning every word.

Shakita was ready to give up twelve years of friendship since Latrice didn't want to commit a crime with her. Latrice felt that if Shakita couldn't see that what she was asking of her was wrong, then Shakita's friendship wasn't worth having anyway. Latrice wished she would have found out that they weren't meant to be friends a long time ago. That would have made their departure from each other a lot easier to deal with.

Latrice extended her arm out even more, trying to hand Shakita the gun, further letting her know that she was ready to disband their relationship.

"I guess I'll see you around," Shakita said as she took the gun out of Latrice's hand.

"Maybe, maybe not," Latrice said seriously with a strained look in her eyes. Without any signal, they both embraced each other and started to shed tears, as the thought of them not being friends began to set in.

"I love you, girl," Shakita said as she started to sniffle and tears dripped down her chin.

"I love you too," a watery-eyed Latrice wept.

Neither one of them could handle the emotional moment well. Everything they shared would be forever lost. Their alliance had finally taken its course and it was time for them to go their separate ways. "I got to get going," Shakita said as she broke their embrace and wiped the tears off her face. She then backed away from her slowly. They shared a stare for a moment, then Shakita turned away. Latrice didn't make any attempt to stop her from leaving, nor did she try to do anything to get her to stay. Shakita got in her car and looked at her ex-best friend for what could possibly be the last time, then sped off.

Latrice got back behind the wheel and began to sob heavily, reflecting how the whole incident would affect the rest of her life. As much as Latrice wanted to get back on the walkie-talkie and let Shakita know that she was down with her until the end, she couldn't. Being there for Shakita wasn't what she wanted in her life anymore. Latrice was becoming a different type of woman and had to relieve herself of any unwanted baggage in order to be successful in her next venture. She was convinced that Shakita wouldn't be a good fit in her new life. Where Latrice planned on going in the music industry, it wasn't good business to have problematic friends around that were always trying to bring you down. She had been certain Shakita would never leave the scandalous world she lived in, and that's why they could not remain friends.

Shakita held her head down in agony. She was frustrated that Latrice had left her high and dry right before they were about to make the hit. Her stress level started to rise as she rushed to think of another plan of attack. She was all alone and couldn't figure out how she was going to rob the van, force the driver off the main road, then unload the money without being seen. Shakita was about to give up and find someone she could trust to help her at another time. Suddenly, she thought of a plan that could possibly work. It had to be done carefully. She started to believe that she didn't need anybody but her damn self and was ready to handle her business. The van would be on its way soon, so she had to get herself at the right location before she missed her opportunity.

The driver finished up his route and was rushing to get back to the depot station, so he could drop his load and get on the Beltway before traffic got too heavy. He hated sitting in gridlock traffic for at least two hours trying to get back to his home. The driver was flying down the street and noticed that the car in front of him slammed on its brakes unexpectedly. Without enough time to react, he smashed right into the back of the old Buick sedan. The crash was so severe that it left both vehicles disabled. The driver wasn't hurt much, but he wanted to see how badly the person in the other car was injured.

When the driver of the van approached the car, he noticed that the driver of the Buick was not moving and appeared to be a young male. He opened the door to see if the driver was still breathing, and that's when he felt a clank on his wrist. Before he knew it, he found himself handcuffed to the steering wheel with a gun pointed to his head. He was scared as hell.

"If you don't do anything stupid, I won't kill your ass. You understand?" Shakita said calmly.

The driver nodded his head in fear, willing to do whatever he was told to prevent from getting shot. "Now I want you to slowly put your other hand on the top of the car and wait for further instruction. You got that?"

The man slowly lifted his hand from his side and placed it on the roof of the car as he was instructed. "Now I want you to turn your body all the way to your left and keep it that way until I tell you otherwise." The man had to think for a second which side was his left so he didn't make a mistake. When the man's right hip was facing her, Shakita removed his gun off his waist and then tossed it on the backseat.

"Now slowly bring your hand back in the car and place it on the steering wheel." The man did what he was told and then felt the cold steel cuff that was already attached to the wheel being slapped on his other wrist.

Shakita then climbed out of the car from the passenger side and headed for the van with her gun tucked in her waist. She ran to the back of the van and was ready to get the money out. She had to move fast in case someone called the police. Shakita swung the heavy doors open, so she could climb in and pull the canisters out.

Boom!!!

The shotgun blast threw Shakita's body to the ground as the officer in the back of the van emerged with a smoking barrel.

Shakita's legs twitched as she gasped for air. The massive hole in her chest was making it hard for her to breathe, as thick blood spewed from her mouth. Shakita's heart had already stopped beating before she realized what had happened to her. The armed officer jumped out of the van and stood over her dead body. He saw that the man's mustache was hanging off his face, so he assumed it was a fake, and when he looked at the man even harder, he realized something else about him when he pulled the mustache all the way off.

"You're just a young girl," the officer said under his breath.

The officer started to put the pieces together, and figured out that she was probably the same woman that robbed the very same van a week before. He had hoped she wouldn't try it again, wanting to avoid the tragic event that had currently taken place. If Shakita would have been watching the news lately, she would have known that the BERK van robbery set off a security breach that couldn't be allowed to happen again. Each van that was transporting money had to have a backup officer on board to add an extra layer of defense. Shakita's addiction to gambling resulted in more than her simply losing endless amounts of money and her best friend in the world. She lost her life and it was too late to ask her was everything she'd ever done worth it. The officer walked over to the smashed-up Buick to see if his fellow officer was all right as squad cars rushed to the scene.

Latrice sat on her couch and tuned into the five o'clock news wanting to see if there was anything about another BERK van robbery. Latrice didn't think Shakita would have the heart to do it by herself, and even if she did attempt it, she would be caught and thrown in jail. She thought that if Shakita had a change of heart and decided not to go through with it, then they could possibly be friends again. Deep down inside, she really couldn't see not being friends with Shakita again and truly hoped she'd made the right choice. But when Latrice heard the special news report with Shakita's face posted on the screen, she suddenly broke down crying and screamed from the top of her lungs.

"You're so stupid! Oh, you're so fucking stupid, why! Why, Shakita! Why! Why! Why!" she yelled as she hit the floor and cried while banging her fists against the couch. Latrice was so hurt that Shakita had gotten killed and part of her wanted to blame herself. Latrice felt like if she would've tried to stop her, she would've still been living. She realized if they would have stayed together, both of them would have been dead. Latrice couldn't help but to cry out in devastation over her fallen sister. It was almost hard to believe that her best friend was gone and never coming back. Ironically, Shakita Marshall was dead at the age of "21." She always believed it was her luckiest number.

Eric had called Latrice as soon as he heard the news about Shakita. He wondered if she knew what really happened. Eric found out where she lived and rushed over to her apartment. He really wanted to be there in her critical time of need. Shakita was a big part of his life and he, too, would need to be comforted. When Latrice opened the door for Eric, she fell into his arms and sobbed heavily. He tried to get her to calm down, but nothing he did or said worked. Tears started to flow down his face. Being around an emotional Latrice was becoming harder and harder for him to bear. All he could hear was her crying in his ear as he held her up to keep her from falling. Eric realized that Latrice was too traumatized and didn't expect to get much out of her in the delusional state of mind she was in. All he could do right now was hold her, support her, and prayed that they would both be able to get through this tempestuous time—together.

CHAPTER 29

TWO DAYS UNTIL BAY GETS OUT

Everyone had gathered for Shakita's funeral. Eric paid for all the arrangements so that Shakita would have a proper burial. The viewing of the body and the actual service were done all in the same day, since Shakita didn't have much family or friends that could attend her untimely death. Shakita's mother was a homeless drug addict and her father was a man she wouldn't have known, even if he had been an old customer of hers. Shakita had very few relatives and the ones she did have, Latrice was unable to contact them. Even with the national broadcast of Shakita's killing, that still didn't bring out the support of her estranged family members.

The only other attendees at Shakita's passing besides Latrice and Eric were a few employees from the spa, a couple guys she used to date, and Cotton. Cotton was informed by Eric about Shakita's entire situation after she had been killed. She felt somewhat responsible for driving Shakita to the point where she had to commit armed robbery. She thought that if it wasn't for her, Shakita never would have gone to jail and lost her job at the spa. It was too late for Cotton to say sorry to her, so the least she could do was pay her respects.

During the beginning of the service, two unknown men came in to pay their respects as well. Latrice thought that the two men looked doubtful and presumed they were feds. She thought that they might attend hoping to find the other girl associated with the first van robbery, so she made certain that Eric didn't put her name anywhere on the obituary. She didn't want any additional reasons to get questioned about the robbery. Latrice made sure not to give them too much eye contact either, not wanting to draw attention to herself. With Bay coming home in two days, she couldn't afford to go to jail, especially not now.

Latrice stood over Shakita's casket at the Oak Hill Cemetery and spent precious time with her before she was lowered into the ground. Latrice's face quivered as she cried, staring at the metal casket that held her best friend, still not wanting to believe she was gone. The only time Latrice had dealt with a loss of this magnitude was when her mother died when she was only fourteen. Even then she was too young to truly understand death. All she really understood was that she would never see her mother again. She was older now and with Shakita absent from her life, she had only one person to worry about. A life without Shakita would be such a bore and she wasn't looking forward to it. Eric was saying goodbye to Cotton, when he noticed that Latrice was the last one left at the gravesite and decided to see if she were all right.

"Are you going to be ready to go soon?" Eric asked as he stood behind her and started rubbing her shoulders.

"Yes, in a minute. I still can't believe she's gone, Eric," Latrice said, wiping her tears away.

"Me either. I wasn't expecting this at all," Eric said as he tried to hold back tears.

"It feels like this whole thing ain't real. I'm waiting for her to jump out the casket, and be like *I got y'all bitches.* I would be mad as shit at her for scaring us like that, but I would be so glad that she was here. I know it's not a joke though…I felt her arm at the viewing…and it was hard as a tree branch…There's no way she's coming back from that. I miss her so muchhhh." She burst out in tears as her body shook against Eric's strong chest.

"I do too," Eric said as he handed her more tissue, while unable to hold back his tears any longer.

"I really wish I could talk to her one last time. There's so much that I have to say. We left each other on such bad terms and I could've done more to stop her." Latrice cried even harder as Eric turned her around to comfort her with his embrace.

"I know how you feel," Eric said softly in her ear. "I wish I could change the result of my last meeting with her, too. There was so much I could have done," he said, shaking his head wishing he could have been better to her. "I should have helped her." He began to whimper.

Eric's frustration with himself was starting to get the best of him. He cried even more thinking about all the damaging actions he'd put Shakita through. He felt terrible about the foul deeds he allowed Shakita to do at the spa, but at the time, he had justification for all his actions. Shakita had inadvertently broken his heart shortly after they'd met, and he had never been able to get over his emptiness. There was something about Shakita that caused an unexplainable effect, which drove him to the critical point in his life where he had been unable to erase. Eric felt as if he'd placed his heart in her coffin right along with her. He then realized that was the only way he would be able to move on. He had to give her his old heart and get a new one. They both slowly walked out of the cemetery not knowing how they would be able to move on without Shakita.

"I'll only be a minute," Latrice said as she got out of Eric's car so she could go into Cap Cap's store. She walked through the door and saw Cap Cap behind the counter watching TV as usual. Latrice stepped to the counter and Cap Cap continued to watch his movie.

"Here's the money I owe you," Latrice said as she laid a stack of money on the countertop.

"I'm sorry to hear about your friend," he said sadly, finally giving her eye contact.

"Thank you, Cap. I appreciate it."

"You know. It don't matter how much you plan shit out. Sometimes it doesn't always go our way. I'm glad it wasn't both of y'all. But let me ask you this, young girl." Cap Cap stared into her eyes, hoping to get the truth as Latrice listened. "All that money y'all got, was it worth it?"

Latrice paused before she spoke. "I don't know yet."

Cap Cap didn't know how to respond, so he didn't say anything. Latrice felt like she had said enough and needed to go. "I gave you a little extra on top of what I owed you. I'll see you around, Cap."

"You take care of yourself."

"I'll try," Latrice said, looking back at him before she hit the door. She hoped she never had to go into his store again, and if she did, it would only be for some candy.

After leaving Cap Cap's store, Latrice felt for some odd reason she should go see Fantasy. She hadn't thought of her since the last time she'd been to her club and didn't know why she had come across her mind all of a sudden. Latrice had Eric turn onto K Street, and when she got down in front of the Fantasy Lounge, she was totally stunned.

Latrice got out of the car and walked over to the Fantasy Lounge and saw a sign on the door that read "Bank Foreclosure." She didn't understand how Fantasy had allowed the bank to take away her club when she was making so much money on concerts every week. She thought there had to be a good explanation as to why Fantasy had let herself get in that situation.

"I guess you're going to have to find somewhere else to party because that shit hole is no mo'."

Latrice looked to her left and saw a skinny man holding a beer can in one hand and a cigarette in the other, while wobbling trying to maintain his balance.

"Did the club move? Do you know who Fantasy is?" Latrice asked without thinking about who she was asking.

"Yeah. I should know her. That's my sister."

"What happened? How come the club's not open anymore?"

"'Cause us crackheads can't keep shit open," the man said as he took a sip from his beer. "Do you know where she is now?"

"Yeah, I know where she at. She's getting us some shit. She was supposed to been back," the man said, checking his surroundings for her.

Latrice still couldn't believe the man knew what he was talking about and was about to leave when she saw a shabby-looking Fantasy coming around the corner.

"Did you get the shit?" the man asked Fantasy.

"Yeah, I got it. Just calm down," Fantasy answered, not even noticing that Latrice was standing there.

"Fantasy." Latrice called out her name so she could get her attention.

"Hey. How you doing? Long time, no see."

"Yeah. What happened to your club?"

"Awe, it ain't nothing," Fantasy said as she brushed it off her shoulders. "I owed the bank a lil' money. It'll be going up for auction next month. I'mma try to get it back then."

"Try to get it back, my ass," the man said, interrupting her. "You done smoked all your damn money up with me. That shit's gonna go to someone else. Now come on here, so we can get high," he said, nudging her.

"All right, girl. I got to go. But don't believe what my stupid-ass brotha says. I'm gonna be back on top. You wait n' see. Ol' Fantasy gonna be back," she said convincingly as her brother pulled her away.

Latrice couldn't believe that Fantasy had been a crackhead all along, but when she thought back to all her strange behavior, everything started to make sense. Latrice figured that Fantasy was never going to be able to get the club back, and thought that it was so unfortunate for someone to lose everything they had over crack. She never understood what was so important about the drug that caused people to lose their damn minds. Latrice watched as two lost souls wandered down the street not knowing if it would be their last time getting high. Latrice realized that drugs were Fantasy's addiction and gambling was Shakita's, and she eerily wondered what she was addicted to.

Later on that evening, Latrice didn't want to be bothered with anybody, so she had Eric drop her off at her apartment where she could be alone. She was tired and wanted to relax, so she decided to pour some wine and lay back on the couch. With the television off, it made her surroundings extremely quiet and she was about to drift off to sleep when her house phone rang. She looked at the caller ID and saw that it was a county jail number. She was convinced it could only be one person: Bay.

"Hello," she answered, waiting to accept the call.

"Hello," Bay said after the automated system went off.

"Yes, Bay. I'm here," Latrice said despairingly.

Once he heard her voice, he busted out in laughter. "Yo! I saw the news, young! Your girl went out like a mothafucking gangsta!"

"Bay, could you please not talk about her like that. Her funeral was today. Please have some fucking respect for her."

"Damn. You a sensitive-ass bitch, ain't you? I was actually glorifying her ass. You need to lighten the fuck up or something. What's wrong with you? You need some dick?"

Latrice rolled her eyes. "No I'm good. Is that the only thing you think about is pussy?"

"Hell yeah. What the fuck you think? I've been holding my dick for three months in this bitch. Besides my money, what else is there to think about?" Latrice didn't respond. "I know you're going to give me that pussy soon as I get out, right?"

"I don't know. I haven't thought about it yet."

"What the fuck you mean, you haven't thought about it yet? You better get that motor running under that bald-ass head of yours and stop playing with me."

"You know you really need to learn how to talk to women."

"Well, when you find one, let me know. Then I'll try."

"You are such a fucking asshole. I'm about to hang up. Do you have anything else you have to say?"

"Girl, if you fucking hang up on me, I'll wreck ya lil' ass when I get out. Don't forget who the fuck I am, girl." Latrice realized that she had stepped over the line and decided to watch her tongue. "I'm ready to get off the phone with your lil' dumb ass anyway. But I'm going to need you to be up here early as hell on Friday, so you can pick me up. Can you do that?"

"Yeah. I'll be there," Latrice said, sounding defeated.

"All right. I'm 'bout to be out. Make sure you keep that pussy tight for me. You know I'll be able to tell if you been fucking anybody. "

"I hear you, Bay."

Bay hung up first and Latrice held the phone to her ear as tears streamed down her face.

She hated the way Bay talked to her and wanted the grasp he had on her to be ultimately lifted. She so badly wanted to leave him alone, but there was still unfinished business that had to be handled. There was no way Bay would get out and let her live the type of life she wanted. He had to have complete control over her. Latrice slammed the phone on the floor and then balled herself up on the couch and cried dramatically. Latrice decided she didn't want to be involved with Bay anymore, but since she wanted into the music industry, she had to hold out a little bit longer.

Latrice tossed and turned all night on her couch in a cold sweat. She had nightmares about the days when Bay used to beat on her severely. She replayed in her mind the day that Bay punched her in her mouth for turning up the volume on the stereo in her car while he was on the phone. The strike to her mouth left a small gash on her lip that didn't go away for weeks. She then pictured the night Bay beat her down for not wanting to have sex with him while he was drunk. The battering caused her eye to close up and left her with several engorged ribs. Latrice told Shakita at the time she had been in a car accident. She continued to relive several more incidents when Bay would choke her while she slept and she would wake up fighting for her life.

Latrice jumped up on her couch as she held her throat. She heavily gasped for air as the thought of Bay choking her felt so real. Her heart raced as if she had finished running a marathon. She was extremely shaken as tears penetrated her eyes. She tried not to have those same bad dreams about Bay, but the closer it got to his release date, the more frequently they occurred. She hated the constant battle of having to deal with a man that was so physically abusive to her, but at the same time trusted her with everything. Bay was getting out of jail in one more day, and she hoped that they both would be able to be on better terms where she wouldn't have to fear him.

CHAPTER 30

ONE MORE DAY UNTIL BAY GETS OUT

"I got one more wake-up and I'm out of this bitch!" Bay shouted, trying to taunt the passing officer.

"Don't be so fucking happy, punk. You do so much as hug a bitch too tight, and your ass will be right back up here for good. You fucking woman beater," the officer threatened before walking away from Bay's cell.

"You fucking cocksucker," Bay said under his breath.

Any other time he would have put up an argument with anyone who called him a woman beater. He had one more day of lockup and decided to give the officer a pass without giving him a beat down. Bay lay back on his cot and started thinking about Latrice. It'd been three long months since the last time they'd had sex, and he couldn't wait to get inside her chocolate thighs. He hadn't jerked himself off to any magazines lately, so he really couldn't wait to bust a big load on Latrice's plump ass. Bay's thoughts of fucking Latrice were suddenly cut short when his celly on the bottom bunk started rapping out loud.

"You ain't got no flows, nigga, so shut the fuck up with all that bullshit," Bay said jokingly.

"All, nigga, quit playing. You know I'm the best you ever heard," Love Boat Brad proudly stated. Love Boat Brad was a tall, over-weight dark-skinned cat with a thick beard. He called himself

Love Boat since he was a big PCP dealer in Southeast D.C. and Bradley was his real first name.

"Yeah, you like the best I heard. I got plans for you when you get out."

Love Boat Brad stood up beside Bay's bunk. "So you really trying to get this music thing cracking, huh?"

"Yeah, man. I'm going to be big out here and you are, too. I know you got another year up in this bitch, but we gonna make sure you hella known before you even get out. You're gonna be a guaranteed platinum artist before your record is even pressed. Believe that."

Love Boat Brad was feeling everything that Bay was spitting to him and couldn't wait to tell the world what was on his mind. By the time Love Boat Brad finished his bid, he planned on having at least fifty songs already done to give the streets. His thoughts of success were quickly interrupted when the sounds from an officer's baton rattled the bars to his cell.

Love Boat Brad looked out his cell, then over at Bay. "Yo, Bay. It's ya boy."

Bay lifted up his head and saw that it was Officer Stevens. He was expecting his visit and got up to go holler at him.

"What up? You do that thing for me?" Bay whispered to the officer.

Officer Stevens looked around to see if any other officer was near before he started to speak. "Yeah, I did it. I put it right where I told you I would," he said in a murmured tone.

"Good. So what are you gonna do about the diversion?"

"I got Pam and Glow to take care of that."

"Why you get them two faggots? I don't want them up in my shit."

"It's going to be cool, man. They don't want anything from you.

They want to have a place to fuck each other without being bothered. I can take care of that for them."

"How did you talk them into gettin' involved?"

"They only want to see some drama. You know how it is."

"All right, man. Those little gay hoes better not fuck this up."

"It's already fucked up. They're trying to make sure your ass
doesn't get caught. Nigga, be thankful."

"You don't understand, nigga. I got a lot to lose fucking around
with those faggots."

"If you got so much to lose, then why do it? You're getting out
tomorrow, man. You still can call this whole thing off."

"Make sure everything work out," Bay said, walking away, not
giving Officer Stevens' suggestion a second thought. Officer Stevens
understood that Bay was serious about what he wanted to do, so
he didn't try to hold him back any further. He looked around
before he walked away from Bay's cell. The coast was clear, so he
walked back to his duty post and waited for everything to later
unfold.

The shower room was filled to the max and Timbo had managed
to bully a young white boy for his shower slot. Timbo turned
around and laughed at how he handled the kid while he adjusted
the water pressure. He didn't even notice that Bay was at the opposite side of the shower wall watching his every move. Bay started
to shower again until Pam and Glow started arguing with each
other about who cheated on whom first. Everyone watched as the
two men's words turned physical and they started pushing and
grabbing each other. Fists started to fly and the two lovers were
going at it with everyone in the shower room observing. They
then took their scuffle all the way near the doorway as they chased
each other around the room, and then finally wrestled each other

out of the inmates' view. A lot of the inmates who were showering wanted to continue to see a fight, so they followed the two gay men to see how long they were going to go at it.

Timbo saw enough of the altercation and didn't want to run and see no gay men fighting ass-naked like some bitches. He grabbed his bar of soap and started to build up a thick lather all over himself. Bay lifted up a loose floor tile that was under his foot. Underneath was a long flat razor that was left for him by Officer Stevens. He gripped the razor tightly in his hand and then crept up behind Timbo. Timbo couldn't hear Bay approaching over the loud water and continued to lather himself up.

"This might sting a little," Bay grimly whispered to Timbo, as he put him in a one-armed headlock, and pressed the razor down in his throat. Timbo was struggling to free himself as his feet dangled off the ground. He was losing consciousness from the amount of blood that poured from his carotid artery.

Timbo's fight came to an end when his pulse faded as blood-mixed soap foam dripped off his feet. Bay didn't feel Timbo putting up a struggle, so he let his body slump to the wet shower room floor. Bay dropped the dirty blade down the drain as the remaining inmates stood and watched the tragic incident take place. Bay looked at all the inmates and smiled, showing them exactly how crazy he was. The inmates didn't want to be a witness to the murder, so they turned around and finished their showers. A few of the inmates were scared to turn their back to Bay fearing they would be attacked next. Bay didn't think any of them would snitch on him, so he turned around and washed all the blood off his body.

After Bay was fully clean, he grabbed a towel off the rack and walked out of the shower room laughing hysterically. Bay left a cold and uncanny presence amongst the other inmates, as water from the showerhead continued to pour onto Timbo's lifeless body.

CHAPTER 31

THE RELEASE DATE

Word got around quickly throughout the jailhouse that Timbo had committed suicide in the shower room. There was no witness that saw what had happened, so Officer Stevens didn't have anything to go on when he filled out his report. Bay acted like he couldn't believe what had taken place and was thankful he was getting released. He believed you could easily lose your mind in jail and suicide was sometimes the best option. He was glad his time was minimal in there, and now he could focus on all that was waiting for him on the outside.

"Hey, Bay. It's time to go," Officer Stevens said, standing in front of his cell waiting to process him out. Bay couldn't do anything but smile as he jumped off his cot and looked at himself in the mirror.

"Hey, dirty-ass mirror. This is the last time you're going to see this pretty face."

Love Boat Brad got off his bed, so he could say goodbye to his short-term celly. "Make sure you write a nigga, young. We got to make sure we stay up, so I can see what you're doing."

"Don't worry, big homey. You a true-ass nigga, so I got to fuck witchu. I don't trust too many niggas, but I can say me and you cool. I'm about to be a star and I want you to shine with me," Bay said, extending his hand to give Love Boat Brad some dap.

"Take care of yourself out there, boy," Love Boat Brad said, giving Bay a hug.

"Nah, nigga. Don't worry about me. I'm going to be all right. You're the one still behind the wall."

"I feel you. My turn coming soon."

Bay was ready to roll out, so he had to say his last words. "I'll make sure to get at you as soon as I can, big homey. I gotta make sure I send you pictures of all the groupie love you can expect to get when you come home."

"Do that, young, for real."

Bay walked out of his cell with Officer Stevens, and soon as the cell door was slammed shut, Bay gave Love Boat Brad a head nod, and then started to make his way out of the facility.

"You're still going to get me on as your bodyguard whenever you get started, right?" Officer Stevens whispered in Bay's ear as they walked side by side.

"Yeah, you good. Don't worry; I got you," Bay whispered back.

Bay and Officer Stevens were almost to the area where he would get processed out as Officer Hoke was walking toward them. Officer Hoke was looking straight at Bay. Bay's jaw clenched as the officer steadily approached. Officer Hoke was the same one who'd broken up the quarrel between him and Timbo. Bay and Officer Stevens suspected he knew something odd about Timbo's alleged suicide. They had to play it cool as they attempted to walk past him.

"Hold on one fuckin' minute, Stevens. I have to ask this piece of shit here a question or two," the white officer said as he folded his arms, trying to intimidate Bay.

"Make it quick, Hoke. I got to get his ass down to processing."

Officer Hoke stared at Bay before he spoke. "Listen here, you little low-life fuck. I was there that day you and that dead inmate got into it, and I'm willing to bet part of my own ass that you killed him."

"I'm sorry, officer, but if you can recall, that inmate tried to attack me first. I heard he committed suicide anyway. You can't put that on me. I'm innocent."

Officer Hoke stared into Bay's dark eyes trying to find one reason to believe that he was lying. He didn't have any concrete evidence that placed Bay in the shower room at that time, so he had to let him go for now.

"Hoke. Are you finished yet, man? We got to keep moving," Officer Stevens said, trying to get Officer Hoke to end his pointless interrogation.

"Yeah, I'm done." Officer Hoke still looked at Bay. "But let me tell you this, you stupid fuck. When that autopsy comes back and shit don't add up right, I'm going to have your ass back in here faster than you can pull your fuckin' dick out to get some pussy. This ain't over." Officer Hoke turned and stormed off.

"Don't worry about his ass. He ain't going to find out shit," Officer Stevens assured.

"I hope you right. That mothafucka sound like he trying to put my ass under the jail. You just make sure he doesn't."

Bay couldn't afford to go to prison for murder and needed Officer Stevens to keep the heat off of him. Officer Stevens was going to do everything he could to keep his golden ticket to a better life out of prison. He hoped he wouldn't have to go to that extent.

Bay was processed out and given back all his belongings. He checked to make sure all his items were there before he left. Everything was in his pack except for his money clip, but he wasn't going to trip or make a scene that would end up with him back in jail for disorderly conduct. With all the money he was about to touch in the music biz, he wouldn't have much use for a money clip anyway. "All y'all good people of the law have a nice day," Bay said, laughing his way out the door, hoping to get under the skin of the officers that were within earshot.

Bay got outside and took a deep breath of all the city air that was waiting for him. He was glad to be free and even happier when he saw Latrice sitting on the hood of her car waiting for him.

"What up, baby girl? Your favorite nigga's out of that bitch. Come here and show me some love," Bay said as he walked toward Latrice with open arms.

"Hey, Bay." Latrice gave him a tight hug and felt that his arms and chest had gotten bigger since the last time she'd seen him. Bay took a step back and noticed that Latrice seemed to be a little thicker than he remembered.

"Damn, you got some ass n' titties I ain't never seen before."

"You really think so? I ain't been doing nothing but eating. You like this, huh?" she said, doing a little pose for him.

"I see you stopped rocking that short hair, huh?" Bay noticed she was wearing her long black weave.

"I decided to try something different. You like it?" She smiled as she played with her hair. All Bay could do was stare and lick his lips at her. He couldn't tell if Latrice was that damn sexy to him or the fact that he hadn't had any pussy in a long time. His dick started to bulge out of his pants and he had to have her soon.

Bay hadn't had anything to eat since he was released, so he wanted to go to his favorite food spot, The Diner in Adams Morgan, to get something in his stomach that was anything but some nasty-ass jail food. At the restaurant, Bay wanted to tell Latrice about what had happened to Timbo while they were at the table, but he decided to wait until another time. Bay didn't want to tell her the truth, feeling that she wouldn't be able to handle it. He didn't want to make her aware of anything she didn't need to necessarily know about, so he was going to keep that secret from her as long as he could.

Latrice was getting along with Bay so much that she wanted to spend the entire day with him. Bay wanted to be with her too but didn't want to do no walk-in-the-park-type shit. He wanted to take Latrice to a room somewhere and give her dick all night long. He also wanted to find out what was up with his money and company that she was taking care of for him. He was going to get down to business after he first took care of his pleasures. After they left the restaurant, Bay's quest for lust seemed to be ending when Latrice unexpectedly pulled into the Bottom Dollar Inn's parking lot, which was right off New York Avenue. Bay was eager to get his fuck on, but didn't think they were going to end up at a fleabag motel that was locally known as the "hoe hostel." He didn't want to go to a motel where prostitutes could be seen parading in and out any time of the day. He wanted something better.

"Aye, young. What the fuck are we doing here?"

"I got a surprise for you."

"You couldn't surprise me at the damn Radisson or Hilton or some shit? What the fuck is this?"

"Bay, calm down. I got you. I need you to trust me so I can do something nice for you, okay? If you don't like what I'm doing for you, we can leave. Please give it a chance first."

Bay didn't know what she had in mind, but whatever it was, he hoped it would be worth him lying his ass on some funky sheets. Bay began to think she had another woman coming for him to have a threesome. He was willing to give it a chance to see what was going to go down. He told Latrice before he got out the car that the whole thing better not be some bullshit or he was going to fuck her up. She promised him that he wouldn't be disappointed.

Latrice had Bay open up the door so he could go in the room first. He suspected the reason she wanted him to go in the room first was that she had thrown him a welcome-home surprise party. He realized it couldn't be that. He didn't have any friends that she could invite, and the only ones that would be more than willing to show up were his enemies. Bay wanted his curiosity to cease on what was behind the door, so he opened it up slowly and found nothing but a well-decorated room. There were "Welcome Home, Bay" posters that covered the room from wall to wall and flower arrangements placed neatly about the room. Bay didn't think that the rooms at the motel could be hooked up and never imagined Latrice surprising him like that.

"Damn, girl. You did this for me?" Bay felt overjoyed.

"Yeah. Do you like it?" Latrice asked, smiling bashfully.

"Damn, girl. I wasn't expecting nothing like this. You really came through for a nigga on his first day out."

"You sit down right here and relax 'cause I ain't did nothing yet," she said, taking his hand and leading him over to the bed.

"I need you to get yourself right for me. I got some weed and D'Ussé to help ease your mind," she said, pointing at the bag of weed and bottle of cognac sitting in a half-melted bucket of ice on the nightstand.

"I'm going to go take a shower and put something sexy on for you. You're still going to be here when I get out, right?"

"Hell yeah. Everything I need is right here. You just make sure you hurry up."

"I will. Take a shot for me," she said, smiling before walking into the bathroom. Bay watched her strut across the room and was getting excited.

"Fuck this. I'm 'bout to get bushed," he said as he took off his button-down Akoo shirt, so he could feel more comfortable in his wife beater. Bay removed the bottle of cognac from the bucket and scooped out some ice and put the cubes in a plastic cup. He filled the cup up to the brim and took a long swig. "Woo! I needed that shit. This shit here is going to have me feeling right in a minute. I'mma be doing some rhinoceros-type fucking when I go through the rest of this bottle." Bay hadn't drunk alcohol in so long and felt a slight buzz coming on already. He was really trying to get fucked up, so he picked up the bag of weed and took a whiff of the contents.

"Woo wee! Where the fuck she get this from? This is some of that stanky stank. It looks like some of that Blue Ivy OG Kush everyone been talking about," he said admiring the bluish-colored marijuana.

Bay cracked open a blunt and then began to fill it up with the strong-smelling sticky buds. He lay back in the bed and turned on the television, so he could settle into his surroundings. He heard the shower starting to run in the bathroom and couldn't help but to think about Timbo.

"To all the bitch niggas who ain't here." He tilted his cup and poured some of his drink on the carpet. "Rest in piss pussy," he said, busting out in devilish laughter. Bay had an evil soul and didn't care who he made miserable with his demented ways. In his world, he was the only one that mattered.

Bay felt Latrice had been in the bathroom almost forever and wanted her to come out. He had drunk almost the whole bottle already and was ready to get his smash on. Before he could get up to see what was taking her so long, Latrice was coming out of the bathroom. She was wearing the same orange dress she wore during the van robbery, along with her black leather stilettos. Bay saw how good she looked in her tight-fitting dress and got aroused immediately. Now he really wanted her badly.

"Guess what I'm trying to do?" Latrice asked as she slowly walked over to him with her hands behind her back.

"I ain't the smartest nigga in the world, but I guess you're to trying fuck like I am."

"Yeah. But I'm trying do some kinky shit," she said, dangling a pair of handcuffs in front of him with her leather glove-covered hands.

"Damn, bitch. I just got out da mothafucka and you trying to have a nigga locked up already?" Bay joked.

"Don't worry, baby. These cuffs are for both of us. I'm trying to do the bid with you."

Bay loved the fact that Latrice was his down-ass chick no matter what. Bay was the type of man who thought that being submissive to women was a sign of weakness, and he never showed vulnerability. Latrice was the only one he could trust and Bay felt he was the strongest man she had ever known. Bay thought that it would be fun to see where her game was going since he trusted her so much and really wanted some ass.

Clink! Clink! Latrice slapped a cuff on his wrist and then the other one onto the bedpost. "Before we do this, let me show you the big surprise I got for you." Latrice blew him a kiss and then climbed off the bed.

"Nah, whatever it is can wait. Now bring your ass back over here, so we can get this shit started."

"It's only going to take a minute. Hold on," she said as she opened up a dresser drawer under the television. Bay didn't want any more surprises and only wanted her to show him what it was, so she could stop the bullshit.

Latrice pulled out a white gift box with a red ribbon wrapped around it. She walked it over to him and held it out so he could take it. "Open it."

Bay pulled off the ribbon and then lifted the top off to see what was inside. "What the fuck is this? Is this supposed to be some type of joke?" Bay asked confused as he took out a Bible and threw it on the bed.

"That's only part of your gift, Bay. The rest of it is still in the box."

Bay moved away some of the wrapping paper and saw a large thick envelope with a gold label on it that read: *Everything You Need to Start a Record Label.* Bay was so worried about fucking Latrice that he almost forgot he was even starting a company. He was so pleased to see the package that he cracked a big smile.

"Thank you, baby. This is what the fuck I've been waiting for. We're about to get this thing cranking." He ripped open the envelope, so he could review everything that was inside. The first item Bay pulled out was a document from the United States Patent and Trademark Office. He couldn't wait to see his label's name and logo for the first time. His eyes enlarged as he progressively searched for it.

Bay found the company name and logo and couldn't believe what he saw. His eyes filled with rage as he quickly turned to Latrice.

"Do you like it?" Latrice asked sarcastically.

"Bitch! What the fuck is Bangspot Records?" he yelled.

She simply smiled. "It's the name of my new label."

Bay was furious. "What the fuck happened to my Lonely Thug

Entertainment? Answer me, bitch!" Bay tried to get over to Latrice, so he could choke the shit out of her, but remembered he was handcuffed.

"Bay. Calm down, so I can tell you what's going on."

"Bitch, you got ten seconds to tell me; all this is some bullshit!" Bay said, throwing the envelope across the room.

"No, Bay. Lonely Thug was some bullshit and that's why I couldn't let it come into existence."

"You? What the fuck you mean, you? That's my shit!"

"I guess you don't see what's happening here, do you, Bay? Look around the room…Today's your funeral."

Bay didn't know what the fuck she was talking about, until he looked again at all the flower displays around the room. He then scanned over all the writing on the walls again, and the phrase "Welcome Home, Bay" held a whole new meaning. Latrice then pressed the play button on the stereo that was beside the television, and Donnie McClurkin's "Order My Steps" came blaring out of the speakers. Latrice went back into the drawer and pulled out a black .38 revolver and pointed it at Bay.

"You're going to pull a gun on me? Are you fucking crazy, bitch?" Bay yelled from the top of his lungs.

"Bay. All that barking ain't necessary, baby. It's been your time for a while now, but I never had the heart to do it. I'm glad you got out of jail when you did. If you would have done something stupid in there, I don't know when I would have been able to kill you. You did so much fucking damage to me that you don't even know. Now, for all my pain, I'm taking what's mine." Latrice stared dead into his eyes as he still tried to free himself from the headboard.

Latrice finally had Bay right where she wanted him. The thought of killing Bay had crossed her mind many times after he'd either choked or physically beaten her. She had to find a way to get Bay out of her life for good without him coming after her. Latrice's prayers were finally answered when Bay had to report to jail for a separate battery charge, where he'd left her over a million dollars to hold until he got out, which he intended to use to start up Lonely Thug Entertainment. Latrice's mother always told her that if a man gave you something, then it's yours. Bay had entrusted in her all his money, along with the key to his musical dreams, as she turned what he'd started into her own vision. Bangspot Records was the future and she was going to make it happen all by herself.

Latrice put every legal document, copyright, and trademark in her name and exclusively owned the record label she'd created. She had legally eliminated Bay from what was once a team venture, and left no evidence that he was ever a part of what she built. She had signed her own name instead of his, which allowed her to be the sole proprietor of Bangspot Records.

Latrice's plan was almost doomed when she found out that Shakita had taken from the stash she secretly had hidden. Latrice thought about aborting her plan to kill Bay thinking it wouldn't work since she was missing a lot of the money he'd given her. She had planned to take all his money and run, but was convinced by Shakita to rob the van. She already had enough money that both she and Shakita could live the rest of their lives off of, but she wanted to first teach Shakita a lesson.

Shakita wasn't only playing around with Bay's money. She was really digging into Latrice's future investment. Latrice made Shakita believe that the money she took was all Bay had. She let her know exactly where she kept it, only to see if she would fall for the trap. Latrice felt really bad when Shakita was killed. She could have stopped her test of friendship game at any time, but she didn't. Without her good friend by her side anymore, she had no choice but to kill Bay, since she had lost the most important person in her life. She had nothing else to lose. She thought if they got caught in the process, she could at least use that as her advantage to gain herself street credibility while serving her time in prison. Street credibility was what any music mogul or rapper needed most to survive in the world of gangster rap.

"You ain't got the heart to shoot me, bitch!" Bay screamed, trying to break himself from the headboard as he smashed holes into the wall.

"It's not my heart that's telling me to kill you, Bay; it's my mind. Now pick up your Bible so I can send you home," Latrice commanded as she raised her gun up higher as it trembled in her hands.

"Is there anything I can do to change your mind about this shit?" Bay asked as his fight to free himself from the headboard wasn't successful. He needed to take another route in trying to save his life.

Latrice shook her head as a tear fell from her eye. Bay was disappointed with Latrice's decision, knowing now she was really going to do it. "Well, fuck it then!" he said before spitting on the Bible. "Heaven ain't my home anyway. Hell is, bitch! So take me there!"

Without any further thought, Latrice pulled the trigger and struck him in the head on the first shot. She unconsciously shot him four more times to make sure he was dead, fearing he could come back to get her. He hung off the bed with only the support of the handcuff holding him up. Latrice stared at Bay's lifeless body and couldn't believe the bloody mess she had made.

Latrice dropped the gun on the bed and looked at her shaking hands. After Bay busted up her nose the day he left for jail, she decided to go to the gun range and learn how to shoot. She wanted to know what it was actually like to fire a gun before she could attempt to kill Bay. Even though she was comfortable with shooting a firearm, her nervousness still got the best of her. Now it felt like she had never shot a gun, and she could still feel her hands vibrating as if she were still holding it.

Latrice began to cry uncontrollably as she covered up her face. She wasn't in tears because she'd killed someone. She bawled out of relief that her abuser was no longer going to give her nightmares. She grabbed her overnight bag out of the bathroom and put her gun in it. Before she left the room, she took one more look at Bay the way she wanted to remember him most—dead and gone.

"Thanks for giving me my life back. Thanks for the money, too. You can keep the Bible. And take one of these with you," she said as she removed a flower out of a vase and tossed it at his feet. Following her last words, she walked out of the room and never looked back.

The next day, Latrice stood on the busy Woodrow Wilson Bridge, which stretched over the Potomac River, and peacefully watched dozens of workers at National Harbor help construct the new MGM Casino. She thought that it was amazing how people could look at a blueprint and build something so precise from a simple design or model. Latrice thought about her own project that was in the works, and like the casino, she was also going to need some assistance. She had a whole slate of hungry artists who wanted to help build up her empire and make a name of their own in the process.

Latrice reached into her purse and pulled out her gun. She kissed the top of the cold barrel and hurled it into the river. She then took off her gloves and threw them over as well. Latrice had no more use for her gun or gloves, and was now putting more thought into starting her life over as she continued to watch the casino being built. She now had a new life without pain, without fear, and most importantly, an existence without Bay Jackson. What else could she ask for?

OUTRO

Judge Tomlin saw Shakita's death on the news, and was perturbed by what had taken place, and he even felt somewhat responsible for what had happened. He should have given her a harsher sentence, but at the time, he thought that the young woman needed a break. He thought if he gave her a chance to turn her life around, then that would help her more than driving her deeper into the system, where she may not have been able to find her way out. From now on, Judge Tomlin would make sure that he would have the young women who came before him in the future, seek treatment for counseling to try and prevent their lives from spiraling out of control. Judge Tomlin was really thankful that his two daughters were still in school pursuing their academic futures. He didn't have to worry about them making any critical decisions at this point in their lives. He also had his lovely wife to contribute for that.

After Shakita's funeral, Cotton started to think about what she was doing with her life and where she was going. She was losing her morale for prostitution and wanted to explore something different, but didn't know what. One night, Cotton got in the car with a john she'd never met and felt strange as she rode off with him. When they finally parked in an alley, the man got upset that Cotton wouldn't give him free sex and started to punch her and rip her clothes off. Cotton was raped, followed by being strangled to death and then robbed of all her money. Cotton's body was later found in a Dumpster on the Southwest side of the city, with her blood-stained panties stuffed in her mouth and her wrists bound together by her bra. Cotton had sensed the possible danger she was in before she'd gotten in the car that night, but didn't go with her gut feeling and decided to go with the money instead.

Officer Stevens had been refused bail and was now facing one count of conspiracy to murder, a count of third-degree murder, and a count of acting as an accessory to murder, in the murder of Timothy Sellers. Officer Hoke found out from the autopsy that the laceration on Timothy's neck was impossible to be self-inflicted, proving that Timothy didn't commit suicide and that Bay had more to do with it than he'd alleged. Officer Hoke went from inmate to inmate that was in the shower room that day, and held an extensive interrogation process until he got the information he needed. In a matter of hours, Glow got spooked into telling the authorities everything about the plot to kill Timothy "Timbo" Sellers, and everyone who was involved. Officer Hoke later discovered that Bay was found murdered and the next person in line to take on all the charges was Officer Stevens. Former Officer Larry Stevens, Adam "Pam" Clark, and Walter "Glow" Montgomery, were all convicted and sentenced separately from fifteen years to life in prison for their involvement in the murder.

Fantasy got down to her lowest point in her life and eventually found herself living in a homeless shelter. She'd tried to get herself together enough to try and buy back her club, but the money that was needed to purchase it was unattainable. She later discovered that her club was sold, causing her to go into a depression phase, which took her to using harsher drugs. Her brother was jailed for trying to shoplift at Macy's, so she had to fend for herself to now support her multiple drug habits.

For the last five months, Fantasy had been working for a "confidential company" that recruited homeless people to pass as their exasperated workers to picket in front of various law firms and government offices. Fantasy and her crew had been picketing at the corner of Nineteenth and M Streets for over a week and believed they were making a change. Yet, they had no idea the company they picketed for weren't even in the same building they were causing so much commotion in front of.

Two years later, Bangspot Records had made mainstream success and turned the entire music industry on its ear. Latrice's idea for distribution allowed the music world to see record sales skyrocket for the first time in three years and still kept ringtones as a profitable tool for the artists. Clarity's debut album titled *A Clear View* held the number one spot on the *Billboard* Hot 100 for two consecutive months in a row, going 6X platinum worldwide. Her top singles "Diamond District," "I Can See Thru These N——s," and "Never a Dull Moment feat. Dull," all sold more than two million downloads each.

Clarity soon lost her number one spot to her label mate, Teyron. His debut album entitled *Teyronimo* sold one million albums in his first week and his downloaded songs had sold eight millions times already. His songs "Teyronimo" and "No Break Up" were both up for Grammy nominations.

The N.A.R.C. album had been pushed back due to Killa D carrying out a jail sentence, for being charged with a gun, a small amount of marijuana, and cocaine that had been found on his tour bus on *The Bang'em While It's Hot* Tour. With Killa D being jailed, N.A.R.C.'s fan base had increased and when they finally dropped their highly anticipated album *Legal Narceteering*, they were expected to move 1.5 million albums in the first week of its release.

Latrice and Eric had a story all of their own. After Shakita's passing, they both decided to take their friendship to the next level, and ended up having a wild night of sexual bliss after Clarity's album release party. They continued to "touch bottoms" with each other, until they both decided that business and pleasure wouldn't mix, unless they became a "super couple." They then decided to purchase the Fantasy Lounge together at a private auction, and named it 20/20 Vision, which had been doing extremely well since its opening.

Soon to come, with every Black Emporium that opened up around the country, a 20/20 Vision Club would be built right next door, along with a Mark & Jay's Italian Café right across the street.

Latrice decided to make Clarity a business partner of hers, since the name of the club was Clarity's idea, which had been inspired by her album. Latrice's decision to make Clarity a stockholder in the club really came about when Clarity threatened to write a tell-all book about her come up in the rap game, and their spicy relationship they'd had together.

The crookedness continues…

THE END

Crooked Envy coming soon…

ABOUT THE AUTHOR

S.K. Collins was born and raised in Pittsburgh, PA and is now living in Washington, D.C. This former aspiring rapper-turned-author brings out the heartfelt emotion in his writing from an edgy street-life perspective that leaves the reader begging for more. S.K. describes himself as a fortunate new author to have received guidance, words of encouragement, and advice about the publishing industry from some of the veterans like Keith Lee Johnson, author of the series *Little Black Girl Lost,* and Teri Woods, author of the trilogies *True to the Game* and *Dutch.* S.K. already has numerous books in the works that he can't wait to feed the hungry audience out there waiting to feed on something new and fresh. Connect with the author on Facebook, Twitter, and Instagram.

Tell S.K. what you thought about his book.

CONTACT INFO
thewritersk@gmail.com
Facebook: SK Collins
Twitter & Instagram: @thewritersk

ALSO COMING SOON BY S.K. COLLINS
Unforgiven Love: Wide Open 2
Anything But Good

DISCUSSION QUESTIONS

1. Who was your favorite character(s) and why?

2. Who were the character(s) that you hated and why?

3. What was your favorite part of the story?

4. What do you think Shakita could have done to get the money she needed instead of robbing BERK ?

5. Now that Eric and Latrice are a couple, what do you think will happen with Teyron?

6. Do you know anyone who has dealt with an addiction like Shakita?

7. Shakita's addiction was gambling. What addictions did the rest of the main characters have?

8. If *Crooked G's* became a movie, who do you think could play Shakita and Latrice?

9. Why do you think Eric didn't want Shakita to work the purple and black floors? What do you think happens on those floors?

10. Do you think Latrice could've found another way to get Bay out of her life for good?

11. Do you have any friends that have dealt with physical and mental abuse like Latrice?

12) How do you feel about Latrice and Eric becoming a couple? Do you think Shakita and Eric would have made a better couple?